SHE CAN RUN

MELINDA LEIGH

SHE CAN RUN

Printed in the United States of America.

Published by Montlake Romance
P.O. Box 400818
Las Vegas, NV 89140

ISBN-13: 9781612181516
ISBN-10: 1612181511

DEDICATION

This book is dedicated first and foremost to my husband and kids, for believing in me from the beginning and for willingly eating tons of takeout.

To my agent, Jill Marsal, for her tireless efforts on my behalf.

To Jeff Belle, Alex Carr, and everyone else on the Amazon publishing team for giving me this amazing opportunity.

Additional thanks to the other founders of Liberty States Fiction Writers: Gail Freeman, Rayna Vause, Caridad Pineiro, Michele Richter, Lois Winston, Kathye Quick, and Anne Walradt for generously sharing their combined wisdom with a newbie; and to my critique partners Dale Mayer, Walt Mussell, and Beverley Bateman.

I couldn't have done it without all of you.

PROLOGUE

Beth's hand trembled. Her knuckles hovered an inch from the recessed oak panel. The office door was closed, which meant Richard didn't want to be disturbed. She glanced at the box in her hand, delivered by messenger just moments before. It must be important. Would Richard be angry if she interrupted him? Or angrier if she didn't? Her stomach clenched. He'd be angry no matter what she did.

With a hitched breath, she rapped lightly. The latch hadn't caught properly and the door swung open. Beth froze, paralyzed by the scene before her.

Confusion shifted into comprehension, and fear turned her insides to ice water.

Could she slip out before he noticed her? She eased backward, but Richard sensed her presence. He turned and stared. Their gazes locked for a few seconds, his feral, hers panicked. The lion and the gazelle.

Then he grabbed the crystal letter opener on his desk and lunged.

Beth ran.

She couldn't leave the house. Her children were upstairs. She needed a weapon. Her eyes locked on the kitchen doorway ten feet away.

His Italian loafers scraped the wood floor of the hall behind her as he fought for traction. The rubber soles of her sneakers fared better. She almost outran him. Almost.

At the threshold, he caught her in a flying tackle. She flung her hands out. Pain shot through her wrists and palms as she braced her fall before her face slammed into the tile.

After all this time wondering if he'd eventually kill her, there was now no more doubt. If she didn't get away, she was dead.

Panting, on all fours, he pulled on her legs. She donkey kicked backwards, catching him on the side of the face. He grunted. His grip loosened, and she belly crawled forward a few inches before his hand closed around her calf.

She raised her chin and eyed the knife drawer, an impossible ten feet away on the other side of the room. In a frantic visual sweep, her peripheral vision caught the cordless flashlight plugged into the outlet on her left.

She kicked at his fingers. They jerked open. Pulling a knee under her body, she pushed forward and yanked the flashlight from the wall. Richard crawled closer and slashed at her middle. Her skin registered a flash of agony, then went numb.

Without losing momentum, she turned over and swung the flashlight in an arc toward his head. Metal clanged against bone.

His eyes widened in shock before his body went limp.

Shaking, Beth scrambled out from under his torso. Blood seeped through her silk blouse.

Lungs heaving, she rooted through the odds-and-ends drawer and pulled out a roll of duct tape. She rolled him to his side, forced his wrists behind his back, and taped them together. As an extra precaution, she secured his hands to a heavy table leg, then bound his ankles. She slapped a final piece of tape across his mouth. Richard wasn't going anywhere until the cook arrived in the morning.

Adrenaline and nausea coursed through Beth as she glanced at the clock. She had exactly ten hours to vanish.

CHAPTER ONE

Ten months later

Beth stopped the car in the middle of the street and stared at what was supposed to be her family's new home. *Uh-oh.*

"Why's there a hearse parked in front of the house?" In the passenger seat, her son, Ben, chewed on his thumbnail. At twelve, he was wise beyond his years, and that was all her fault.

"That's a really good question." Her gaze shot to the rearview mirror. The road behind her was empty. Satisfied that she hadn't been followed, she nudged the gas pedal with a toe, turned off the estate's private road, and parked at the base of a circular drive. She stared through the windshield at the strange vehicle two cars ahead. Mild queasiness from a seven-hour drive and a greasy rest-stop cheeseburger churned into full-blown nausea. The fragile hope she'd nurtured all day evaporated in an instant. Just once she'd like something to work out the way she'd planned. Just once.

"Are you sure this is the right place?" Ben asked.

"This is it." The Dutch Colonial mansion looked exactly the same as when she'd interviewed for the caretaker position two weeks ago—except for the hearse. That was definitely new.

"Weird."

"Yeah." And weird was so not what they were looking for.

Ben lowered his hand and picked at the cuticle. "What do you think it's doin' here?"

"Only one way to find out."

She peered over the seat back. Katie's eyes remained closed. Her head rested on the side of her booster seat. Behind her seven-year-old daughter, luggage and boxes crowded the rear of the wagon. Beth turned back and contemplated the black-curtained vehicle again. "Maybe you should wait here while I check it out."

Ben shot her a "duh" look. He clearly had no intention of coming in with her.

"Lock the doors." She covered his hand with hers and squeezed. "It'll be OK."

He nodded as he opened the car window a few inches. His gaze shifted back to the hearse. She couldn't blame him. It drew the eye like Gorbachev's port wine birthmark.

Rusty metal protested with a grating squeal as she wrenched the door open and slammed it shut. Thick clouds kept the sun's rays at bay, but midsummer humidity clung to the evening air. She picked her way across a crabgrass-and-weed-encroached gravel path.

Stopping at the base of the walkway, she lifted her eyes to study the house's facade. One faded black shutter hung askew on the gray Pennsylvania fieldstone. Against an overcast, late afternoon sky, the house looked shabbier than on the sunny day she'd previously visited. With a deep breath she climbed three steps to the peeling front porch. Her finger hovered over the doorbell. Moisture pooled on her lower back, saturating the waistband of her dress slacks.

Just do it already.

Chimes broke the silence, followed by the muffled bark of what sounded like a large dog.

The front door opened. Instead of the elderly gentleman she'd expected, a forty-something man in a rumpled polo shirt and jeans greeted her. Even slouched over a crutch, he towered over her by at least a foot. A metal brace enveloped his leg from mid-thigh to mid-calf. A glass of amber-colored liquid hung from the fingertips of his free hand.

"Can I help you?" He lowered his hand from the doorknob to the handle of the crutch.

Beth's gaze rose, traveling up his long legs and narrow hips, over the muscular wall of his chest, and settled on his well-defined biceps. Horrified by her gawking, she jerked her gaze up to his face and cleared her throat. "I'm looking for Mr. O'Malley."

"I'm Mr. O'Malley." Alcohol fumes wafted over the space between them.

Eyes stinging, Beth pulled back. "No. You're not."

He raised his brows and grinned. "I'm not?" The mussed hair and boyish humor in his expression were at odds with a square-jawed, masculine face, which sported several days of beard growth. His eyes were deep brown, the color of dark chocolate, and just as tempting. Even in their current bloodshot state, they captivated her for a few seconds longer than was polite.

Refocusing her attention, Beth stammered. Heat flooded her cheeks. "I'm sorry. Of course you know who you are. I mean, you're not the same Mr. O'Malley. I'm looking for Daniel O'Malley."

"Oh, right. My uncle. I'm Jack. You're just in time. This way." His eyes flashed in understanding. "You almost missed him." Jack turned and disappeared through the doorway.

Beth followed, pulling the door closed behind her. She exhaled in relief. Daniel O'Malley was here. Thank God. Maybe his nephew, Jack, worked for a funeral home. That would explain the hearse parked outside in a nice, neat way that did not involve any dead bodies.

Her heels clicked on the wood floor as she crossed a wide, two-story foyer heavy with the scent of flowers. Jack lurched through a set of French doors. Beth turned the corner and stopped dead. In the room beyond an open casket sat amid a field of floral arrangements.

No.

In front of the coffin, two black-suited men maneuvered a wheeled dolly.

It can't be.

Jack set his glass on a small table.

"Hold on a minute, guys. We have one last toast." He turned to two disheveled blond men sprawled on an overstuffed sofa. One snored, his head tipped back at an awkward angle. "One of you bums get the lady a scotch."

The conscious blond unfolded his long frame and staggered over to a wheeled cart in the corner. Dirty glasses and empty bottles cluttered the bar's surface. He broke the seal on a new bottle of The Macallan and reached for a clean tumbler on the second shelf.

"Thank you, but I don't drink." Beth squared her shoulders and crossed to the casket. Her heart stuttered.

Resting on a bed of pillowed ivory satin was the elderly man who'd hired her.

The air left her lungs in a quick whoosh. Her knees wobbled, and she reached for one of the tables flanking the coffin.

A shadow fell across her as a hand grasped her elbow. Startled, Beth took a jerky step away, bumping the table with her hip. A brass vase of carnations wobbled. She reached for the flowers and steadied them with a shaky hand.

"OK." Jack pulled his hand away and lifted it in front of his chest palm out. "Take it easy." Blondie handed him a glass. Jack passed it to Beth without moving any closer.

"I'm sorry. I thought you were here to pay your respects, but you're not, are you?"

While he surveyed her, from her cheap shoes to her home dye job, Beth held the glass to her lips. Whisky vapors burned her nose, and she lowered her hand. She shook her head, staring at the whisky. Her throat tightened. What was she going to do?

Her eyes filled, but she blinked back the tears. Dammit. She could not get a break, no matter how hard she tried.

Under the haze of scotch, Jack's shrewd brown eyes narrowed. "Let's start again." He held out a hand. "Jack O'Malley." He nodded toward the blond man pouring an inch of whisky into his glass. "My cousin, Sean Wilson. The guy passed out on the couch over there is his older brother, Quinn, who never could hold his liquor."

"Freakin' embarrassing." Sean sighed.

"And your name is?" Jack's hand beckoned.

"Beth Markham." Uncomfortable with physical contact, she gritted her teeth and allowed their palms to touch for a nanosecond before tugging free from his grasp. "I don't understand."

Jack frowned down at her as she pulled her hand away. "Uncle Danny planned his own funeral. The family viewing was this morning. The burial's tomorrow. This afternoon the three of us held our own private send-off. We were sort of like Huey, Dewey, and Louie to Uncle Danny's Scrooge McDuck. He was eligible for a full military funeral, but he didn't want the fanfare. Just this."

"Get pissed with me one last time, boys," Sean added in a thick, fake brogue as he collapsed on the sofa. He raised his glass. "To Uncle Danny. Wherever he is, may the scotch be old and the women young. Not the other way around."

"To Danny." Jack picked up his glass and tossed back a half inch of whisky. He gave his head a quick shake.

Beth barely wet her lips on her glass and her stomach cramped. She had no job. They had nowhere to live. "But he just hired me. What happened?"

Jack hiccupped. "He had a heart attack. Don't get me wrong. We'll miss the old bugger, but he was eighty-seven. It wasn't exactly a surprise, especially when you consider how much he loved his scotch and cigars."

"I guess not." She couldn't go back to her uncle James's place in Virginia, where they'd been hiding all this time. He'd said it wasn't safe, which was why she'd driven all the way to the northeastern corner of Pennsylvania today. She had thought this job would be perfect. Secluded, remote, secure. Dotty old Daniel O'Malley hadn't been a threat. He hadn't even asked her many questions during her job interview. James had talked her into the arrangement, and he was the only man in the world Beth still had faith in.

But this man…She raised her eyes to meet Jack's bloodshot gaze. He cocked his head to the side and studied her. Even with more scotch than blood coursing through his veins, he saw too much. And she had so much to hide.

"You said my uncle hired you?"

Beth nodded.

"For what position?" He and his cousin exchanged a glance.

Beth hesitated. Oh, what the hell? She didn't have anything to lose at this point. She reached into her purse and pulled out the letter confirming her employment. Thank God she'd asked to get her offer in writing.

Jack opened the envelope and pulled out the letter, squinting as he scanned the text. His eyebrows shot up when he reached the second short paragraph. "You and your kids were supposed to live here?"

"Yes."

"Where are they?"

"In the car. With the hearse and all…I thought they should wait outside." Beth paused as her new reality struck her again. "I'm glad I did. Now that Mr. O'Malley's gone, I suppose I won't be needed. Can you direct me to the nearest motel?"

"Christ, I can't even think straight." Jack scratched his head. "Look, Ms. Markham…"

She interrupted, "Beth." She hated using her last name. There was always the risk she'd forget to answer to it. Which people tended to notice.

"Beth. This is a huge house. Why don't you and your kids stay the night? The only motel nearby isn't fit for human occupation. We can talk again tomorrow afternoon, after the funeral, and get everything straightened out. Right now I just want to go to bed." He dragged a hand through his already rumpled hair. "Besides, it looks like a storm's rollin' in."

Beth glanced out the window, where black clouds were gathering on the horizon. The wind whipped leaves across the side lawn. She had to get to Katie before the storm broke. Her gaze swung back to Jack. Good-looking men were not to be trusted.

"The funeral tomorrow morning is just family. Maybe a dozen people. You're welcome to attend." Jack lowered his voice. "Or you can stay out of sight if you like."

Beth hesitated. The fact was they had nowhere to go. She was suddenly bone tired, so weary that even holding her eyelids open was a chore. Even if she managed to find a cheap motel, she wouldn't be able to leave all their stuff in the car. And she didn't want to drive through a thunderstorm with Katie in the car. Never a good idea. Neither was running without a plan. Even a simple act like renting a motel room or filling her gas tank could have fatal consequences. The more people who saw them, the greater the chances that Richard's men would find them—again. Her stomach knotted. She bit her lip. "OK. But just for the night. Thank you."

He swung around on his crutch and headed back into the hall. "Drive your car around back and park it in the garage. You can come in through the kitchen so the kids don't have to watch them wheel Uncle Danny out. Do you need any help with your stuff?" At the front door, despite his handicap, he opened the door for her. Barking erupted from the back of the house as he stepped backward far enough so she could pass without touching him.

Oh, yeah. He saw way too much.

His gaze swept over the front lawn to her beat-up Taurus wagon then dropped to his braced leg. His mouth tightened. "I'm useless, but Sean would help you with your things." He inclined his head in the direction of the living room.

She shook her head. "No, thanks. I've got it." They wouldn't need very much for one night. If she chose, they could be gone long before Jack had any opportunity to talk to her.

– – –

Jack closed the door and headed toward the kitchen at the back of the house. Pain sang through his knee. God damn. Even a quart of scotch hadn't dulled it one bit. Thumps and the sound of rolling wheels came from the front hall.

"Funeral home guys are gone," Sean announced a few minutes later from the doorway.

Through the glass door off the kitchen, Jack watched the piece-of-shit station wagon pull up to the six-bay garage. He pressed a button on the wall to open the overhead door to an empty bay. The vehicle disappeared into the building.

"Should I go help her?" his cousin asked.

"No. Seems she'd rather go it alone."

"She's kind of jumpy." Sean scratched his unshaven chin. "Do you think the letter's legit?"

"Looks like." Jack sighed. "I've seen enough of Danny's scrawl over the past couple of days to recognize it. She did walk in on three guys getting drunk with a corpse. Some people might find that disturbing."

"Good point. People who didn't know Danny anyway," Sean conceded. "But why would Danny go and hire a caretaker after refusing to do just that for the last ten years?"

Jack pinched the bridge of his nose. "Why would he make us all believe he was broke when he was rolling in coin? And why is this place so rundown? It's not like he couldn't afford the repairs."

"No fucking clue." Sean shook his head. Then he pointed at Jack. "You didn't tell her you're in charge now."

"I haven't officially accepted." Damn his uncle for adding a residency requirement to the inheritance. Westbury was a nice place to live—if you were into small towns in the middle of no-where. He wasn't. Except for summer vacations at his uncle's estate, Jack had lived on the outskirts of Philadelphia his entire life. He'd been a city boy and then a city cop. Wasn't it bad enough his career had been yanked out from under him? Did he have to abandon his entire life?

"Yeah, yeah. Whatever. We both know you're going to. A year's not that much time. Face it, Jack." Sean glanced down at Jack's knee. "You're not going back to the force any time soon."

The surgeon had given Jack the bad news the day before Uncle Danny died. There was a good chance he was permanently disabled. A fucking cripple. Five years in the army and twenty on the force without a single injury, only to be taken out by an old man running a stop sign in his '87 Olds. "You going to put your disgrace of a brother to bed?"

Sean sighed. "Somebody has to. He's such a Nancy."

Jack snorted. "Stick him in the den. I'm sending my house-guests upstairs. I don't want her sneaking out on me before I know what she's up to."

"Think she was conning Danny?"

"Could be. She looks broke. He was a sucker for a pretty woman."

"Aren't we all?" Sean turned and headed for the hall.

Jack turned back to the window. Across the downward slop-ing expanse of green, Beth and two children emerged from the garage. The adolescent boy, a full head taller than his mother, held a carry-on sized suitcase. The little girl clutched Beth's hand.

Thick, dark clouds hovered overhead as Jack opened the door and stepped out onto the patio. A warm, wet wind blew across his face.

"Damn it, Henry!" Sean's voice boomed from the house. "Look out, Jack!"

Behind Jack, nails scrambled on hardwood. He lunged for the door just as one hundred pounds of barking German Shepherd leaped over the threshold, knocking him backward. He grabbed a patio chair to recover his balance.

Shit! He'd forgotten he'd locked Henry in the den after he'd tried to jump into the casket. Henry had liked Uncle Danny. A lot.

"Henry, heel! Sit!" The enormous blur of tan and black fur streaked across the patio onto the back lawn and made a beeline for the trio walking up the path. "Get back here!"

Jack hobbled after the dog. Fifty feet ahead, Beth's eyes wid-ened with alarm when she saw Henry barreling toward her like a freight train. She stepped in front of the children.

"He's friendly," Jack yelled. "Really friendly. Brace yourself."

Beth held her right hand in front of her body in a crossing guard stance and commanded, "Sit!" in a firm voice. Stunned, Jack watched Henry slide to a stop, haunches tucked under his body like a champion barrel racer. The huge dog's butt bounced on the grass in barely contained excitement as she reached down and scratched him behind his enormous ears.

Son-of-a-bitch. Damned dog did know a command.

Panting, Jack hobbled over and stopped just short of them. "I'm sorry about that. Henry has no manners. I hope he didn't frighten you."

She stood maybe an inch over five-foot, somewhat elfish, with a slim body and long black hair that seemed unnaturally dark for her complexion. Even in her current travel-worn state, there was no denying her beauty: large eyes, smooth skin, delicate features. Still scratching the dog behind his ear, she straightened her shoulders and looked up at Jack. Her face softened with the hint of a smile, and Jack felt an unsettling pull deep in his loins. "I'm not afraid of dogs."

No shit. Henry's lips parted in a goofy smile as he listed to one side, his back paw twitching in circles.

"Henry's a police dog reject. Officially, his file's stamped re-tired, but he's only four." Jack grinned, remembering an embar-rassing incident involving a high school drug raid, a locker, and a hoagie. His buddy, Mitch, in narcotics, hadn't thought it was so funny. "I'm pretty sure he has ADD."

Jack glanced at the children. Both had light brown hair, green eyes, and a wary stance, two white-tailed deer poised for flight. The boy squared his shoulders and extended his hand to Jack.

"I'm Ben, and this is Katie." He shook Jack's hand firmly, keeping his slight body angled between Jack and his sister. He had the awkward, overgrown look of a baby giraffe, knobby knees and elbows, long limbs ending in oversized hands and feet. The little girl studied her pink Hello Kitty sneakers as she sidled a few inches farther behind her brother. At least five or six years younger, she could've doubled for Tinkerbell, with her diminutive body and enormous eyes.

"Why don't we go inside?" Jack started hobbling toward the house. The dog pranced in excited circles around the group and bumped Jack's knee. Jack gritted his teeth as pain shot up to his hip. "Henry, would you relax?"

He led the way into the kitchen. "Do you need anything? Are you guys hungry?"

In the distance, thunder rumbled. Katie turned and hugged her mother's leg, burying her face into Beth's side.

Beth lifted the child onto her hip. "Thank so much for the offer, but I'd just like to get them settled for the night, if that's OK. It's been a long day."

"Sure." Jack led them through the kitchen into the hall. In the foyer, he nodded toward the curving staircase, grabbing hold of Henry's collar. The dog whined. His tail slapped at Jack's thigh.

Beth and the kids kept their distance as they crossed to the foot of the stairs.

"Left at the top of the steps. Take any of the bedrooms you want. They're all empty. I apologize for not going up, but that's a lot of hopping." Jack pointed to his knee. "My housekeeper will be back later. Don't be alarmed if you run into her."

Halfway up the steps, Katie whispered in her mother's ear.

Beth smiled tentatively. "Is it OK if the dog comes upstairs with us?"

"He's all yours." Jack let go, and Henry bounded up the stairs.

Beth turned and looked directly into his eyes. "Thank you." Hers were a deep emerald green, and Jack was riveted until she turned away.

"No problem," Jack murmured, and remained in the foyer, staring, until they climbed the steps and disappeared into the upstairs hall. His chest tightened, and something inside him wanted to follow, something instinctive, primal, and discomforting that stirred his blood. He shook it off, returned to the kitchen and poured a tall glass of water. No more booze tonight.

"Diluting the scotch?" Sean asked.

"Worth a try." Jack's head throbbed. "I'm too old for this shit. I feel hungover already, and I haven't even gone to sleep yet." Popping the cap off a bottle of ibuprofen, he swallowed two and washed them down. "You get Quinn settled?"

Sean nodded. "You get your new employee settled?"

"Christ." Jack drained his glass and refilled it at the tap. "What am I going to do with them? I haven't even decided if I'm staying."

"Where were you planning to go? Back to that shitty little apartment? Even for a bachelor pad, that place was pathetic." Sean shook his head. "Think of it this way. If you only stay the year, at least you'll have a caretaker for this place when you leave." His cousin paused and scratched his jaw. "But I still can't figure out how Danny hired her without any of us knowing. Quinn and I both came by here a couple of times a week. He never said a thing. Did he place an ad? Use an agency?"

"Beats me." Jack set his empty glass in the sink. Lightning flashed, illuminating the kitchen. "But I intend to find out."

CHAPTER TWO

Something cold and wet touched Beth's face. She sat bolt upright, her pulse quickening. She struggled to free her legs from the confines of the twisted sheets and sucked in a deep, shaky breath. Her eyes darted around the room as she fought to orient herself. Slowly, her brain registered the simple furniture, the white drapes, the soft bed, the sleeping face of her daughter next to her, all illuminated by the faint pale gray of first light.

They weren't in Richard's house.

Henry set his head on the mattress next to her and licked her hand.

Just a nightmare. Not real. At least not anymore.

Relief washed over her like cold rain. Shivering, she pulled the blanket up to her chest.

She should have killed him.

Just a few more blows after he'd collapsed unconscious at her feet would have done the trick. It wasn't the first time that thought had bubbled up inside her. Like all the previous times, she tamped it firmly back down. She would have gone to prison and lost her children. There was no way anyone would have believed her story. Correction, no one *had* believed anything she'd said. Richard had money and power and the complete control that came with them. And he'd made sure his wife was utterly defenseless.

Through the open doorway, Beth could see her son shift on the couch in the sitting room. Beth pushed her sweat-dampened hair from her face and pressed a palm to her forehead. The dog thrust his nose against her hand and whined softly.

"Thank you, Henry. I didn't need to see the rest of that dream," she whispered. Henry took her comment as an invitation and jumped onto the bed. Settling his head next to her pillow, he stretched his warm body out alongside her and blinked his brown eyes at her expectantly.

"I'm sorry if I woke you." She stroked his broad head.

Henry thumped his tail on the bed a few times and closed his eyes. Beth rolled over and leaned her head against the dog. She ran her fingers through his fur, feeling her heart rate slow, her breathing ease. The steady rise and fall of his chest and the soft snore that accompanied each breath soothed her raw nerves.

Beth glanced at the clock. She'd slept almost four hours. Not bad, considering her current state of employment and housing limbo, as well as the thunderstorm that had raged until after midnight.

She glanced toward the window. Dawn slowly brightened the sky.

The dog sighed. With one arm around his massive neck, she rested her head next to his and closed her eyes.

"Mommy?"

So much for getting another hour of sleep.

"I'm hungry." Katie sat up beside her, both arms curled around a ragged stuffed giraffe. Brian had bought it the week before he died, for their daughter's first birthday. Katie didn't remember her father, but she knew about the animal's link to him.

"Well, then. We'd better get dressed and go see what's in the kitchen." Beth kissed Katie on the nose. Just then Ben stepped through the doorway. He'd put on jeans and a T-shirt, but his hair still stood up on one side of his head. She tossed clothes on the bed for Katie and headed into the bathroom to see how much havoc one more sleepless night had wreaked on her face.

The black hair was still startling, so different from her natural light brown and a sharp contrast to her pallor. God, she just wanted to be herself again. A few splashes of cold water barely added enough color to mimic faint life signs. She smoothed her hair back into a ponytail and tugged on a pair of worn jeans. She looked like Morticia Addams on casual day.

What the hell were they going to do next?

It was barely light out. They could pack up their stuff and be gone before anyone else even got up. On the other hand, she still harbored a small hope that there might still be a job here for her. Someone needed to run this place, even if it was only on a temporary basis. That could buy her some time to figure out the next step. There was no reason not to hang around at least until she could talk to Jack.

It wouldn't be a problem to make themselves scarce during the funeral. The place was huge, a couple hundred acres. The barn was the logical choice. She and the kids loved animals. Even if they skipped out before the end of the day, spending the morning with the horses would be therapeutic for all of them.

The estate's isolation had been one more reason she'd wanted this job. When they'd stayed with James, they'd had to spend almost all their time indoors. Here they could run free.

But she was getting ahead of herself. First, she needed to get the kids some breakfast.

Katie perched next to Henry on the bed, stroking his head. "Mommy, can we keep Henry with us?"

"I think that's up to Henry. Mr. O'Malley doesn't seem to mind if he follows you around."

At the sound of his name, Henry raised his head and thumped his tail. He shifted his weight and placed his head in Katie's lap. Ben reached over and ran a hand down the dog's back. Henry rolled over and presented his belly to be rubbed.

"Let's go downstairs and see what we can find for breakfast." Beth removed the travel doorknob alarm and pushed the antique Shaker dresser she'd slid in front of the door before going to sleep out of the way. It moved easily on the hardwood floors. Too easily to have done much except slow an intruder's entry, but she'd never have slept without a barricade of some sort. James had taught her to add layers of security whenever possible.

"Let's be quiet, OK? It's really early. Everyone else may still be asleep."

The group headed quietly down the stairs, and the dog zoomed ahead of them.

Despite the early hour, Jack was already in the kitchen, drinking coffee at the farmhouse table. His braced leg rested on a chair. A beat-up T-shirt and khaki shorts hugged a long, lean body. As they entered, he set his newspaper down, dropped his reading glasses on the table, and leaned back. Gray feathered his military-short hair at the temples, lending a distinguished look to a face that wasn't classically handsome, but immensely appealing in its strength and masculinity. Beth refused to squirm as he surveyed them one by one, then settled his gaze on her. His eyes were clear. Too clear. Maybe this wasn't such a good idea. "Everyone sleep OK?"

"Fine, thanks." The morning sun streamed through the French doors. Beth squinted.

"I bet you're all hungry." Jack flattened one palm on the table and reached for his crutch with the other. His mouth tightened as he lowered his left foot toward the floor. "What would you like for breakfast?"

"Oh, please don't get up." Beth took a step forward. "I can get it."

Jack frowned and sank back into his seat. "OK. Then you can help yourselves or wait for Mrs. Harris." He crossed his arms over a peeling Hard Rock Cafe logo. "Dishes are in the cabinet behind you, Beth. There's milk and orange juice in the fridge. Cereal's in the pantry." His eyes shifted back to the children, who stopped just inside the doorway. His jaw tightened.

Beth hesitated at his clipped words. Nerves twisted in her belly. He'd acted more hospitable the night before, but he'd been intoxicated. She had no idea what this man was really like. He could be a drunk. He could have a terrible temper. He also seemed to sense something was off with the children. Maybe they should just be on their way right after breakfast.

Before she could regain her composure—or plan her exit strategy—the back door opened and a woman in her mid-sixties stepped through, a stack of white bakery boxes in her arms. She kicked the door closed with one heel. The boxes wobbled.

"Let me." Beth jumped forward to take the top half of the stack.

"Why, thank you. You must be Ms. Markham." The house-keeper's tall, sturdy frame was draped in a stylishly tailored black pantsuit. Short, beige-blond hair fell in waves around her face.

"I'm Betty Harris." She set the remaining boxes on the counter and held out her hand. "I apologize for not being prepared for you. Danny must have forgotten to tell me he'd hired you."

"It's OK." Beth shifted her pile to one arm to accept the housekeeper's firm handshake. The woman's no-nonsense, friendly demeanor tugged at the tight knot in Beth's belly, loosening it just a hair.

"Jack told me you had children. I picked up some doughnuts with the order for the reception. It's the box on top."

"Call me Beth, please. And thank you. I hope we haven't put you out."

Mrs. Harris waved the comment away and patted Beth on the shoulder. "Nonsense, this place needs some kids to liven it up. It's too big and quiet for my taste. I have twelve grandchildren. So don't worry about these two bothering me."

Henry pushed past Beth's legs, planted himself at Mrs. Harris's feet, and focused on the white boxes. A string of drool dropped from the dog's mouth onto the wide-planked floor.

"Go eat your kibble, Henry. Doughnuts aren't good for dogs."

The shepherd sighed and ambled over to a stainless steel bowl in the corner, but he kept one eye on the bakery box as he crunched through his dog food.

Beth set her stack of boxes on an outdated laminate countertop. The kitchen was clean and spacious, but its décor was two decades past needing a remodel.

"Did you get some coffee, dear? It's in the pot next to the refrigerator." The housekeeper nodded at Ben and Katie, still standing at the kitchen's entrance. "I'm Mrs. Harris."

Beth stepped to their side and slid an arm around her daughter's shoulders. The child leaned into her. "This is Ben and Katie."

"I bet you're hungry."

"Yes, ma'am." Ben nodded. His eyes darted in Jack's direction for a second. Katie stared at the floor.

"Then let's get you some breakfast." With one eye on the children still standing near the doorway, Mrs. Harris pulled a frying pan from the overhead rack and called over her shoulder. "Jack, shouldn't you be getting ready?"

Beth poured coffee in a mug and took a sip. After yesterday's java binge, her stomach cramped in protest. She set the mug on the counter.

"We have hours before we have to leave. The sun's barely up," Jack insisted. Mrs. Harris propped a fist on her hip, raised a brow, and stared at him. "OK then, I'll go get dressed." He folded his paper and grinned up at her. "Good to know someone's in charge."

"Someone has to be." The housekeeper crossed her arms in mock authority, but Beth could tell she fought a smile.

"Game, set, and match to Mrs. Harris." Jack heaved to his feet and tucked the crutch under his arm. Swinging forward, he leaned down to Beth and lowered his voice. His breath caressed her neck. "You can expect us to return at about ten. The family'll stay for a couple of hours. The coast should be clear by one."

She forced herself not to move, but her spine stiffened as he loomed over her. A woodsy aftershave drifted down and teased her senses. For a moment, she felt the heat from his body just inches from her skin. The flutter in her belly had nothing to do with the coffee and disconcerted her as much as his proximity. To her surprise, instead of recoiling, her body leaned a centimeter closer to his, as if pulled by a huge magnet.

Unsettled by his size and shocked by her response, she acknowledged his statement with a tight nod before stepping away. Moving past the scarred table, she stopped in front of the French doors. Her eyes skimmed over the vista. Forest fringed a broad expanse of sloping lawn shaded by towering oak trees. In the distance, a valley dipped off to the right, revealing a glassy lake through the trees. Beyond, green and brown mountain peaks and valleys rimmed the horizon.

The secluded nature of the estate had appealed to her two weeks ago when she'd stood in this very kitchen, but Daniel O'Malley's death had changed everything. The safety she'd perceived here was an illusion, a mirage that had evaporated the moment she arrived yesterday. She felt like she was lost in the desert, unsure whether safety lay ahead or behind her. Her life, and those of her children, depended on her making the right choice. That is, if she even had one. So far this morning, Jack hadn't mentioned the will, her job, or anything at all about her possible future on the estate. He just might make that decision for her. Then what?

"What are your plans this morning, Beth?" Jack's deep voice sounded behind her. His voice startled her out of her thoughts. She thought he'd already left the room. Had he just been standing there staring at her?

"The kids like horses, so we'll spend the morning in the barn if that's all right."

"That's fine." Jack nodded. "Let me know if they look OK. One of the neighbors has been looking after them since Uncle Danny died, but I don't know the guy very well. And I know absolutely nothing about horses."

"OK." Maybe if she showed him she was capable of taking care of the horses, he'd keep her on as caretaker.

Finished with his breakfast, Henry barked and scratched at the French door. Jack pulled it open and let him out with a sigh. "It would be helpful if you kept the dog with you. He's hell on a buffet table." He turned and limped toward an open doorway at the rear of the kitchen. Halfway through, he paused. "We'll talk later."

That's what she was afraid of.

– – –

After a quick breakfast, Beth led the kids to the French doors off the kitchen. Jack and Mrs. Harris had withdrawn to prepare for the funeral. Standing to one side, she peered through the glass panes and scanned the open area of grass and the tree line beyond. Nothing looked out of the ordinary. She opened the door and listened. The quiet was punctuated only by the rustle of the morning breeze through the woods and the chirping of a robin.

Unfortunately, there were dozens of places to hide between the house and the barn.

She stepped through the doorway and out onto the patio. The kids and the dog followed. Beth kept one eye on Henry. Would he know if someone was waiting out there?

A path led through a small copse to the barn and pasture. The air smelled organic, redolent with the heavy odor of grass layered over clean pine. Fifty yards from the barn, Henry spotted a squirrel and tore off through the woods. The squirrel raced up a tree. Henry ran circles around the base and barked.

Ben turned off the path. "I'll go get him."

"Me too." Katie skipped after her brother, breaking into a jog to keep up with his longer strides. Ben took her hand.

"Don't go any farther than that tree and stay together," Beth called after them.

Ben waved over his shoulder. It was already clear that both kids enjoyed the freedom afforded them by the estate's seclusion.

Beth strode into the cool barn and smiled at the welcoming nicker. A head bobbed over the half door of the closest stall. An impatient hoof rang against wood. The smell of hay and sawdust reminded her of the time before Brian's death, when she'd had time for hobbies like the horseback riding that had been a part of her life since her teen years. Long before Richard's deceit had destroyed their lives.

A shadow to her left moved and Beth jumped.

"Hello." A figure stepped out of a doorway.

Beth's heart seized. "Oh." She placed a palm over her pounding chest.

The neighbor. Please let this be the neighbor.

He was in his early thirties, on the short side and slight of build. His red short-sleeved polo shirt was buttoned all the way up the front and emphasized his ruddy complexion. *For Christ sakes, chill.* A pocket protector away from nomination to the Geek Squad, this fellow hardly looked like a threat.

"I'm Jeff Stevens. My farm is just over the hill there." He pointed to the buttercup-dotted meadow that rose on the other side of the barn. Sweat beaded his brow. "Are you all right?"

Get a grip. "Just surprised, that's all." *So much for Henry's superior canine hearing.*

"I'm sorry if I frightened you." He tucked his hands into the front pockets of his jeans and slouched. "I didn't mean to."

"It's fine. I'm Beth." She backed out of the aisle into the sunlight. In the open space of the barnyard, she took a deep breath. She knew she should probably explain who she was and what she was doing in the barn, but she hardly knew herself. She just hoped he wouldn't ask. "Jack said his neighbor was taking care of the horses."

"That's what neighbors are for. I liked Danny." Jeff followed. Sunlight glared off his balding head as he stared at his work boots. "I just finished feeding the horses. Waiting for them to finish their breakfast so I can turn them out."

Beth forced a smile. "I can do that this morning. I'm here anyway."

"OK." As he raised his eyes to her face, they paused fleetingly on her breasts. Then his face flushed as he stammered. "D-do you want me to show you where everything is before I go?"

She hesitated. Had that been a leer? Beth did not like the idea of being alone in the barn with him, but it wasn't his fault she was paranoid. He was Jack's neighbor. He didn't work for Richard. "I'd appreciate that, thanks." She stepped toward him.

Henry shot across the clearing, barking. He bounded up to Beth, jumped up, and placed both paws on her chest. She stumbled backward. "Henry, relax."

The shepherd circled her legs and head butted her hip, putting his body between Beth and the neighbor.

"I'm sorry, Jeff. He's a little rambunctious."

"It's all right," Jeff insisted, but he moved back a half step and frowned at Henry. "He could use some obedience training."

Ben jogged up and grabbed the dog's collar, pulling him away from Beth. "He's mad. The squirrel wouldn't come down."

Katie ran up beside her brother. When she saw Jeff, she ducked behind Ben and the dog.

Beth blew out a breath. The man was going to get suspicious if they all cowered away from him. And, really, he was only trying to be helpful.

Jeff stared at the kids and opened his mouth. Beth cut him off before he asked to be introduced. She didn't like to give out their names if it wasn't necessary. "You were going to show me around the barn."

"Yes." Jeff brightened and straightened his shoulders. "I was."

Henry strained at the hold on his collar. Ben's feet slid a few inches in the dirt. "Give it up, Henry. You're never gonna catch that squirrel, buddy."

Inside the barn, a horse's kick rattled a loose door.

Jeff turned toward the barn. "Probably Lucy. She's impatient."

"We're coming," Beth called out as she followed him inside, waving gnats away from her face. Behind her, the dog whined and Ben talked to him in a low voice.

Jeff stopped at a doorway. "The feed's in here." He continued down the dirt aisle, pointing out the tack room and the ladder that led to the loft. An elegant chestnut head poked out of the first stall as they approached.

"This is Lucy. She was Danny's favorite." Jeff reached up and scratched the mare under her forelock. Lucy rubbed her nose against his chest.

"She's beautiful." Beth stepped up and patted the side of the animal's sleek neck. The warm, horsey smell eased the tension from her shoulders.

"Lucy's the only one that's a handful to ride. The three geldings are fat and lazy." Jeff's gaze caught on her breasts again, and he blushed all the way up to his sparse, receding hairline. OK, that had definitely been a leer. Beth stepped backward and crossed her arms over her chest self-consciously as he introduced her to the other horses. An engraved nameplate hung on each stall door. Smaller identification tags were fastened on the side of each animal's leather halter.

"Thanks so much, Jeff." She stroked the mare's nose as Lucy nibbled at her T-shirt. Beth gently pushed the muzzle away. "What kind of farm do you have?"

"I train dressage horses."

"Really?" Beth was impressed. Dressage was the equivalent of ballet or gymnastics on horseback. Jeff must be a skilled horseman.

"I sold a gelding in '05 that went on to the Olympic trials last year." Jeff's chest puffed out just a little.

"That's amazing."

He blushed at the compliment. "I guess I'll be going then. Don't be afraid to call if you need anything. I'll be back tonight."

"OK. Thanks again." Beth followed him to the back door, where a beat-up Jeep Wrangler was parked in the shadow of the building. He climbed in, started the engine, and drove across the meadow with a short wave. The jeep's engine rumble faded. Beth breathed in the scent of warm summer grass and wildflowers.

If she could stay here, she wouldn't have to deal with strangers every day, just one odd, mildly perverted, and socially inept neighbor. At James's tavern each new customer had been a potential threat. What would it be like to not have her heart seize twenty times a day?

But what was Jack going to say? It appeared as if he were in charge, but had he inherited the estate? Regardless, surely someone needed to look after the place, at least in the short term. He said he knew nothing about horses, so that someone wasn't going to be Jack. She found herself hoping there might be a place for her and the kids here.

Suddenly Beth was looking forward to their afternoon discussion. She was tired of being in limbo. But would he answer the ten-thousand-dollar question?

Would Jack let them stay?

CHAPTER THREE

"I'm surprised you're still here." Jack winced as pain pulsed through his leg. Around the house he managed fine with one crutch, but the uneven ground of the barnyard was a different story. It didn't help that, courtesy of yesterday's scotch infusion, he felt like the sun was boring holes directly through his retinas into the back of his skull.

Beth brushed the gleaming shoulder of a large brown horse tied to the fence in the shade of a tree. Since he'd just gotten off the phone with the attorney, he supposed it was *his* large brown horse. The animal seemed bigger now that he was up close and personal with it. And it smelled like shit. Literally.

"I said I would be." Beth glanced over her shoulder and met his eyes for a split second. Sweat glistened on her forehead and had darkened the back of her T-shirt. She swallowed, her gaze darting to her children a dozen yards away. In the shade of a mature oak, Ben groomed a black horse with a speckled patch of white across its rump. On the other side of the tree, Katie sat on the ground with Henry.

The kids had been talking and laughing before Jack drove up, but as soon as he walked into the barnyard, they'd fallen into complete silence. The boy kept one wary eye on him and the little girl refused to look at him at all. Just like this morning in the kitchen, when the children had nearly climbed the wall to get as far away as possible from him. Normal kids weren't afraid to walk into rooms. Normal kids weren't this meek and quiet. He'd felt like an ogre, especially when Mrs. Harris told him later that they'd settled in fine after he'd left the kitchen.

The afternoon sun beat down on the top of his head. He wiped his brow on his sleeve and sidestepped into the very edge of shade, trying not to get too close to the horse. His toe caught on a rock, twisting his leg. Fire shot through his knee. He breathed through his nose and waited for the pain to recede to a manageable throb.

Crinkling her brow, Beth nodded toward his leg. "Shouldn't you stay off that?"

"It's OK." She was right. He should have his leg elevated and packed in ice. But he'd already sucked up his pride driving the short distance to the barn in Danny's golf cart. Interviewing his prospective new employee from the sofa would make him feel like total waste of space. A man could only take so much humiliation.

She looked doubtful but turned her attention back to grooming the horse, continuing to run the brush rhythmically along the length of its neck.

"I've decided to accept the terms of my uncle's will."

He watched Beth's hand freeze mid-sweep as she waited for him to continue. The arm that poked out of her T-shirt sleeve was way too thin, but her worn jeans hugged a nicely curved ass.

"Which makes me the new owner of this estate," he added.

She jolted back into action without a word, moving away from him, down the horse's body to clean its belly with long strokes.

Most nervous people were prone to chatter. He'd questioned hundreds of scared people: criminals, victims, and everything in-between. Beth had clearly learned to control her emotions somewhere along the line. But when? And why?

When silence didn't provoke a comment, Jack prodded her for a response. "I thought you'd want to know that you still have a job. If you want it, that is."

"Really?" Beth stopped and turned to face him.

Daylight brought out the pallor of her skin and emphasized the dark circles under those fascinating green eyes. Had she looked this exhausted last night? Maybe if he hadn't been totally shit-faced, he'd be able to remember. He must have made a great first impression. Regret nagged at him.

Way to go, O'Malley.

She lowered her voice. "You don't have to do that. You don't even know me."

"Uncle Danny hired you. That's good enough for me." He gestured to the beast standing behind her. "Obviously you can handle the horses. What sort of responsibilities did you and my uncle discuss?" The employment letter Danny had given her was ridiculously vague.

"I have some bookkeeping experience. He wanted me to get estimates for a new roof and some landscaping."

As if unhappy with her lapse in attention, the horse bumped her with its nose. The nudge nearly knocked her off her feet. Without turning, she reached back and patted its neck.

"All of those things still need to be done," Jack pointed out. "I've never even owned a house."

"I don't know." She turned back to the horse, leaning into a bucket of supplies to exchange the brush for a small metal pick.

Was she going to turn him down? And what was the deal with this sinking feeling in the pit of his stomach?

"How about a trial period? Say two weeks? We'll see how it works out for all of us. Then if you're not happy here, I'll have time to find someone else for the job." Jack held his breath as she bent down to lift the horse's hoof. The waistband of her jeans sagged, revealing the top band of a black satin thong. Jack's brain short-circuited and redirected his blood flow south.

Shit. How was he supposed to talk to her now?

As she cleaned all four hooves, Jack averted his eyes and tried to remember the score of last week's Phillies' game. The image had little effect on the pornographic slide show running through his head. With the horse in the background, Jack's mind added a cowboy hat and boots to the stripper ensemble his brain had superimposed on Beth. What the hell was wrong with him? He hadn't gotten laid in months, since before the accident, but his response to Beth was way out of whack.

He was spending way too much time with Sean.

"All right." She straightened and tossed the pick back into the bucket. "We'll try a couple of weeks, but no promises."

And to think he'd come down here under the assumption he was doing her a favor. "Thank you. If you like, you can stay in the rooms you're in now, and we can discuss your responsibilities over the next couple of days. Let's just go with what Danny agreed to pay you. Sound OK?"

"Yes. That's fine." Beth untied the rope and tugged the horse toward the pasture gate a few yards away. The horse followed her docilely as Jack tried not to stare at her ass.

"You'll need to call your neighbor and let him know," she called over her shoulder.

"My neighbor?" He concentrated on an image of his grand-mother in his head, picturing her in church, praying the rosary, lighting a candle. Not working. His brain had developed picture-in-picture capability, running his personal porn flick right along-side the saintly image.

He was so going to hell for this one.

Beth gave him a quizzical glance. "Jeff Stevens? He was in the barn when we got down here this morning."

The vision of his weird neighbor was a definite boner-shrinker.

"Oh. Yeah. Him. I'll call Jeff this afternoon. I'm sorry. I haven't lived here very long either." Jack nodded toward the children. "You know, the kids don't need to work. I don't expect them to do anything. They're just kids."

"Thank you, but they wanted to help. They like animals."

"As long as they know they don't have to do it, it's OK with me. Speaking of animals, did Henry give you any trouble?"

"None. He keeps his distance from the horses, though. I think he's afraid of them." Beth laughed.

"I can't say I blame him, but Henry is the most cowardly ex-police dog I have ever known." Jack paused for a minute, watching her face soften with a smile for the first time. Humor danced in her eyes for only a few seconds, but the image imprinted in his head. He wanted to see it again.

Beth unlatched the gate and released the horse into the pasture. As she fastened the gate, she jumped. "Ow."

Blood dripped down her forearm. Jack swung forward on his crutch. "What happened?"

"I caught my hand on something." She twisted her arm trying to look at the outside of her palm.

"Let me see." Jack reached out and closed his hand around her slender wrist. He'd barely felt the throb of her pulse against his thumb when she started and snatched her hand away. The blood drained from her face.

"Whoa." He released her and took a step back.

Wild-eyed and pale, she trembled in front of him. "It's nothing. Just a scratch." Even her voice shook. A shove from a half-ton animal had no effect on her, but the touch of his hand sent her off the deep end.

"OK. But come on up to the house and clean it out." Jack smoothed any recognition of her fear from his voice as he watched her shove her shaking hands into the front pockets of her jeans. She raised her chin and squared her shoulders, almost defying her body's visceral reaction. Something inside his chest shifted as she struggled to regain control. It wasn't just her body that he admired. Her courage was damned attractive. "It's past lunchtime anyway. There are plenty of leftovers from brunch. I think the heat is getting to you."

She nodded and cleared her throat. "We'll be along in a few minutes."

As Beth walked toward her children, Jack turned and headed for the golf cart parked next to the barn.

Why were they all so afraid of him? They hadn't backed away from Mrs. Harris this morning. Guilt? Nah. If she'd been conning Danny, she probably would have taken off last night. Unless she was considering playing him. Somehow that didn't feel right. Not the way she'd reacted when he'd touched her.

That hadn't been guilt he'd seen in her eyes.

Beth had been terrified.

– – –

On the patio, Beth and the children removed their muddy shoes before entering the house. The air-conditioning that enveloped Beth's body as she walked inside was pure bliss.

"There you are," Mrs. Harris greeted them. "I was about to come looking for you. It's past lunchtime."

"Wash your hands," Beth instructed the kids as she herded them toward the sink. "Lots of soap."

Soap stung the inch-long gash on her palm as she scrubbed her hands, making sure to get all the dirt out from under her nails. Stepping back from the sink, she looked down at her legs, then glanced at the children. All three of them were streaked with mud, cobwebs, and straw.

"Maybe we should eat outside. I didn't realize how filthy we all were." Beth turned to herd the children back outside.

"Relax. This isn't a museum. You look like you could use some cool air. Iced tea, Beth?" Mrs. Harris opened the refrigerator and poured two glasses of milk. "Those children need to eat. Not an ounce of fat on either one of them. Do you like ham?" She directed the last question toward Ben and Katie.

"Yes, ma'am." Ben slid into a chair at the table. Katie sat next to him.

"I can get it. You don't have to wait on us." Beth hurried to help. "I don't want to add to your workload."

"Nonsense. I'm glad you're all going to be moving in with us. But you can set the table if you like."

Beth retrieved silverware from the drawer.

"This place is too quiet." Mrs. Harris set a platter of sliced ham on the table. "I'm used to it, because Danny was practically a hermit the last few years. But Jack needs the company. He was a policeman for a long time, and he's not used to having a lot of free time."

Beth dropped the handful of utensils on the table with a clatter. Mental head smack. Jack *had* said that Henry had been a police dog. Her taxed brain just hadn't connected the dots.

Great. She'd given a false identity to a cop. Was that a felony or a misdemeanor?

"Are you all right, dear?" Mrs. Harris inquired. "You look ill. You have to be careful working outside in this kind of heat. I'll bet you didn't even take water with you. Sit down and drink this." She gently pushed Beth into a chair and handed her a cold glass of iced tea.

Rolls, potato salad, deviled eggs, and a plate of cookies joined the ham. The kids dug in. Clearly no one would go hungry as long as Mrs. Harris was in charge of the kitchen. And she was definitely in charge.

Unfortunately Beth's appetite had gone out the window when Mrs. Harris made her revelation about Jack—who might easily have seen a missing person's report with her face on it sometime in the last year. Acid rose in Beth's throat at the thought of Jack contacting Richard. One phone call. That's all it would take. Her gaze shifted to her children. Would he kill them, too? They were loose ends, and nothing was beyond Richard's cruelty. Or maybe he had other plans for them. Her chest constricted as she contemplated her options, their fate.

Wait. Jack had shown no sign he'd recognized her. He could have been a cop anywhere. She'd dyed her hair black and let it grow out. Thanks to the Stress Diet, she'd lost weight, so her face was thinner. Then there was the corpse-like thing she had going on with her complexion. She reconsidered.

"Aren't you going to eat, dear?"

"I'll get something as soon as I cool off a bit." Beth forced a smile and kept her voice light. "You said Jack was a cop?"

"Yes. Until his accident a few months ago."

She sipped her tea. "Did he see his uncle often?"

"No. He worked about two hours from here, in South Bend. That's a suburb of Philadelphia. When he was younger, Jack spent a lot of time up here, but after he made detective, not so much." Mrs. Harris frowned as she refilled Beth's glass with iced tea.

"Thank you."

Jack hadn't worked in the same jurisdiction where Richard lived. But cripes, it was close.

Mrs. Harris pulled out a chair and sat down. She picked up a cookie and took a bite. "You're still pale. You need to get some food into you after working hard all morning."

Although her belly cramped at the mere idea of eating, Beth forked some ham and potato salad onto her plate. Mrs. Harris was right. Beth needed to eat to sustain her energy. Missing a meal wasn't advisable when she might have to run at any time. If only she had somewhere to go.

– – –

Jack hobbled into the kitchen and pulled out a chair across from Beth and the kids. Ben held his ground, but even with the table as a barrier between them, Katie cringed as Jack sat. Beth looked like she was about to throw up.

Under the table, Jack's knee throbbed with every beat of his pulse. Either someone had stuffed shards of glass under his knee-cap or he'd spent way too much time on his feet this morning. He must've looked as bad as he felt, because Mrs. Harris went immediately to the freezer and pulled out a large bag of crushed ice.

"That leg needs to be put up." She gave him her fiercest do-not-mess-with-me face.

Jack didn't argue as he lifted his leg onto the chair she pushed under it. His knee was roughly the size of a basketball. If he didn't get that swelling down overnight, his physical therapist was going to have a shit fit tomorrow.

He sat back, swallowing the ibuprofen Mrs. Harris set in his palm with the iced tea she put on the table in front of him. "Thank you."

To draw his attention away from the pain, he focused on the other people in the room. The kids were chowing down. Beth, however, only picked at her ham. She needed a good ten pounds on her if she wasn't going to blow away in a stiff breeze. Had she eaten anything at all today?

Henry sat at Katie's feet, giving the child his starving dog routine. Brown eyes tracked the movement of her fork from plate to mouth like a spectator at a tennis match. A string of drool dripped from his black muzzle to the floor. Jack pretended not to see Katie slip him a piece of ham under the table.

They were all filthy and emitted the distinct odor of horse. Sweat glued their hair to their foreheads. It was too hot for anyone to work outside. He hoped Beth didn't intend to return to the barn this afternoon, because he'd have to veto that idea.

"Can you guys swim?"

"Yes, sir." Ben kept his head down as he answered.

"You can call me Jack." *Sir* sounded old. "Well, there's a pool out there. You can use it whenever you want, as long as there's an adult with you. Sure hot enough today. Down at the lake, there used to be a beach, too. I'd like to get it and the dock and boathouse repaired." He glanced at Beth. "We should make a list, and since you're going to be staying a while, you could bring in the rest of your stuff." Jack gritted his teeth. He should be getting up and hauling their stuff into the house for them. But no, he was sitting in a chair like a freaking old man.

Both children stopped eating to stare at their mother.

"We're going to try it for a couple of weeks," Beth explained.

With a grin that made Jack smile, Ben jumped up from the table and flew out the door, calling out, "I'll get our stuff."

At least one of them was happy about the arrangement.

Without her brother's body to shield her, a panicked look crossed Katie's face. Her gaze darted to Beth as if contemplating shifting over a seat, but moving closer to her mother would mean moving closer to Jack. Clearly that wasn't an option. Katie wouldn't even look at him.

Jack had to do something. There was no reason for her to be afraid of him. And, yeah, damn it, it bugged him.

"Katie, I would like to ask you for a favor." Jack made it a point not to even lean in her direction. He kept his voice low and even. Still, her face paled and her fingers trembled at the sound of his voice. It made Jack's chest ache just to watch her, but he continued. "It's about Henry."

At the mention of his name, the dog hauled his furry butt off the floor and rested his head in Jack's lap. Jack scratched Henry's head. Despite having zero work ethic and the attention span of a gnat, Henry was a good soul. The big dope was simply more of a lover than a fighter.

"Henry is a highly trained police dog, you see." *Sort of.* He wasn't exactly lying. Henry had been trained extensively. The fact that none of that training had stuck was another issue. "With my injury, I can't practice with him every day. He might forget everything. That would be a real shame."

Henry's eyes glazed over as Jack rubbed just the right spot behind his ear. Jack focused on the dog, keeping Katie in his peripheral vision. The little girl's eyes were still wide as saucers, but she no longer looked like she was going to lose her lunch.

"Do you think you could take over his practice? It's a pretty big responsibility."

The child's nod was almost imperceptible.

"Can you read?" How the hell old was she anyway? Five or six? A really small seven?

She nodded again.

"OK then. I'll write down all his basic commands for you." Jack picked a small piece of ham off the plate. "You give him a command, like *down*." The dog didn't move. "And you give him the treat if he does it."

Still standing, Henry's whole butt wagged.

"Only if he does it." Jack showed him the ham. Henry drooled. "As you can see, he's already forgotten a lot."

The dog sighed and sank to the floor with a protesting groan. Jack gave him the treat. "That was a little slow, buddy."

Henry swallowed the ham and closed his eyes.

"Do you think you can do that?"

She gave him another minuscule nod and looked at him for the first time. *Baby steps.*

Ben came through the door wheeling a large suitcase, a couple small duffels slung over his shoulder. Katie slipped off her chair to follow him down the hall.

Beth cleared her throat as she stood up to follow the kids. "Thank you." Were her eyes actually misty?

Jack had a moment of satisfaction after Beth disappeared through the doorway before Mrs. Harris burst his Good Samaritan bubble. "Does this mean you're through feeling sorry for yourself?"

He winced. "Was I that bad?"

Mrs. Harris gave him a pointed stare.

"Sorry."

"You're entitled to be angry, even depressed about your injury, Jack. But you're going to have to move on. Why do you think your uncle wanted you to live here? It wasn't like he got a kick out of controlling people. You know he wasn't like that."

Jack shrugged. She had a point. Danny had never tried to interfere with his life. He'd merely kept in touch and invited him to spend the occasional weekend at the estate.

"If you ask the attorney, you'll find out he wrote that stipulation into his will about a month after your accident—*after* Quinn told him he thought your knee was shot."

Jack's mouth dropped open.

"Danny said you needed to come home. You just didn't know it." Mrs. Harris's gaze moved to the glass door. "And I think, somehow, he knew he was going to die."

"I'm going to miss him. I should have visited more often."

"Probably." Mrs. Harris didn't pull any punches. "He worried about you, Jack. Sean and Quinn have families to keep them on track. Danny thought you needed roots, too."

"Maybe he was right." Jack adjusted the ice pack. "So, what do you think of our new houseguests?"

"Something's not right with them." Mrs. Harris stepped to the fridge and pulled out a bottle of Coors Light. She handed it to him and he twisted the cap off for her. "Do you think they're in some sort of trouble?"

"Who knows?" Jack shook his head. "But keep your eyes open. Just in case."

"Don't you worry. Not much gets by me." Mrs. Harris tipped the bottle back for a long swallow.

No shit.

CHAPTER FOUR

Sweat rolled down James Dieter's back as he methodically wiped the kitchen surfaces with glass cleaner. He finished the cabinets and did a quick walk around, checking for any remaining sign of Beth or the kids. He'd disposed of everything that could possibly hold a print or be traced. The place was squeaky fucking clean.

At the other end of the small apartment the window air conditioner groaned. He crossed the worn carpet and switched it off. Summer in Virginia was a bitch, but the heat didn't bother him much. Anybody who complained about the temperature or humidity should belly crawl through a jungle in 'Nam in full combat gear.

Before leaving, he glanced out the window at the street below. Droplets of condensation obscured the view, but so far, so good. There was no sign of the slick, pony-tailed man yet, but he was on his way. Coming for Beth. James had envisioned him in vivid detail just this morning. And the hair on the back of his neck itched. A sure sign fate was ready to collect her due. Well, thanks to some funky wiring in his head, James was ready.

He slipped out the door and down the wooden stairs, letting himself back into the small neighborhood tavern he'd owned for more than a decade.

Ten minutes later, as he perched on a stool tallying the previous night's receipts, the hair on his nape quivered as if the air were charged with a weak electric current. It was an alert system, rather than an indication of fear. His long-conditioned senses recognized when precognition and reality were about to collide. And he knew some major-league shit was about to hit the fan.

Outside, a car door closed.

Slick was here.

He swung his legs over the bar and ducked. The persistent itch felt like an old friend as he strained for a sound that would give away the intruder's position.

Outside, the wooden staircase creaked. A shadow crossed the window as it ascended. James stepped closer and peered sideways through the mini-blind slats. Morning sunlight glinted off the barrel of the gun in Slick's hand. The guy thought he was slick all right, sneaking up on an old man, a woman, and a couple of kids, but Slick had a surprise in store for him this morning.

Mr. Magoo was going Rambo on his ass.

James slipped behind the bar, squatted down, and pulled out a locked metal box. He transferred a handgun to his pocket but kept the razor-sharp Ka-Bar in his hand. His fingers curled around the familiar, thick grip of the knife that had been a part of him for decades.

Footsteps squeaked overhead.

Moving quietly, James crept toward the door. He caught the first whiff of smoke. Through another faint creak, he located the intruder on the steps. James timed his next move. The man moved past the door. James opened it and yanked the slimy little weasel inside by his ratty hair.

"What the fuck?" Slick was surprised all right, bested by a senior citizen.

"Who are you?" James held him by his greasy ponytail, lifting him up onto his toes. He pressed the sharp blade against Slick's throat.

"This place is on fire, man. We gotta get outa here." Beads of moisture trickled down Slick's face and soaked through his shirt.

"Everybody's got to go sometime. I've lived a long life. How about you?" The truth was, James didn't fear death as much as he feared dying. And he'd much rather go out in battle than die piece by piece like Gloria.

"Come on man, let's go outside and talk." Slick licked his lips, eyes darting from the crackling sounds overhead to the door.

"No, I don't think so. I asked you a question, and I suggest you answer it. Who are you? Who do you work for? Why are you looking for the woman?"

Sweat beaded on Slick's forehead and dripped into his eyes. "Look, I got nothing personal against the bitch or her little runts. It's just a job."

"Who hired you?"

"I don't know. I never meet my clients. It's all done online now."

Fucking Internet.

The smoke thickened. A few flames licked down from the rafters. The old structure creaked and groaned. From the intensity of the heat radiating from the fire upstairs, James thought the ceiling would collapse soon.

Slick coughed.

James had already decided Slick wasn't leaving. He would only try again. James removed the blade from Slick's neck. Although an effective interrogation technique, throat slitting was messy, and not at all his style.

Slick breathed a sigh of relief.

It was his last.

James pushed the long, sharp blade upward into his back, neatly puncturing the hired killer's heart. The wound barely bled.

Killing was like riding a bike. Twenty years of retirement hadn't dulled his skills. But then, the government had trained him well.

James looked around the burning bar. There was nothing here for him now. It was time to go. He wiped his blade on Slick's pants, then reached down and removed the dead man's wallet and keys from his pockets—anything to delay the official identification of this Anthony Cardone.

Sirens approached. James left by the back door and climbed into Slick's black SUV. Three blocks from the bar, he parked the truck right in front of a local chop shop. He left the windows down, the doors unlocked, and the keys inside because spray-painting "steal me" across the windshield would be a little too obvious. Within the hour, the local boys would strip it like a school of piranhas.

His small bungalow was a fifteen-minute walk away. Once there he packed a small duffel bag. Until Beth showed up last spring, he'd been holding this place, and Gloria's memory, in a tight fist. Not really living, just existing, idly passing his remaining time on Earth. Now, anger kindled emotions he hadn't felt in a long time. He'd missed this rush of adrenaline through his veins.

He sat on the edge of his mattress and opened his nightstand. With a sigh, he pulled out the silver saint medal he'd found under her couch. Remembering Beth's tears the day she'd lost it, guilt pricked his conscience. He flipped it over on his palm to reveal the figure and writing on the quarter-sized disk. Saint Florian, the patron saint of firemen. Someday he'd return it to her, but for now he needed it. Weak visions were stronger if the object had personal significance. He curled his fingers around it and waited.

The vision hit him like a blow to the head. Pain. Fear. A faceless man loomed in the darkness. A knife flashed. Blood flowed, warm and wet. Terror rose in his throat and choked him.

A suffocating weight held his body down. His arms were yanked over his head and pinned in the dirt. A blow to the face blurred everything.

His hand opened. The pendant dropped to the wood floor. The sunlight pouring through the window burned his eyes. Squinting hard, James used a handkerchief to pick up the pendant. He stuffed both into his pocket.

He hadn't survived twenty years in Special Forces—and worse—on luck and skill alone, but his *gift* had some definite drawbacks. It had been a real bitch knowing ahead of time which of his men weren't going to survive the mission.

The details of the dream were still vague, and he didn't know how much time he had. Whether his dream described an event that was a few days or weeks ahead was hard to say, but as the time drew closer, his visions tended to gain clarity and intensity. When they rolled through his head in high definition, Beth was in imminent danger. Given the power of the one he'd just had, he'd better get moving.

He gathered his things. After a detour to his kitchen for a bottle of ibuprofen and water, he slid into his sedan.

Beth and the kids were four hundred miles away with a man no one would ever connect with him. Hell, he hadn't seen Dan O'Malley in over thirty years. But he had no doubt O'Malley would do as he'd asked. O'Malley owed him, big time, and for Beth, James would collect. As Gloria's niece, she was almost family.

Or would have been if he'd married her aunt. But enemies were a natural by-product in his former profession. And how could he have married a woman when he couldn't even tell her his real name? Ironically, it was the fact that he wasn't actually related to Beth by blood or marriage that had made their relationship hard for anyone to trace—and his house the perfect hiding spot. He'd lost Gloria to a faceless disease he hadn't been able to fight. But with a little luck, he could save Beth.

James mentally kicked himself. Beth had refused to tell him why she needed to stay with him. Or why she needed to use a fake last name. But he could've, should've found out what she was running from when she had shown up at his door with her two kids in tow. Only after the visions started last month did he discover that her situation was more complicated than a nasty, high-publicity divorce.

She'd had no contact with that politician dickwad she'd up and married, and from things that had slipped out of the kids' mouths, James knew her ex was to blame. Unlike cancer, a dirty politician was a flesh-and-blood foe. Beth had been Gloria's favorite niece, and Beth and her kids had brought joy back to his life over the past ten months, something he hadn't thought was possible. James was going to fix this for her.

James stopped at the bank to peruse the contents of his safe-deposit box, removed several neat stacks of cash, and stowed them in his duffel. He shuffled through several driver's licenses, all bearing his picture, like playing cards. After choosing one, he selected the accompanying Social Security card and passport. He also transferred a small felt pouch to the duffel bag. James liked his investments to be portable, durable, and untraceable.

When he emerged into the painfully bright sunshine, James Dieter no longer existed. Hello, James Miller.

Time to find out how many skeletons Dickwad had in his closet.

CHAPTER FIVE

Amelia Bentley eased her car into the space in front of the ladies' room entrance, within the weak yellow circle of light generated by the fixture above the door. Darkness encroached from the surrounding woods. The streetlight in the corner of the weedy asphalt rectangle was out.

She stared at the surrounding forest. A shiver of unease snaked up her spine, and despite the warm, humid air, goose bumps rippled up her arms.

In hindsight, the super-sized Diet Coke she'd purchased at the last rest stop in Maryland hadn't been a good idea. Amelia contemplated her options. Her bladder was strained to bursting, but her parents' house was another half hour away. She squeezed her thighs together. She definitely couldn't hold it that long.

She scanned the empty lot. What she wouldn't give for a family of six to pull up beside her right now.

Her parents were nuts. Moving to the Poconos at their age. Why hadn't they retired to Florida like everybody else? Then she could spend her vacations with the big mouse or on a sun-drenched beach like a normal person.

With a deep breath she reached for the armrest and unlocked the car. Her belly tightened as she stepped out onto the cracked blacktop and glanced around one more time.

The lot was still empty.

She hurried into the squat brick building. Florescent light glared off dirty yellow walls and cobwebs hung in the cinder-block corners, but the facilities worked. Amelia washed her hands and dried them on the leg of her jeans because the towel dispenser was empty. On her way out she glanced in the broken mirror over the sink and automatically brushed her hands over her hair.

– – –

He cruised down the interstate. Although he'd taken the last one only a week ago, the urge tugged at him. He usually waited several weeks between engagements to ensure he didn't get sloppy. Carelessness invited suspicion. But his last date hadn't satisfied him. She'd been too easy. She'd caved almost immediately, before he'd even gotten warmed up. That was the problem with preying on whores and the homeless. In a way they were already broken.

And so the hunt was on tonight. He'd thrown a dart at his wall map of the tri-state area and so here he was, searching for prey.

Women were his addiction, their screams his drug of choice.

He was determined to find a new playmate tonight. But this time, he was going to change the game again. No more whores. Maybe upping the stakes would put some excitement back into his hobby, restore that high he'd been missing lately.

He glanced down at the speedometer. He'd never gotten a ticket and didn't intend to start now. He wasn't worried about the police. Then again, he saw no need to draw their attention.

The orange low fuel indicator glared at him. He should have taken care of that earlier in the day.

It would serve him right if he spent tonight alone. He deserved to be punished for this lapse. If tonight's dart toss didn't yield a target, so be it.

Despite his frustration, he grinned. Let the cops figure out *that* pattern.

He credited his success to this random method of selecting the location for his hunts. In addition to confusing the authorities, this technique introduced an element of chance to the game. Although he wasn't a gambling man, it had added to his amusement. For a while.

Unfortunately, boredom had edged in on his game again.

It was time to bump up his game from *Wheel of Fortune* to *Jeopardy*.

He took the next exit and pulled into a gas station. Choosing the pump farthest from the kiosk, he paid in cash. Although he didn't see any other customers around, he kept his baseball cap pulled down to shadow his face. The pimple-faced attendant in the booth was watching a small portable television and didn't even look at him when he accepted the money.

He briefly considered turning around and going home. Tonight's oversight could be a sign he wasn't ready yet. Perhaps he should regroup and plan the next hunt more carefully. Mistakes could get him caught, and he enjoyed his "dates" far too much to give up the game. After all, he hadn't found the ideal woman yet. That perfect blend of courage and beauty still eluded him.

Still undecided, he drove toward the access road that led back to the interstate. A short distance ahead, a sole pair of taillights disappeared to the right, following a sign for the restrooms. He slowed as he reached the same spot and followed, flipping off his headlights as he left the highway.

Maybe his luck had changed.

Across the lot a woman emerged from her car and entered the small brick building that housed the bathrooms. She was small and had long dark hair.

Perfect. Everyone knew blonds were stupid and redheads were bad-tempered. But brunettes were natural and wholesome. He supposed he'd never lost his adolescent fixation on Mary Ann from *Gilligan's Island*. She'd been pure and sweet, with just the right amount of spunk.

Just the kind of woman who would be a pleasure to break.

He squinted into the darkness. The energy in her movements suggested she was young, and his predatory instincts went on alert.

He carefully scanned the surroundings. Thick foliage surrounded the rest area and blocked even the moonlight. The men's room was on one side of the building, the ladies' entrance was on the other, and the back of the brick structure was completely shadowed.

Excellent. A thrill tripped up his spine.

Lady Luck had returned him to her good graces.

He parked a few spots away and quickly formulated a plan. After removing a small metal bar from his glove compartment and slipping it into his pants' pocket, he stepped out of his car. He walked casually toward the door, but instead of going inside, he ducked around the building and waited patiently in the darkness behind the ladies' room door.

She emerged from the doorway. He grabbed her smoothly around the throat. Covering her mouth with his free hand, he dragged her backward into the darkness. She struggled, striking him in the shins with her sneaker-clad feet. In the darkness of the trees, he released his hold on her neck, palmed the metal bar, and immediately brought it down on her head.

Her pathetic struggle ceased instantly, and her small body collapsed.

Pressing his nose against her neck, he inhaled the scent of fear. His groin swelled at her pungency.

Unconscious, she was heavier than she appeared, but then they always were. *Dead weight*, he thought with amusement. He carried her quickly around to the passenger side of his car and set her in the reclined seat, pulling the seat belt across her lap. He arranged her to look as if she were sleeping. Luck was still on his side, and the lot remained deserted as he closed the passenger door and walked around to the driver's side of the car, whistling. Once inside, he opened the glove box to retrieve the syringe he'd already filled. With a stab, he plunged the needle through her jeans into the large muscle of her thigh. She'd be out for hours.

The entire episode had taken less than a minute. Before fastening his safety belt, he fanned her beautiful hair around her face. She was lovely, and he was going to thoroughly enjoy their time together.

He steered the car toward the highway that would take them back home to Westbury.

CHAPTER SIX

Jack opened his eyes as the wall-mounted control panel emitted a half dozen low-toned beeps. In the dark bedroom, bright green lights blinked in unison with the sounds.

Someone was disengaging the alarm system.

He awakened in an instant, conditioned by years of interrupted sleep.

He glanced at his digital clock. Four thirty was a little early for anyone to be up and about, which suggested his early riser had an illicit activity on this morning's agenda. The only other people who knew the code were Mrs. Harris and Beth. Jack doubted Mrs. Harris was moving around this early. And even if she were suffering from a bout of insomnia, she wouldn't be going out. She'd make herself a cup of tea and watch reruns of *CSI* On Demand. Beth had been here less than a week and had avoided solo contact with him whenever possible. He had no idea what she would do if she woke in the middle of the night.

Nevertheless, he needed to know. He slipped into a pair of gym shorts. Leaving his crutch by his bedside, he fastened his knee brace and hobbled barefoot into the hall. Pausing, he listened for any sound of movement. All his senses kicked into high alert as he heard the back door squeak open then close with a soft click.

Had Beth let someone in or gone out? Or had someone broken into the house? The estate's ancient alarm system wouldn't be that difficult for a professional to disarm.

Just in case, Jack detoured to his nightstand to retrieve his gun from its locked box and then returned to the doorway. The hair on his neck stood on end as he twisted his upper body around the doorframe.

The kitchen was empty.

The refrigerator hummed as he limped through the dark room to the window, keeping his body out of sight. He peered through the glass. The moon cast the yard in an ethereal glow, illuminating Beth's white-robed figure on the path near the pool.

She was alone.

He exhaled in relief. Jack snagged one of Danny's old rubber-tipped canes from the umbrella stand by the door. Adrenaline pumped through his veins like water through a fire hose as he stepped outside and followed her.

From the shadow of the house, he watched her enter the pool enclosure and slip out of her robe in the dark. Silvery moonlight bathed her slender limbs. Jack's groin tightened. Tossing the cover onto a patio table, she walked down the steps into the water and began to swim slow, steady laps. Jack eased through the wrought-iron gate and lowered his body into a chair facing the pool. Putting on the safety, he set his gun on a side table.

A bullfrog croaked from the direction of the lake, but his ears honed in on the sound of Beth sliding through the water. The surface glistened with a trail of reflected moonlight as her body cut through the black water in a smooth freestyle. Even though he knew she wasn't naked—he'd seen the outline of a dark-colored tank suit—it was still erotic as hell.

He had a really good imagination, which had no problem peeling the suit from her wet body. In his mind she begged him to touch her. Jack shifted his weight to ease the pressure in his groin. Pain shot through his knee, bringing reality back with a vengeance.

He sucked in a deep breath and let it out slowly. Sweat trickled down his bare back, and his leg ached from the earlier adrenaline rush and the exertion of getting out here. He was going to have to chill if he was really going to retire. Obviously Beth didn't have any criminal intentions this morning. But really, who the hell went swimming outside before the sun came up?

"You almost gave me a heart attack." He spoke to Beth's moving form when she reached the end of the pool where he sat.

She stopped swimming abruptly, spun around with a soft cry, and started treading water in the deep end of the pool.

"Don't you know it's dangerous to swim alone? What if you got a cramp?"

"I...I'm sorry." Eyes wide open with fear, she stammered. "I didn't mean to wake you. I tried to be quiet." The words tumbled from her mouth as her gaze darted back and forth between him and his gun.

He'd scared the crap out of her. Just what she needed.

Good going, O'Malley.

"Sorry, Beth. You didn't do anything wrong. I reacted instinctively. Cop habits die hard." He sighed and decided to take a direct approach. "I won't hurt you or the kids, Beth. You guys don't have to be afraid of me." He rubbed the back of his neck to ease the tension.

"I know." With choppy strokes, she swam toward the ladder. Water sluiced down her slim form as she climbed out of the pool.

She turned toward him and moonlight bathed her skin. She was still too skinny, but nicely shaped, curved in all the right places. Her breasts were just the right size to fill his palms, and despite the warm air, her nipples poked through the wet fabric of her suit. She caught him staring and quickly wrapped her robe around her body.

Jack swallowed and blinked.

As she sank into a chair a few feet away, she clamped her trembling hands together and tucked her legs under the calf-length wrap, covering every inch of lovely skin.

Guilt pricked Jack's conscience. Maybe he could kick a puppy later to round out his day.

"I couldn't sleep and didn't want to wake the kids." She glanced over at him. "You came all the way down here without your crutches! Did you hurt yourself?"

Great, he scared the bejesus out of her while she looked out for his welfare. If he hadn't felt like a total shit before, he did now.

"No, I used a cane." And wasn't that a hit to his already whimpering ego. "No harm done."

She nodded. "I'm glad."

"You know, it's Friday. You've put in more than forty hours already this week. Take the day off; spend it relaxing with the kids. I can handle the place for one day." Jack stretched his long legs out in front of him. "There's a movie theater and a small shopping mall about ten miles down the interstate. It's not exactly a metropolis, but you haven't taken the kids anywhere since you got here. You can take the pickup in the garage anytime. No offense, but your car doesn't look very reliable."

"None taken. It's a piece of shit." She surprised him with that response, and his lips pulled up at the corners. "We don't need much entertainment." She hesitated, then added, "The kids like it here." And it was true. While she'd been working with the horses and tackling the bookkeeping, the kids had spent long days swimming in the pool and touring the grounds with Henry.

"I'm glad to see them settling in. Ben seems to be getting comfortable, but I don't think I've heard Katie say one word."

"She's a little shy, especially around men. She's not used to them. Ben still remembers his father, but Katie was a baby when he died." Beth spoke softly, her voice thick with emotion.

"How did he die?" Jack asked.

"He was killed in a car accident on his way home from the gym. Very ironic, because he was a fireman and I was always so afraid when he went to work. I never thought to be worried when he was off duty." She stopped abruptly.

Jack glanced sideways. Her eyes took on a distant look, and moisture gathered in the corners. She wiped a hand across her cheek.

Now he'd made her cry. *Nice going.*

"I didn't mean to upset you. It's none of my business. I just wondered why they were so quiet all the time," Jack said.

The expression that flashed across her face was one of complete devastation. She had loved her husband very much. A short burst of longing gathered in Jack's chest. If he died tomorrow, no one would miss him like that.

"It's all right. He's been gone seven years now. We coped. Ben had the hardest time understanding. He kept asking when Daddy was coming home. His memories fade a little every year. I wonder if he'll remember his dad at all when he's an adult."

Pale gray colored the horizon. As if the approaching dawn made her uncomfortable with revelations best left in the dark, she rose to leave. "I'd better get dressed. The kids will be up soon."

Jack watched her stride purposefully up the path toward the house. Then he hobbled over to the pool. Ripping open the Velcro of his brace, he set it on the edge and lowered himself into the cool water, easing the duel fires in his knee and groin.

He doubted that seven-year-old grief, no matter how heartfelt, was the reason for her predawn swim. What was the demon that drove her from her bed in the dark? He'd have to walk a careful line to avoid scaring her away.

But he would uncover her secret. And something told him he'd better do it soon.

– – –

After a short soak, Jack limped his way back to the house and changed into dry shorts. As he pulled a faded T-shirt over his head, something crashed in the kitchen.

He poked his head through the doorway. Katie stood in front of the open refrigerator in a large puddle of orange juice. The jagged pieces of the broken glass pitcher were scattered around her bare feet. Juice dripped from the front of the cabinets, the inside of the refrigerator, the front of her skinny legs, and was spreading across the floor. Raw terror flashed across the child's face when Jack walked into the room.

Afraid she would step on a piece of glass, Jack shouted, "Don't move," as he stepped into his sneakers.

Eyes wide, Katie backed away from Jack, oblivious to the shards around her feet.

As he approached, her darting eyes measured the distances between herself and the door and Jack. The realization that the child's panic was a result of her fear of *him*, and not the glass on the floor, gave Jack a sick feeling in his stomach. He lowered his voice as if speaking to a victim.

Because that's clearly what she was.

"Katie, it's OK. I'm not mad. It's only a little spilled juice. I don't want you to cut your feet on that glass on the floor. Please don't move anymore. I'm going to walk toward you now." Jack kept his voice soft and steady as he slowly moved toward the little girl, who was frozen in place. Her green eyes locked on Jack's. By the time he reached her, she was shaking violently.

"I'm going to pick you up now." He put his big hands under her arms and lifted her, holding her away from his body. His knee screamed in protest as he turned and carried her to the other side of the kitchen. His long fingers completely encircled her thin chest. He set her on the counter, pulled over a kitchen chair, and sat down in front of her both to appear smaller and because his leg was about to give out.

The tremor of her lower lip made Jack's heart ache deep in his chest. His physical injury was insignificant compared to the psychological damage this child had endured. He cleared his throat and swallowed his pity.

"Let me check your feet for glass." He reached for a kitchen towel and dried off her legs. His hands dwarfed the child's feet as he checked thoroughly for cuts. "You look OK to me. Does anything hurt?"

Katie shook her head. She was still wide-eyed, but Jack was relieved that her trembling had subsided.

Henry barked from outside the kitchen door. "Why don't you go outside with Henry while I clean this up? I wouldn't want him to cut his paws on any broken pieces of glass. Put some shoes on."

Katie waited for Jack to rise and back away before she slipped from the counter and bolted out the door, grabbing her sneakers on the fly.

He watched through the window as she put both arms around the big dog and buried her face in his furry neck. The dog stood still and waited patiently. Henry turned toward Jack, and met his gaze through the glass with a look of surprising intelligence.

Jack's feelings shifted from sadness to anger at whoever was responsible for Katie's fear. He had seen a lot of abused children in his long career, but he never ceased to be horrified at the torment an adult would inflict upon a helpless child. He cursed under his breath while tossing paper towels on the floor to sop up the juice. *The human race is truly despicable.*

Looking up, he saw Beth standing in the doorway, her face drawn and tight. She'd changed into jeans and a modest tank top.

"Let me help with that." She crossed the room and opened the pantry, taking out a broom and dustpan. She squatted down and began to pick up the larger pieces of broken glass.

Jack's anger deflated as she looked up at him.

"Who hurt her?" he asked softly.

"No one ever hurt Katie," Beth answered, but she refused to meet his gaze and kept her attention firmly focused on the floor. She pushed the rest of the shards and sopping paper towels into the dustpan. Then she dumped the whole mess into the garbage can.

"Then what is she so afraid of?"

Beth didn't answer right away but continued to clean up spilled juice from various surfaces. She returned the cleaning equipment to the pantry, and with slumped shoulders, she softly closed the door. Her hand clenched the knob, and she kept her gaze on the floor. "It's a long story, Jack. I can't talk about it. Please give her some time."

"If you think she needs counseling, I know some good people."

"Not yet." Beth turned to face him. She straightened her shoulders and stood as tall as her tiny frame would allow. "I'm sorry. I know you mean well, but I can't do that right now. I can't explain either. Please don't ask me any more questions. I'm doing the best I can."

"All right," Jack said softly. He knew a futile argument when he saw one. "But remember, I might be able to help."

On impulse he reached out and gave her shoulder a gentle squeeze and was shocked when she didn't flinch. Her eyes widened slightly. Then her gaze shifted from his hand, still resting lightly on her shoulder, to his face. Not only was there no trace of fear in her expression, but he could see that fact surprised the hell out of her, too. Her pupils dilated. His fingertips moved, just an inch, a nearly imperceptible caress across her delicate skin. With a quick intake of breath, Beth drew her lower lip between her teeth, and Jack went hard as stone in one heartbeat. Need began to pulse deep inside him, thrumming through his veins, each beat of his heart urging him closer. To touch. To taste. To take.

With his eyes locked on hers, he leaned toward her. Her scent enveloped him, fueling the primitive longing that flooded through him. His hand slid across her collarbone to encircle the delicate column of her throat, where her skin was like warm satin and her pulse throbbed under his thumb. His gaze dropped to her mouth.

The instant he broke eye contact, Beth blinked. Her jaw tightened and she backed away from the physical contact *almost* before he could register the undeniable surge of heat in her eyes.

Almost—but not quite. Her body wanted him, even if her brain wasn't on board. Jack's hand itched to touch that smooth, bare skin again.

"Beth." He took a half step forward. Beth backed up double that distance, and he let his hand fall to his side. *Shit.* He'd pushed her too far. She dropped her gaze to the floor, her retreat and refusal to look at him clear signs she regretted the moment that had just passed between them.

Moment? Hell, it'd barely been a few seconds. Damned good seconds, though.

"I'm going down to the barn to feed the horses. Ben's already down there." Beth turned away from him and toward the door, pausing at the threshold. "I wish things were different. If you want us to leave, say the word. I understand how we could make you uncomfortable. We're not exactly the Cleavers. You had no idea what you were getting yourself into."

"Beth, I don't want you to leave. I'm not the one that's uncomfortable. This is a good place for kids."

Without turning to face him, she nodded. "You're right. This is a good place. Thank you." She went out the door and onto the patio.

Jack watched her stride down the path toward the barn. Katie and Henry raced to meet her. Beth swung Katie up and hugged her tightly before setting her down and continuing to walk. Beth held her daughter's hand on one side and reached down to scratch Henry's head with the other. The big dog pranced neatly at her side as if he hadn't failed obedience school twice. They entered the grove of trees that separated the barn from the house and disappeared from view.

Jack threw the towel across the kitchen. He wished he knew how to help them. Without information, however, he was powerless. It had taken nearly a week before he could touch her without sending her through the roof, and this latest move had only made things worse. One step forward, twenty steps back. Christ, at this rate, it'd be years before she'd trust him.

His gut told him she didn't have years. She needed help now.

— — —

"Are you OK?" Beth squeezed her daughter's hand as they entered the patch of trees between the house and barn. This early in the morning, the shaded copse was cool, even in midsummer. She inhaled the scent of fresh pine and felt her jagged nerves smooth over—and let the breeze chill her out-of-control libido.

Jack asked far too many questions. And every time he looked at her, she could see the suspicion swimming in his eyes. But there'd been much more than just suspicion in those deep brown eyes this morning. A heated look that sent a quiver through her belly even now. Her skin still tingled where he'd touched her. His hand had been warm and solid, and it had taken all of her resolve to move away from it when she'd really wanted to get closer. He'd been about to kiss her, and God help her, she'd wanted to let him do that and more. She could practically feel his mouth claiming hers, his strong fingers roaming the rest of her body. Her nipples tightened and damp heat pooled between her legs as she pictured the unmistakable desire in Jack's eyes. The impressive torso she'd seen this morning at the pool wasn't helping matters. Jack had a runner's body, broad shoulders, long and lean muscled limbs, the kind of hard physique that made a woman feel soft and utterly feminine.

She realized with a pang of regret that they should go. Find somewhere else to hide. Somewhere she wasn't tempted to let her defenses down again.

"He's not mean." Katie's answer pulled Beth out of her thoughts.

"No, he isn't." Beth's heart squeezed at the surprise in her daughter's voice.

Katie continued, "He's kinda like Uncle James."

It had taken James a while to relate to the kids. Like Jack, the older man had never had any children of his own. After her aunt's death, James had closed himself off. But he'd cared, and eventually Ben and Katie softened his hardened heart. James and the kids had grown close.

"So you're OK staying here with Jack for a while?" Emerging into the sunlit warmth of the barnyard, Beth stopped and turned to face Katie. Her daughter blinked up at her.

"It's nice here." Katie draped one arm around Henry's neck. The dog turned and licked her face. "And I don't want to leave Henry. We don't have to go away, do we?"

Beth closed her eyes and swallowed the lump in her throat.

They really should go. Things here weren't turning out quite the way she'd planned. With a sigh, she raised her eyelids. Katie's lower lip trembled. Beth's resolve crumbled.

Jack might be curious, but she didn't think he posed any danger to them. Not the life-or-death kind she was worried about right now anyway. Still, she should keep her distance.

"No, sweetheart." Beth smiled. "We can stay, for a while anyway."

Katie's grin made Beth's heart ache. "Good. It's pretty here."

A hoof banged against wood.

"We'd better get the horses their breakfast."

Katie turned and skipped toward the barn door.

Eventually she'd have to take her little girl away from here. This wouldn't last forever. Nothing good ever did.

Just as her daughter passed into the barn's shadow, Beth paused, her gaze inexplicably drawn to the thick woods on the far side of the pasture. A naked and vulnerable feeling settled over her, as if she were being watched. The hair on the nape of her neck rose in primitive warning. She pivoted to scan the rest of her surroundings. The only sign of life were thumbnail-sized white butterflies hovering over dandelions in the weedy pasture. She inhaled deeply through her nose and blew the breath out through her mouth.

"What's wrong, Mommy?" Her daughter's voice drew Beth's attention back to the barn entrance, where the little girl waited, eyes opened wide as she read her mother's anxious expression.

Beth smoothed the alarm from her face. "Nothing, honey. Nothing at all."

But as she joined her daughter, goose bumps rose on her arms, and her gaze was pulled back to the dark fringe of forest.

— — —

He lowered the binoculars and sank deeper into the underbrush. The woman couldn't have seen him. Not only was he too far away to be visible to the naked eye, he was completely concealed behind thick foliage like a hunter in a deer blind.

Yet she'd seemed to look right at him.

He raised the binoculars again and watched her turn her attention back to the little girl. After a moment of conversation, they both vanished into the barn.

Sure looked like her, but that wasn't his call.

He had his orders. Follow up on all promising inquiries. Make visual contact. Obtain photos. Report.

On to step three. He had two more possibilities that still needed to be checked out.

He pulled the high-powered digital camera from its case, screwed the super telephoto lens into place, and attached the tripod. Even though the image would be small, with twenty-one megapixels of resolution, the photo could be cropped and enlarged. By the time he was done editing the shots, he'd be able to count the crows' feet around the woman's eyes.

He aimed the camera at the barn door and adjusted the settings. He settled in and waited for her to reappear.

CHAPTER SEVEN

The saddle creaked as Beth trotted Lucy down the forest trail. A thick layer of pine needles blanketed the path, cushioning the horse's footfalls. Settling into a steady two-beat rhythm, a sense of peace washed over her. A half hour on horseback was the best possible therapy. Guilt nagged at her for slipping out alone, but she pushed it away. The kids were content baking cookies with Mrs. Harris. Besides, she needed to recharge. And she *really* needed to think.

There was no question that she had to get her shit together after this morning's back-to-back debacles with Jack. The next time she woke up before dawn, she'd stay the hell in bed and stare at the ceiling.

He'd scared the shit out of her and—worse—he'd known it. Then she'd gone and spilled the beans about Brian. Strike two. Then there'd been Katie's freak-out in the kitchen. Strike three. Beth's chest still hurt when she thought of how Jack had calmed her terrified daughter. For a bachelor, he was surprisingly good with children. He hadn't pressed Beth for answers, but he'd wanted to. She'd seen the questions in his eyes, cop eyes that saw so much more than she wanted him to know. For instance, he probably noticed she hadn't exactly recoiled at his touch. No, she'd barely resisted the urge to wrap her body around his. From now on she'd keep her distance. She couldn't afford to have any personal attachment beyond her children.

Jack wasn't the type of man to let something go. On a positive note, she was fairly sure he wasn't the kind of man to take orders from a dirty politician either. She also couldn't picture Jack raising his hand to a woman—although she no longer trusted her own character assessments. After all, she'd picked Richard. No, Jack would have to be kept at arms' length. If he was developing any personal interest in her, she needed to put a damper on that immediately. Although she doubted flying under his radar was possible at this point, she could at least keep their relationship professional and appropriately formal.

She was sure of only one thing right now. One more screw-up and they'd have to leave. She couldn't afford to have Jack discover her true identity. Richard had too many connections in the police and FBI. If anyone started asking questions, even with the best of intentions, Richard would be sure to get wind of it. He couldn't afford to let her live, not now that she knew his secret.

Breaking Katie's heart—again—would be better than getting them all killed.

A tug on the reins and the sound of rushing water brought Beth back to the moment. Anticipating a good splash, Lucy snorted and picked up the pace as they approached a shallow stream. As the mare pranced, Beth's body flowed with the movement. She stretched her legs farther down Lucy's sides, heels down, seat snug in the small English saddle.

At the water's edge, Beth loosened the reins so the mare could paw the water and gave her elegant neck a pat. She allowed the horse a few minutes to play before turning back. Quiet time was almost up. A hay delivery was scheduled for this morning.

Beth let out some rein, and Lucy lengthened her stride. When they broke free of the woods into the meadow that sat below the barn, she let Lucy have her head. The horse responded with a surge of speed, galloping up the hill. Beth savored the feel of the muscles smoothly shifting beneath her, the mare's long strides eating up the ground. The wind pushed against her face, and her eyes teared. When Lucy headed for the fallen tree, Beth let her go. Together they sailed through the air and landed lightly on the ground on the other side.

Halfway up the slope, the barnyard came into view, and Beth pulled Lucy back down to a trot. A large white truck labeled "Martin's Feed" was backed up to the double doors. She eased Lucy into a walk to cool her down. The mare stretched out her neck as they climbed the slight incline to the barn.

The driver leaned against the fence. His forearms sat on the top rail, and one booted foot rested on the lowest plank. As Beth watched, Jack's golf cart emerged from the trees and stopped next to the barn. Jack got out, using his cane to hobble over to the deliveryman. They shook hands.

Lucy eyeballed the truck and danced sideways as they entered the barnyard. Beth took up the slack in the reins as she steered the horse toward the two men. The visitor was in his late twenties and a few inches shorter than Jack, maybe six-foot, but instead of Jack's tall, rangy body, this man was built like a gorilla, with over-sized biceps and no neck. Dark steely tufts of body hair poked out from the V-shaped neck opening of his tight T-shirt. He wore dark sunglasses and a baseball cap pulled over his short black hair.

"Good morning," Gorilla-man called out. His voice was too smooth, his posture too arrogant.

"Morning," Beth responded but steered Lucy away from him. Instinctively, she wanted as little contact with this slimy guy as possible.

"Hey, Beth." Jack's cell phone rang as he greeted her. He excused himself and took a few steps toward the barn to answer the call.

Gorilla-man glanced at Jack and lowered his voice. "You have a great seat."

Beth paused. Had that comment been laced with sexual innuendo? Or was her imagination getting the best of her?

Dismounting, she loosened the saddle's girth before leading the horse toward the men. Perspiration dripped into her eyes, and she wiped a hand across her brow. Though it had been cool when she'd set out on her ride, the humidity had risen with the sun. She glanced down at her soaked T-shirt, which had molded to her breasts. Thank God she'd worn a padded bra. Although the way this man stared at her, she might as well be topless.

Gorilla-man held out a thick hand. "Will Martin from Martin's Feed Store. Nice to meet you."

Beth gritted her teeth and extended her hand. Just as their palms touched, Lucy snaked her head over Beth's shoulder and pulled her away, cutting the handshake off abruptly.

Beth made a mental note to bring the mare some extra carrots that evening.

"Lucy was Danny's favorite. He didn't ride, but he liked her because she's feisty," Martin commented as he walked around the horse, his eyes traveling over the animal's body, then back to Beth. He gave the mare's shoulder a hard pat. Lucy stomped her foot and swished her tail, pinning her ears back in warning when Martin slapped her rump.

"Nothing like a sassy female." Martin stepped back with a laugh. "Nice lines. Looks like fun to ride." With his face turned away from Jack, Martin leered at Beth.

Her skin crawled.

"If you ever want to sell her, I've got a stud that'd love to service this girl."

Beth's empty stomach rolled. She tied the animal to the fence and took a deep breath. She straightened her shoulders. The sooner she got this over with the better.

"Let's get that stuff unloaded. I'm sure you have other deliveries today." Not waiting for Martin, she strode toward the barn. His stare burned her ass as she climbed up the ladder into the loft. She could hear the murmur of Jack's voice from where he stood near the barn door.

Walking to the edge, she looked down into the aisle. Martin had backed the truck into the barn. He climbed into the back and began tossing hay up into the loft.

Beth dragged the bales to the rear of the space and stacked them neatly against the wall. Martin finished unloading the truck bed and moved up the ladder to help her stack the remaining bales.

"You're pretty strong for such a little thing." His voice was low enough that Jack wouldn't hear him down below. Martin's smile was a sly, teeth-baring smirk.

All the better to eat you with, my dear.

A chill slithered up Beth's spine, and she kept several feet of empty space between her and Gorilla-man. With his help, the remaining hay was stacked in minutes.

"I'm sure you want to finish your deliveries before it gets any hotter." Beth stepped toward the ladder, but Martin maneuvered himself between her body and the exit. She moved to the side, intending to go around him, but he mirrored her steps, blocking the way.

"You're the one that's looking hot." His eyes roamed her body from head to toe. She felt exposed and threatened, like he was mentally stripping her right there in the loft. All the moisture evaporated from her throat.

"Excuse me." She ignored his comment and smoothed her shaky voice. Jack was just outside the door. Surely Martin wouldn't try anything with someone else so close.

"Anytime, sugar." He stepped closely around her, rubbing his hips against hers as he passed. Beth froze at the forced contact with his thick body. Her stomach turned over as his hardened groin brushed her belly, but she refused to back down.

Cowering gave bullies a rush and fueled their cruelty. This she knew from personal experience.

He smelled of sweat and testosterone. Lightheaded, Beth inhaled through her mouth. The hot, stale air in the loft was stifling, suffocating. Exhaling slowly, she willed her heart to slow its frantic beating. As she held her ground, she concentrated on the dust motes floating in the sunbeams streaming through the window.

"I'll get back to you. Thanks." Jack's voice, followed by the sound of his cell snapping shut, floated up to the loft.

Martin nodded. "After you. Ladies first." He stepped aside, but his eyes traveled over her body again, lingering on her breasts. He licked his lips and bared his teeth in another feral grin. Beth broke from her trance and covered the distance to the ladder in a few long strides. She descended rapidly, missing the last rung and landing hard on her heels in the aisle. Her teeth snapped together. Pain ricocheted through her jaw. She felt a hand on her back, steadying her. She glanced over her shoulder at Jack standing behind her. Heat spread from his hand all the way up her spine.

Jack raised his eyebrow in a silent question as she regained her balance. Then he looked up at the big man following her down and narrowed his eyes. Clearly he suspected something had happened up in the loft because he used the large hand still splayed on her back to steer her away from the base of the ladder, behind him. Beth didn't fight it. She backed away, stuck her shaking hands into her front pockets, and focused on calming her frayed nerves. She felt Jack's gaze on her face, but she refused to look at him.

Will whistled a tune as he descended the ladder. "That's it." He grinned at Beth and raised an eyebrow, as if they shared a secret.

Bile rose into her throat, and her heart raced on.

"Nice to meet you, O'Malley. See you next time, Miss Markham." Martin strode out of the barn, got into his truck, and pulled away without waiting for a reply.

Leaning on his cane, Jack followed Martin out into the yard.

Jack didn't say anything for a few moments. He stared down the road at the retreating truck, his mouth a grim, tight line.

Walking out of the barn to finish untacking Lucy, Beth avoided his gaze when he looked back at her. Her body tensed as Jack approached.

"You all right?"

"I'm fine." As if to dispute her statement, her hands shook as she unbuckled the saddle's girth and lifted it off the horse's back.

"What happened up there?"

"Nothing, really. I'm overreacting. Probably the heat." She turned away and set the saddle on the fence rail. Returning to Lucy, she began to brush the mare's back, removing the outline of caked sweat and dirt where the saddle had been.

To Beth's surprise, Jack picked up a brush and stepped closer to the horse—closer to Beth—close enough that she could feel the warmth from his body. If she moved three inches to her left, their arms would touch. The warm spot on her back reminded her how strong and solid his was.

Beth retreated to brush splatters of mud from the mare's hind legs, putting a few feet of space between herself and Jack. His shadow enveloped her. She caught a whiff of his scent on the breeze, coaxing her to turn toward him instead of away. Not far enough. She moved to clean the horse's other side.

Jack was talking to the horse as he ran the brush down her face, his voice deep and soothing. Though directed at the mare, Jack's voice calmed Beth, too. As she worked and Jack talked, her hands gradually stopped shaking. He moved to stand in front of the horse and brush dried sweat from behind the mare's ears. Lucy leaned against him, rubbing her big head up and down his side. Beth envied the horse. She wanted to lean into Jack and let him wrap his arms around her. But that wasn't possible.

Jack scratched under the mare's thick mane. "Once you get past the size, horses are OK. They're like really big, extra-smelly dogs."

Unable to respond, Beth concentrated on a spot of dried mud on Lucy's foreleg. Her children's lives depended on keeping their identities a secret. She couldn't afford to trust anyone.

"Beth."

She stood and turned to face him. Especially not an ex-cop who still had strong ties to the police force.

"Listen, next time Martin comes, let me handle the delivery. Or we can look into getting another supplier."

"No. It's OK. I can handle it." Beth raised her chin and met his gaze head-on. If she started giving into her fears, she'd be overwhelmed in no time. She'd never be able to get up each morning.

"Some guys are assholes, Beth. You can't change them, but you don't have to be alone with them either. There's no sense in making yourself an easy target. Martin's a big guy. If I'm not here, make sure someone else is around." Jack stroked Lucy's nose. "Maybe I'm paranoid, but I'm a cop. Was a cop," he corrected with a brief tightening of his mouth that he quickly smoothed over. "There are some nasty people out there, and I have a feeling Martin's one of them."

No kidding.

"Thanks, I'll be careful." Beth knew all about nasty people.

Jack nodded. "I trust my instincts about people. You should do the same."

Yeah, right.

Her instincts were the last things she could rely on. Her instincts wanted to turn to Jack for comfort. Her instincts wanted Jack's hands all over her naked body. Those same instincts had gotten her into this mess.

– – –

Jack tossed his magazine onto the table and glanced outside at the setting sun. Over the mountains, the cloudless sky had faded to pale pink. He turned back to the kitchen to watch his housekeeper pull a stick of butter and a carton of eggs from the fridge. A wild Friday night on the O'Malley estate.

"I wonder where Beth and the children are?" Mrs. Harris glanced up at the clock before turning her attention back to assembling ingredients on the counter. "I told them I was baking cookies, and it doesn't usually take them this long to feed the horses."

Jack followed her eyes to the clock. It was nearly eight. Since they'd arrived, Beth and the kids had been back from their evening barn chores by seven thirty. Jack's gut clenched as a sudden spark of suspicion coursed through him.

Had they run away?

Martin had done something to frighten Beth this morning. Had that asshole scared her so much that she'd bolted? She was already so tense. It wouldn't take much to set her off.

"Maybe I should go see what's keeping them." As he hauled his butt out of the chair, the kids and dog emerged from the patch of trees between the house and the barn. No Beth, but they were still here. Suspicion gave way to curiosity. What was keeping her? It'd be dark soon, and he didn't like the idea of her being alone in the barn.

Ben stepped inside. Katie slipped through the open door behind him, trying to keep one eye on Jack while checking out what Mrs. Harris was doing at the counter. Henry ran to his bowl to check for food, although he'd already been fed. Always the optimist.

Ben cleared his throat. "Mom wants you to call the vet."

That can't be good.

Jack turned to Mrs. Harris. "Any idea where I'd get that number?"

"Check your uncle's Rolodex. The vet's name is Dr. White. If it's not there, you can call Jeff Stevens. He'll have it."

Jack faced Ben again. "What should I tell him?"

"Lucy's colicking."

"He'll know what that means?"

Ben nodded.

"OK." Dr. White's number was not in Danny's Rolodex, so Jack called his neighbor, then the vet. When Jack returned to the kitchen, Mrs. Harris had enlisted the children's help with her baking. Katie was perched on a stool, stirring batter with a wooden spoon. Ben was rooting through the pantry. Henry stretched out on the floor behind the kids, waiting for someone to drop something.

Katie froze for a second as Jack passed through the room. Then she went right back to stirring. Jack fought a smile. Progress.

"Vet's on his way."

Ben set a bag of chocolate chips onto the counter and moved toward the door. "I'll go tell Mom."

Outside the sun had dipped behind the treetops, casting long shadows across the yard. Children shouldn't be running around in the dark either.

Jack brushed past him. "It's OK, Ben. I've got it. They're my horses. Time I learned something about them." He hobbled down to the garage, stowed his cane in the golf cart, and drove to the barn. The stable was quiet as he entered. Some hay rustled and an animal snorted. Beth leaned on Lucy's half door, resting her chin on her crossed arms. Jack checked the stalls as he walked through. The other horses had been turned out into the pasture for the night.

"How is she?" He stepped up beside Beth and looked over the stall door. His arm rested against her shoulder. Beth, too absorbed in watching and worrying about the horse, didn't move away from him.

A ridiculous sense of satisfaction bubbled up in Jack's chest.

The mare stood in the center of the dim stall. An unhealthy sheen covered her copper flanks, and her sides heaved. She turned her head around and nipped at her belly, then paced a nervous circle.

"So far, not too bad." Beth didn't take her eyes off the horse. "Did you get hold of the vet?"

"Yeah. Anything we can do in the meantime?"

Beth shook her head. "As long as she's quiet, I'll just watch her."

They stood in silence for a few minutes. The horse turned in another circle and pawed at the ground.

"Shit." Beth grabbed a rope hanging on the wall and slipped through just as the horse lowered herself onto her knees, then her side.

"What are you doing?" Jack's breath locked in his throat. He didn't know much about horses, other than they were fucking big, but he was pretty sure going into the stall wasn't the best idea.

Beth moved toward Lucy's head. "Can't let her roll."

Which was exactly what Lucy had in mind. The mare turned onto her back. Hooves flailed in the air. Beth jumped to the side, but not before a thrashing hoof caught her on the calf. Her leg went out from under her, and she fell onto her hip in the straw. Another hoof missed her skull by inches. Beth ducked and rolled out of the way, coming up against the wall hard.

"Get the hell out of there!" Jack's heart jackhammered. He opened the door and stepped inside, looking for a way to get between Beth and the horse. Not possible. Beth was on the other side of a thousand pounds of thrashing animal. Jack wasn't carrying his gun. No chance of shooting the horse before it smashed Beth's head in.

Beth pushed herself up on her hands and knees. The horse rolled back to its side and gathered its body to turn over again. Beth launched herself at the mare's head and grabbed hold of the halter. She clipped the lead rope into place and gave it a sharp jerk. "Come on, Lucy, Get up."

The mare resisted, shaking her head and trying to use it as leverage to turn over again. Beth yanked the rope up, stopping her. "Up!"

Chin up, Lucy balked, rolling her eyes and exposing the whites.

"No, you don't." Beth pulled the rope behind her butt and used her weight to pull on the mare's head. With a huge groan, the horse shifted forward, gathered her long legs under her body, and heaved to her feet.

The air rushed from Jack's lungs.

"Good girl." Beth crooned words of praise, cradling Lucy's head in her arms and rubbing her nose in obvious relief. Straw stuck to the mare's damp coat. The giant body gave a slight shudder.

As his panic subsided, the blood rushed from Jack's head, making him lightheaded. "You could have been killed!" His voice came out louder than he'd planned.

"Keep your voice down. I'm trying to calm her down." The admonishment was delivered in the same soothing tone she'd used on the horse.

Beth led the mare out of the stall, up the aisle, and out into the barnyard, where she proceeded to walk in a large circle. Both of them seemed to have forgotten about the previous, terrifying moments, which had burned into Jack's memory for eternity.

"She wasn't doing it on purpose. She's in pain. If I let her roll, she could twist an intestine. Then she'd have to be put down." Beth stroked the wet neck as she continued to walk the horse slowly around. Lucy's skin quivered. "Can't let that happen, can we, sweetheart?"

If it were up to him, he'd put the beast down before he ever let Beth take another risk like that. He liked animals and all, but not enough to sacrifice a woman with two small children. The idea of losing Beth made his chest hurt.

Where was the damned vet?

An engine rumbled behind the barn. A minute later, Jack was surprised to see Jeff Stevens hurry into the barnyard. What was he doing here? Jack had called him for the vet's number, but he hadn't expected Jeff to rush right over. He didn't know Jeff very well, but he knew the guy lived alone in that big farmhouse. Guess he didn't have anything else to do. Didn't seem to have much of a social life.

The neighbor didn't pause to greet Jack but hurried immediately to Beth's side, his attention riveted on the horse. "How is she?"

"Not too bad right now." Beth stopped walking.

Jeff curled back the horse's lip and pressed a finger to her gums. He lifted an eyelid; then he pressed his head to her side and nodded. "She's prone to spasmodic colic every so often. It's usually not too serious, but she works herself up." He gave her neck a light pat. "Any Ace in the tack room?"

Beth shook her head. "I didn't see any."

"I have some back at my place. If the vet doesn't show up soon, I'll run home and get it," Jeff said, "but I'd rather Doc White looked at her first."

The mare began to paw again. Beth pulled on the rope and resumed walking, this time with a subtle limp. Christ, Jack had forgotten the blow she'd taken to the leg.

He shook himself out of his stupor. Something about Beth, and his reaction to her presence, kept all of his neurons from firing. "Jeff, can you walk the horse for a few minutes? I'd like to talk to Beth for a minute."

"Sure." Jeff took over.

Beth limped over. "What is it?"

He raised his eyebrows and looked down at her leg. No blood, but her jeans were torn. "Let me take a look at that."

"It's nothing. Just a bruise."

"If you have a cut, it needs to be cleaned right away." Lucy's hooves were covered in manure and dirt. Visions of tetanus and sepsis swam in Jack's head. Who'd have thought a few horses could be so much trouble? Why the hell had Danny bought them? Christ, when normal people wanted a pet, they got a cat, not four animals that outweighed compact cars.

Beth's jaw tensed. Her weight shifted back a hair as she fought the urge to move away from him. Maybe he'd scared her earlier when he'd shouted, but she'd been too concerned about the horse to react. Or maybe she was more afraid she'd respond to his touch the way she had in the kitchen. Didn't matter. Either way, he had to make sure she was OK.

She exhaled and nodded. "You're right."

Jack lowered his body onto a wooden bench next to the barn door and set the emasculating cane aside.

Beth bent to pull her pant leg up, but her calf had already begun to swell. She cut off a soft gasp of pain. The jeans wouldn't budge. Jack grasped both sides of the tear and ripped the denim all the way to the hem. Beth jumped, but Jack ignored her. If she was going to pull stupid stunts, she had to expect to get hurt.

He wrapped one hand around a slender ankle and turned the injury to the light cast by the fixture over the barn door. Sure enough, a bruise was already coloring the side of her leg and had swelled into a softball-sized lump. The skin wasn't broken, so no fear of infection, just an insult to the otherwise perfectly smooth skin on which his hand lingered.

He lifted his eyes to look at her face. She was staring at his hand on her ankle, too. She met his gaze and blinked. Her face flushed as she realized he'd caught the look, which held no trace of alarm. Desire, however, was a distinct possibility. His thumb stroked the soft skin just above her anklebone. Under his fingertips, her pulse quickened. He couldn't be sure in the dim light, but her eyes seemed to darken.

Headlights appeared on the access road to the barn and swept across the barnyard.

With his fingers still wrapped around Beth's delicate ankle, Jack cleared his throat. "You should put some ice on that."

"Later." Beth pulled her leg from his grasp, shook her torn pant leg down, and returned to the horse's side. A plain white van pulled up into the yard, and a gray-haired man stepped out. Dr. White's six-and-a-half-foot frame was clad in extra-large green coveralls and huge muck-covered work boots.

Jeff introduced Dr. White to Beth and Jack. For a split second, Jeff's gaze met Jack's with surprising venom, then smoothed over. Was he jealous? Did Jeff have a thing for Beth? Not hard to believe. Jeff was a semi-recluse, more comfortable with his horses than humans, and Beth was beautiful—and nice. Most good-looking women wouldn't give a guy like Jeff the time of day, but Beth treated him with kindness. A crush on Beth would certainly explain why Jeff had rushed over here tonight. It didn't really matter. Beth didn't show any signs of reciprocating.

The vet gave the horse a quick examination, devoting considerable time to listening to her belly with a stethoscope. He rubbed her neck. "Same old, same old, huh, Luce?" He returned to his van, filled a syringe, and injected it into Lucy's neck. "Gave her a very light dose of Ace. She should start to improve in the next thirty minutes to an hour. Walk her twenty minutes every hour…" he glanced at his watch. "Until 'bout midnight. Then, as long as she's quiet, you can put her into her stall, but keep an eye on her. Call me if she gets any worse. I'll leave you with another dose in case you need it. I'll send the bill to the house, Jack. Gotta go see a sick cow over at the Walsh place."

That was it? He was leaving? Jack looked to Beth, then Jeff. Neither of them seemed the least bit shocked that the vet was going to leave them with this sick and possibly violent horse.

Jeff took over walking so Beth could follow the vet to his van. The doctor handed her a plastic bag before climbing in and driving off. Beth stowed the package in the barn and returned to the horse, taking the rope from Jeff.

They walked for another twenty minutes. Full darkness had descended on the yard, which Jack decided needed better lighting. And he was calling tomorrow to have a phone installed in the barn. Damned cell service was too spotty out here. Finally, Beth checked her watch and stopped. Lucy's head hung lower. She didn't paw or snort, and her breathing seemed to have eased.

Beth's head seemed to hang lower, too. She looked tired, but she'd probably walked a couple of miles with the horse. Food might perk her up. "You gonna be here for a few minutes, Jeff?" Jack called. "I have to run up to the house real quick."

"Yeah, I'll stay till you get back."

Beth stroked the horse's jaw and called out, "Would you check on the kids while you're there?"

"Sure. Be right back."

Katie had fallen asleep on the sofa in the living room. Her hair was still damp, and she was in her pajamas. Mrs. Harris sat next to her, watching television.

"Ben's in the shower." She kept her voice low and anticipated his next question. "There's a thermos of coffee and some cookies in a bag on the counter."

"Thanks. Sounds like we're going to be there a while."

Mrs. Harris nodded. "Colic can be an all-nighter."

Wonderful. By the time he returned to the barn, food in hand, Beth was sending Jeff on his way.

"I'm a phone call away if you need anything." Jeff gave the horse a gentle pat on the shoulder.

"Thanks, Jeff. You were a big help."

His dorky neighbor seemed to expand at the compliment. Did she have to sound so grateful? And why didn't she use that appreciative tone with him instead of Jeff? Jack set the bag of food down on the bench and walked Jeff to the beat-up jeep he'd parked behind the barn.

After Jeff's taillights had started bumping their way across the meadow toward his farm, Jack turned his attention back to Beth and the horse. They lapped the barnyard a few more times, then stopped to rest again.

"Here." Jack handed her a travel cup of coffee. "Sit down for a few. There are cookies in the bag." He reached for the lead rope.

Beth paused, obviously unsure of his ability to handle the animal, even now that it was drugged and compliant. "You sure?" Her doubt was understandable, but it still stung.

He nodded. A wry smile pulled at his face. "I think I can handle standing still with her for a couple of minutes since she's quiet."

"Thanks." Beth sank onto the bench in an exhausted slump.

"I should be thanking you. This is my horse you've been walking all evening." The mare's muzzle was soft as velvet under Jack's stroking fingers.

"It's my job, remember?" Beth worked her way through several cookies, chasing them down with long swigs of coffee. The single, dim overhead light deepened the shadows under her eyes. How long would she insist on watching the horse?

"Really, you've gone above and beyond."

"You obviously don't know many horse people." Beth grinned. "This isn't all that abnormal."

Jack gave the mare a rueful look. "Who'd have thought something so big could be so fragile." He shifted his gaze back to Beth.

Or that something that looks so fragile could be so strong.

Somewhere around midnight the horse left a steaming pile of manure in the barnyard and emitted several unladylike digestive sounds that inordinately thrilled his new caretaker. Beth smiled and rubbed Lucy's neck. "She'll feel much better now."

"That was it?" Couldn't be. Beth couldn't possibly have risked a hoof in the head because the horse had gas.

Beth led a placid Lucy into her stall. The tranquil mare stood with her head in the corner, eyes closed. "If we're lucky."

Horses were a pain in the ass.

Beth leaned on the half door and rested her head on her forearms. Exhaustion had drained her face of all color and animation. That was when Jack realized she had no intention of leaving the barn for the duration of the night. Which meant he was in for a long night, too. There was no way he could sleep in his comfortable bed while Beth played nursemaid to his sick horse and possibly tried to maim herself again. He limped into the tack room and grabbed two chairs. The wooden seats wouldn't be very comfortable but were way better than standing up for the rest of the night. His knee ached like a mother.

The look of surprise on Beth's face when he set them in the aisle was well worth losing a night's sleep. After barely a second of thought, she sat down next to him, too tired to move the chair further away. And when his arm settled against hers, she didn't move.

No more than thirty minutes passed before her head dropped onto his shoulder. While she dozed, Jack leaned closer and did something he couldn't do when she was awake. He inhaled the scent of her. Under a layer of hay dust, she smelled like strawberries and woman, a heady mix that sent extra blood rushing to his groin despite the pain in his knee and the uncomfortable chair.

In his imagination she turned her face to his, her eyes open and filled with desire. And, of course, she was naked.

If only there was some way to turn his dream into reality.

CHAPTER EIGHT

Thump. His cargo shifted in the trunk as the car passed over a large pothole.

"Sorry, darling," he called aloud to the empty vehicle—as if an apology was meaningful at this point.

He lowered the car window and breathed the damp night air deep into his lungs. What a wonderful evening! Of course, his date hadn't had quite as much fun, but then he hadn't intended for *her* to enjoy herself. He chuckled to himself as he slowed the car, looking for the narrow gravel lane that led to his favorite dump site.

A half mile after passing the green sign announcing he'd entered South Bend, Pennsylvania, he put his foot on the brake and made the turn.

An owl hooted from the depths of the dark forest as he pulled his sedan into the clearing and parked. No one lived in the old two-story saltbox anymore. Built too close to the water in a low area prone to flooding, the riverfront home had been abandoned years earlier. Wind and rain had stripped the paint from the once-white porch. Windows that weren't boarded up were broken. Weedy vines claimed the foundation and the first few feet of faded yellow clapboards.

Beyond the house, a decaying floating dock pointed out over the dark water like a bent, arthritic finger.

He got out of the car. Letting his eyes adjust to the darkness, he hefted the large, tarp-wrapped bundle from the trunk and threw it over his shoulder. It was lucky he preferred his dates to be petite.

Since storm clouds smothered the moonlight, he fished a flashlight from his pocket and trained the narrow beam of light directly on the dock in front of him. At the end, he set the bundle down, spreading his feet to balance himself on the undulating dock.

Without the additional weight, the trip back to the car to retrieve three cinder blocks took only a minute. He used to use only two, but a few weeks before, one of his previous packages had broken loose and drifted downstream to be discovered near the public access ramp just days after he'd dumped her. He didn't mind them popping up, but the longer the bodies stayed under-water, the better.

Quickly unwrapping the bundle, he secured the blocks with nylon rope and rolled the body into the water, temporarily dis-turbing the thick layer of greenish-brown scum on the surface. The head went under first. Long, dark hair swirled in the beam of his flashlight. A pair of slender bare feet tipped out of the water briefly before sinking in an eddy.

Yes, he knew for a fact that his date hadn't enjoyed her eve-ning.

He swatted absently at a mosquito on his arm as he folded up his tarp and jogged back to his car. Thunder rumbled. The com-ing storm would wash away any trace of his visit, but he gave the ground a quick scan just in case.

Humming cheerfully, he headed back toward Westbury on the interstate, satisfied with a job well done. The ride wouldn't take more than ninety minutes, much better than the long distances he used to travel. Despite the fact that he'd reduced the size of his hunting and disposal circle, the police were no closer to identifying him. They were totally clueless. What did he have to do to make eluding them a challenge?

He'd take a few weeks off, a well-deserved rest. Then it would be time to decide on another beauty. Just to keep things interesting, no more random selections. He'd already made a list of likely candidates.

Now, he only had to make up his mind which one was going to be the lucky woman.

There was one who'd caught his eye. Westbury's newest resident was beautiful and brunette, with equal doses of spunk and timidity to spice things up. She was very close to home, though, which posed a whole new level of risk. As did the fact that she lived with an ex-cop.

Was he ready to up the stakes?

CHAPTER NINE

Jack sat on the padded table, legs extended, hands gripping the sides.

"Pull," Barry, physical therapist from hell and sadist extraordinaire, ordered Jack in a tone that would've impressed Sergeant Hulka. Oversized biceps bulged beneath the sleeves of his skintight polo. Barry's juice of choice probably wasn't orange.

Jack braced himself for the pain and pulled his heel toward his butt. Bending his knee should not be this difficult. Surgery number two had been about as useful as a cap gun in a shootout.

"Come on, Jack." Barry would've wowed 'em in the Spanish Inquisition. "Harder."

Jack panted. Sweat rolled down his temple into his eye. But no amount of willpower could make his knee bend any farther. Barry "helped" him, putting one hand behind Jack's knee and grasping his ankle. Bright colors exploded behind Jack's eyelids as the scar tissue gave another inch.

"Not bad." Barry nodded with satisfaction. "At your age, you can't expect miracles."

Dick.

"Now let's straighten it."

Oh, goody. Jack bit back a gasp as he pushed his foot toward the foot of the table. His lungs worked like a fireplace bellows, and his kneecap exploded in pain. Unbelievably, extending his leg hurt more than fucking bending it.

"That's great, Jack." The condescending little shit patted Jack on the shoulder. "Good job today."

Great wasn't the word on the tip of Jack's tongue.

"All right. Let's get you up and moving."

Jack swung his legs over the side of the table and lowered his feet to the floor. At least he was motivated for the next part of his PT session. His career might be in the tank, but he would walk again. And he'd do it without the effing cane.

Barry wrapped the brace around Jack's leg and fastened the Velcro straps. "I loosened the hinge so your leg can bend sixty degrees. This is mainly for lateral stability."

Barry handed him the crutches. "Last time we did seventy-five percent of your body weight. Let's try a couple of steps without any assistance. The crutches are only there if you feel like you're going to fall." Barry stood in front of him. "Take it easy now."

Jack stepped forward and transferred his weight to his injured leg slowly. Stability was more of an issue than strength, and walking was not as painful as the flexion exercises. He rolled his weight forward and stepped through with an exhalation of relief. The leg held, but he wouldn't be appearing on *Dancing with the Stars* next season.

Or any other season for that matter.

After twenty minutes of quality time with a jumbo-size ice pack, Jack showered, changed, and limped out to his Explorer. Heaving his exhausted body into the driver's seat, he dragged his left leg into position under the dashboard. Pain shot through the joint.

Shit.

It was time he faced it. He was never going back to the force. The captain had made noises about a transfer to a less physically demanding position, but a desk job or spot in public relations appealed about as much as an IRS audit. Maybe less.

He started the truck and switched the air conditioner on full to combat the assault of the midday August sun.

As he leaned back against the headrest, a picture of Beth's pale face at breakfast this morning popped into his mind. The episode with Lucy in the barn last night had taken its toll on her, as had yesterday morning's incident with Will Martin. The horse couldn't help being sick, but Martin made a conscious decision to be an asshole.

Could it have just been the heat that had unsettled her so thoroughly? No. Definitely not. Her hands had been shaking. When she'd ridden into the barnyard, her face had held an attractive flush from exercise and the obvious pleasure riding brought her. After she'd finished in the loft, a mere fifteen minutes later, she'd looked traumatized—no, victimized. Afterward Beth had pulled herself together by sheer force of will, but Jack had been acutely aware of her vulnerability.

What had Will Martin done up in that loft to intimidate Beth? Anger rose in Jack's chest.

He made a mental note to talk to Mike O'Connell, the local police chief, about Will Martin. In the meantime, he would find out if there were any other feed suppliers in the area. He wondered if Beth knew anything about self-defense. He could show her a few moves, but she wasn't comfortable with physical contact. Jack had a bad feeling deep in his gut that Beth was in danger. He'd learned to trust his instincts. He'd get Beth a canister of pepper spray. That stuff could take down a bear. If all else failed, well, there was always Sean, who would have no qualms with helping Jack give Martin a very private message.

– – –

The mystery surrounding his new employee made the back of his neck itch. But he still couldn't put his finger on what exactly was wrong. Nothing about Beth's actions set off his criminal-ometer. She and her kids acted like victims. It was far more likely she was running away from something. Or someone. She was a smart woman, so she must have a good reason. But, damn it, he couldn't help them if he didn't know what they were up against. Since she seemed determined to remain tight-lipped, he'd have to start looking for answers elsewhere. He'd have to be careful, though, and keep his investigation firmly under the radar. Who knew what she'd do if she found out he was digging into her secrets.

He didn't have access to records anymore, but he knew some-one who did.

He switched on his Bluetooth and speed-dialed Wes's cell. Jack hadn't set foot in his former station since his injury. But his gut was firmly telling him his new employee needed help, so it looked like the time had come.

He trusted his former partner with his life—and Beth's.

– – –

Two hours later Jack parked in a visitors' slot in front of the butt-ugly concrete square that housed the South Bend Police Department. Despite the pain he was sure to endure later, he left his cane in the car. His former coworkers would feed off it like sharks on chum. Cops protected each other against outsiders, but hazing within the ranks was brutal.

With a deep breath, he pushed through the glass door. The receptionist gave him a finger wave as she answered her phone. Jack skirted the front desk and limped toward the door that led to the main room. As he pushed through, a cacophony of ringing phones reverberated against metal desks, industrial linoleum, and cheap ceiling tiles.

In his head, Jack cringed. How many years had he worked here? Had it always been this loud and dirty?

Working his way through a sea of back pats, handshakes, and "hi, how are ya's," Jack weaved through a maze of cubicles to Wes's desk in the far corner. Wes was on the phone. His friend held up one finger.

Working hard to keep a straight face, Jack nodded to the slim man at the next desk, Wes's new partner, Brandon Stiles, otherwise known as "Jonas" for his resemblance to the lead singer of Disney's boy band. Someone had taped an autographed picture of the pop star to the front of his desk. Although he had to be close to thirty, the baby-faced boy wonder could still pass for a teenager, which had been good for his career. Before Jack's accident, Jonas had been on an undercover narcotics assignment at a local high school.

Jack watched as Jonas grimaced at his computer screen. The corners of his eyes wrinkled ever so slightly. Looked like Peter Pan was going to have to leave Neverland.

Wes hung up the phone and stood up to greet him. Jack leaned in to shake his hand. "If you can ditch Jonas for an hour, I'll buy you a late lunch."

"No problem." Wes snorted and turned to his partner. "Hey, Jonas, why don't you get started on that paperwork from this morning's stiff while you wait for your agent to call."

Jonas flipped Wes the bird without looking up from his screen.

Wes grinned. "He's just pissed 'cause somebody inter-officed him a purity ring."

Jack snickered. He felt bad for Jonas, but what was the kid thinking? He was wearing a fucking pink shirt under a thin-lapelled gray suit jacket. And those tight-legged pants were probably high fashion on the club scene, but with this testosterone-pumped lot, the kid might as well post a "kick me" sign on his back. The police station rivaled a frat house any day of the week.

Of course, today it looked more like a frat house than ever. Was it his imagination, or was everyone in the room at least fifteen years younger than he and Wes? Jack scanned faces, noting that a few familiar ones were missing. "Hey, where's Dan?"

"Retired." Wes snagged his cell phone from his desk. "Took the package the second it was available."

"Phil?"

"Out on disability. Herniated disk."

OK. He and Wes *were* the oldest guys in the room. *Shit.* He didn't belong here anymore, and not just because of his knee. Had the murder and mayhem phase of his life run its course?

Jack followed his friend out into the lobby, struggling to keep pace and ignore the pain now slamming through his leg thanks to his juvenile ego. In the parking lot, Wes automatically headed for his police issue. Jack followed, sliding into the passenger seat of the unmarked sedan. He pulled an empty Subway bag from behind his back and tossed it on the floor, where it joined a couple of Power Bar wrappers. A few chest pains over the winter, which thank God had turned out to be heartburn, had prompted his partner to embrace a lifestyle change that involved eliminating cigarettes and greasy food.

"How's the kid as a partner?"

"OK, I guess. Young." Wes sighed. He glanced at Jack's leg. "You OK?"

Jack looked down. He'd been unconsciously rubbing his knee. "Yeah. Any progress on the case?" Jack didn't have to specify. The body that had been pulled out of the Watkins Rivers a couple of weeks before had been determined to be a victim of the Riverside Killer. He and Wes had handled a number of homicides each year, but they'd never worked a case involving a serial killer.

"Not much." Wes reached into the front pocket of his worn sport coat for a pack of gum. He popped a stick into his mouth and tilted the pack toward Jack.

Jack shook his head.

"South Bend's playin' the ugly stepsister to the Feds, thank God. Some of the guys are pissy about it, but we all know we're just not equipped to do the job right." Wes sighed. "There have been four victims that we know of: all small females between twenty-five and forty, attractive, dark hair. The women were tranquilized shortly before death with acepromazine, also known as Ace, ACP, and Atravet. It's a veterinary sedative, commonly used in cats, dogs, and horses. So we're looking hard at vets in New Jersey and Pennsylvania.

"All the women were raped, tortured, and strangled before being dumped into the water. Bodies were weighted down with ordinary cinder blocks and tied up with plain old nylon rope. Four bodies dumped in two different states, and we're still SOL."

"Any luck identifying the women?"

"No." Wes shook his head. "We're going through missing person's reports again. Three of the women had various STDs and two were users."

"Hookers or homeless?"

"That's the working hypothesis." Wes turned into the parking lot of his favorite Italian restaurant and slid into a spot by the door. It was smack dab between lunch and dinner, so the lot was nearly empty. "We're also pulling files and looking for the usual suspects: paroled and released sex offenders, rapists, etc. There's enough of those on the loose to keep us busy for a long time."

Jack commiserated, "Too bad we can't convict violent offenders on tax evasion. They'd serve more time."

Wes agreed with a disgusted noise.

Inside, they slid into a booth. A middle-aged waitress stopped by with glasses of ice water and took their order. Normally Jack would've peppered Wes with more questions about the investigation. But today, the thought of tracking a serial killer had no appeal. What the hell was wrong with him? This case was bigger than anything he'd handled in his entire career, yet his brain backed out of the conversation. "If you need a break, come on out to the mountains. I have a six-pack of Evian with your name on it."

Wes snorted. "If I truck my ass all the way up to Bum Fuck, PA, there'd better be a beer waiting."

"I thought you quit drinking."

"Shit. Give me a break. I quit smokin' and eatin' anything that I like." Wes reached for the bread basket and selected a hunk of garlic bread.

"Admirable." Jack nodded. "But if you want to lose that spare tire, you're gonna have to visit a gym once in a while."

"Fuck you. I lost ten pounds."

"From where? Your head?" Jack shrugged. "You really think Diane's gonna want to come back to that fat and saggy old ass?" They both knew Diane's departure had nothing to do with Wes's gut.

"You suck." With a disgusted huff, Wes tossed the bread back into the pile. "We'll make it a light beer, then."

"She call?"

"Yeah." Wes picked at his napkin. "Wants me to leave the force. Says twenty-five years is long enough to play second string in a marriage." Wes's chest pains had been a revelation to his wife, too. Apparently, she'd had enough of the same-old, same-old routine.

"She right?"

"I don't know. What the fuck would I do with myself? I don't have any hobbies, and I hate fishing."

"You could just sit around and get uglier."

"Dick." Wes flicked a crumpled napkin at Jack's head. "So how's the knee, really? You ever gonna be useful again?"

"It ain't lookin' good." Jack sighed. "May have to trade in my badge for a rocking chair. Maybe I'll take up whittling."

"Glad I'm not that old." Wes grinned. He was six months older than Jack, but the coal-black hair he'd inherited from his Shawnee mother refused to gray. "So why are you really down here? I mean, I'm glad to see your ugly mug, but you have something on your mind."

Jack scanned the empty dining room. He lowered his voice so the waitstaff in the kitchen wouldn't hear him. "I need you to do me a favor, very quietly."

"How quiet?"

Jack leaned closer. "Cone of silence."

Wes nodded. "OK."

"I need some information on a woman." Jack spelled Beth's full name and provided Wes with her Social Security number and driver's license information as well. "Whatever you can find without attracting any attention."

"No problem. Give me a couple of days." If Wes was surprised by Jack's request, he kept it to himself.

CHAPTER TEN

A flash of color appeared among the trees. He adjusted the lens of his camera. Beth and the children emerged from the woods and walked toward the barn. The little girl skipped by her mother's side, while the boy walked a few paces ahead.

He zoomed in, turning the camera vertically to cut the children out of the picture.

Click.

He checked the LCD screen and zoomed out for a full body shot.

Her jeans were faded and worn, the denim molded to her body by age. Small breasts bobbed under the thin fabric of her T-shirt. He adjusted the focus, pressed the shutter.

Click.

She was definitely the one.

The thought of lying awake thinking about her for another night tormented him. She was going to be the perfection he craved. His heartbeat accelerated as he pictured her lovely face and petite, toned body, forced to submit to him in terror.

Placing her hands on her knees, she leaned forward to talk to the child. His finger slid to the shutter release button. The top of the little girl's head popped back into the frame at the last second.

He waited until the child moved out of the way.

Click.

Through the camera's lens, he sized up the boy. He was taller than his mother, but still lanky, a bit uncoordinated, not much of a threat.

He shifted his position in the tree and zoomed in for a close-up. Her dark hair was bound into a ponytail, which swung with her stride. The breeze gusted. A few tendrils of hair escaped the elastic band and blew around her head.

Click.

She lifted her chin and scanned the overcast sky with a small frown. The delicate bone structure of her face, her wide green eyes, and her full lips were flawless. Classic.

Click.

She pushed a stray hair away from her face and tucked it behind her ear.

Click.

They disappeared into the barn. When they emerged, Beth led a fat bay gelding to the fence and wound the rope around the top rail. She bent over at the waist and picked up one of the horse's hooves. The faded denim stretched across her buttocks.

Click.

He slid the camera back into its case and stowed it in his backpack. Then he took out a notebook and diligently recorded the time of her arrival and departure at the barn. This would be the greatest catch of his career, his own personal playoff. After he finished with her, he'd need to move on to a new playing field. Lady Luck had been supportive of him so far, but he knew if he pushed her, the bitch would turn on him.

He sighed. The last one had given him so very much pleasure. The best so far, but eventually she'd submitted, as they all did.

He relived the memory, the play of the knife upon her soft flesh, her small body squirming in terror and pain under his greater weight. He felt the pulse in her throat cease the moment her heart stopped beating. If he closed his eyes right now, he could still see the glaze wash over her eyes as her soul lifted free. She'd been beautiful in life and in death.

He took a deep breath.

The power over life and death intoxicated him.

Before she'd gone, Amelia had taught him a valuable lesson, and for that he was grateful. It was far more satisfying to break the will of a smart, confident woman. Compared to the lovely Amelia, working with whores was like shooting fish in a barrel.

He finally understood why some hunters trekked all the way to Africa to shoot big game. What was more of a challenge to kill: a deer or a lion?

Closing his notebook, he turned his attention back to Beth. He lifted the binoculars to his eyes to see her more clearly.

He was so excited about their date.

Since he had never planned an event this far in advance, he relished the anticipation. Stalking and watching his victim, planning every detail of the abduction, added so much excitement to his game. Much more tantalizing than trolling for an opportunity to present itself.

He could already see her in his mind's eye: gagged and bound spread-eagle in his playroom. She would be naked, her eyes glazed with terror. He'd tell her everything he was going to do first to increase her fear. There was nothing like the smell of purely feminine panic. Someone should bottle it as perfume.

He smiled as a new thought occurred to him. Maybe he would hold on to her for a few days. Add yet another new element to the game.

Did he dare? Of course he did.

In fact, they could make a weekend of it.

CHAPTER ELEVEN

James stepped back into the crowd of reporters and snapped another picture. Resting the camera on its strap, he brushed aside the fake press pass that dangled from a cord around his neck.

At the ribbon cutting ceremony for a pea-sized patch of mulch converted from vacant lot to playground, Congressman Baker was giving a speech on family values, laying on the bullshit thick as cream cheese. Total media whore. Couldn't get enough press. Which was OK with James because no one noticed an extra reporter.

Dickwad was a busy man, constantly attending charity events and giving speeches, soaking up attention like a dry sponge.

Christ. If James really had to do this for a living, he'd eat a bullet.

Behind the podium Baker hemorrhaged lies; James blocked out the sound. Warm and dry, the early morning sunlight heated his back as he lifted the camera again.

Did Baker really think rolling up the sleeves of a Turnbull & Asser dress shirt magically transformed him into a workingman? There was no way those Ferragamo oxfords would ever be confused with a pair of Dockers.

James glanced around him at the sea of dark blue, tropical weight wool. Didn't matter. This was Washington, DC. No real people here anyway. Even the media looked bored. Nothing less than murder or sordid sexual scandal got their juices flowing. They'd probably heard it all, but they kept the cameras rolling anyway. Meanwhile, up-and-coming Congressman Baker looked like a fucking movie star on TV.

Baker waved to the crowd and stepped down from the dais. James snapped a continuous stream of pictures as the congressman moved toward the black Town Car parked at the curb and conferred with a slightly younger, dark-haired man, his aide, Aaron Myers. The television news crews kept pace, shoving microphones in front of Baker's face in a last-ditch effort to get one more comment.

Baker raised a hand and flashed the press a final, commercial-worthy smile.

So far, James hadn't come up with any dirt on Golden Boy Baker, but it wasn't for lack of effort. He'd researched Beth's supposed disappearance. Baker was claiming his wife had tried to commit suicide then run away. But James knew better. There was no way Beth had ever tried to kill herself. She was too devoted to her children. And there was nothing wrong with her mental state. Baker must have set her up.

But why?

After the police investigation had stalled, Baker'd hired some very expensive private investigators. They were still on his payroll. Evidence to the public that the politician was devoted to finding his unstable, self-destructive wife. Baker was now the media champion of mental health issues, and still milking a good deal of publicity from Beth's disappearance a year later.

Through the lens, James watched Myers nod to Baker and pull a PDA from the chest pocket of his tailored suit jacket. The aide tapped on the face with a stylus. A uniformed chauffeur opened the back door, and Myers slid into the car. Baker turned to give the crowd a last wave before joining him.

James lowered the camera and stared. The back of his neck itched.

The next item on Baker's agenda was a charity luncheon to benefit the homeless. What a world. Only a politician could figure out a way to raise money while eating lobster puffs and drinking champagne.

James knew where Baker was headed because he'd hacked into the congressman's schedule, which was so full for the next few days that he wouldn't be making a trip home to his posh Main Line Philadelphia home.

This morning's vision had been bright enough that he knew he had to get moving. Some nasty shit was headed Beth's way. He still needed to touch Beth's silver medal to start the psychic film rolling, though. So he was fairly sure it wasn't going to happen in the next few days.

James clicked off the digital camera, reached into the thigh pocket of his cargo pants, and snapped the lens cap into place. He'd download today's pictures onto his laptop as soon as he got back to his hotel. Something nagged at him. Something he'd seen this morning just wasn't right.

He'd have to trail Baker for just a little longer and cross his fingers that Beth would be OK.

– – –

Congressman Richard Baker sat at his desk, his opened and sorted mail stacked in front of him. His secretary had also brought him a cup of excellent coffee. He had an hour to kill before the charity luncheon. He'd just begun to skim through the pile when the intercom beeped at his elbow. Anita connected the incoming call.

"Thirty minutes. You know where." The line went dead. The taste in his mouth turned acrid.

Blotting his forehead with a monogrammed handkerchief, he called his driver. Then he gave his aide, Aaron, a quick assignment and asked him to meet him at the luncheon. There was no need for Aaron to get involved. Richard was more than capable of taking care of the situation.

A half hour later, his car drew to a stop next to a sleek Town Car nearly identical to his own in the middle of Arlington National Cemetery. The cars were surrounded by an endless sea of white crosses. Instructing his driver to stay put, he exited his own vehicle and slid into the other sedan.

Privacy glass isolated the rear seat.

A small, lean man sat in the far corner of the back seat, his face concealed in shadow. "I assume, since you paid me last time, that you do not want that DVD sent to the media."

Sweat trickled down Richard's back absorbed by his thick Egyptian cotton shirt as he nodded his assent. The man was unimpressive at first glance, but Richard knew those feral black eyes were as vicious as a jackal's. He'd already taken a chunk out of Richard, and like a true scavenger, he was back for another piece.

"Then you'll need to make another installment." The man spoke quietly, but there was no mistaking the malice in his tone. "Same amount. Next week."

This had all started with one indiscretion shortly after his wedding. He'd been desperate. Staying on the straight and narrow all through his courtship of Elizabeth had proved harder than he'd anticipated. He never should have married her, regardless of the polls. His father had insisted that he needed a family to secure the office. Sure, he'd won the election, but now his secret was out there, floating around with Elizabeth. Ironically, it was a copy of the same DVD this man held that his wife had seen that fateful night when she'd barged in on him.

This asshole was going to bleed him as long as he drew breath. His blackmailer was the only other person who knew his secret, and he knew he'd have to pay up if he wanted to keep it that way.

Richard straightened his tie. "I don't have access to that kind of cash."

"I don't want to hear excuses, and don't get snotty with me, pretty boy. That's your problem, not mine. The folks at CNN would love to get their hands on your debut film."

Richard's throat constricted. He gritted his teeth and nodded.

Back in his own car, he put on his happy face and proceeded directly to the luncheon, where he did what he did best: he acted. He returned to his office later that afternoon grim but determined. It was time he asked for some assistance with this situation. This time next week, his blackmailer would be receiving last rites instead of payment.

Richard pushed the intercom on his desk. "Anita, please phone my father's secretary and find out when he'll be back from New York. Tell her it's important." He sat back in his leather chair. His gaze drifted to the window.

No doubt about it. The man had him by the gonads and was likely to haunt him forever. To add to his load, the men his father hired were still unable to find Elizabeth after that debacle in Virginia. It was all her fault, really. Not only couldn't she satisfy him, but she'd spied on him, her own husband. Then she ran away, publicly humiliating him. Now she was a loose end that he simply couldn't afford to leave untied.

Unforgivable.

As soon as they found her, he would make her pay. Different scenarios flipped through his brain. It had to be painful, and not too quick. She deserved to be punished, and he'd earned the pleasure her punishment would give him. The thought of his father's men taking care of her left him feeling distinctly unsatisfied. His dad's man Johnson could handle the blackmailer. After all, that was business. Elizabeth's betrayal was personal.

A special news report flashed on the television in the corner cabinet of his office. He reached for the remote and increased the volume. The reporter on the screen provided the details of yet another woman's body found in a waterway, this time very close to his Southeastern Pennsylvania constituency, possibly an additional victim of the Riverside Killer.

An image took shape in his mind.

Raped, strangled, and tortured.

Perfect.

He shifted his gaze to Elizabeth's picture, which still stood on his credenza. As he stared, he pictured her naked body under his, his hands wrapped around her neck, his thumbs pressing down on her windpipe, her final breath leaving her lungs as he forced the life out of her body. The vision was the only fantasy he'd ever entertained about his wife.

Fear and pain were the ultimate aphrodisiacs.

CHAPTER TWELVE

"Thanks, Wes." Jack placed the receiver in its charger and leaned back in his chair. After three days of searching, his former partner had found nothing on Beth Ann Markham from Virginia. It was as if she didn't exist.

Wes's call wasn't much of a surprise. But why would she change her name? What kind of trouble could she be in? It didn't seem likely she was on the run from the law. Beth epitomized the whole suburban soccer mom package. All she needed was a mini-van and a PTA bumper sticker.

So now what was he going to do?

If he confronted her, she'd skip. No question.

Would that be such a bad thing? Did he need this hassle in his miserable life right now? He could barely keep his hands off her, but *she* still didn't want anything to do with *him*. Limping around with a semi from dawn to dark was making him irritable.

Why had his uncle hired her?

Jack opened the humidor on the corner of the antique oak desk and selected a premium Dominican. He drew the cigar under his nose and inhaled deeply. The worn leather behind his head was infused with the smell of his uncle's expensive cigars, as was everything in the room. He should look on the bright side of his new life. He'd never been able to afford these on a cop's salary.

Good scotch had been a rare treat as well, reserved for visits to his uncle.

Visits that had been few and far between in the last few years.

Scrubbing a hand over his face, he rose, limped to the credenza across the room, and poured two fingers of single malt into a crystal tumbler. Jack wandered to the far wall, covered in framed photos of his uncle's life. A multitude of familiar faces smiled at him, pictures from weddings, christenings, and other family events. There was a section devoted to Danny's travels and his army career. His uncle had toured Europe and South America extensively. At the far side of the room, Jack's eyes lit on a few grainy images of Danny's unit in Vietnam. His uncle had never, ever talked about that war. Not once. Jack had sensed Danny's experiences in Southeast Asia had been the stuff of nightmares. There were a half dozen photos, though, all placed at eye level. Danny hadn't wanted to forget that chapter in his life, however painful it had been.

Jack found his uncle easily in five of the pictures. Danny had been career military, somewhere in his mid-forties during the Vietnam War. According to Jack's mother, Danny was injured in '68. Though his physical injuries hadn't been serious, he'd retired. Would've made colonel if he'd stayed in longer.

The last picture didn't seem to fit the others of Danny and his fellow officers, men he'd been close to, in off-duty type activities. The last shot was a small group of men, taken from a distance as they gathered next to a helicopter. There was something different about these guys. Something edgy. Jack leaned closer, but the images were too small and he couldn't see much detail.

With a sigh, he paced back to the desk and lifted out the tray from the humidor in search of a cigar cutter.

An envelope rested on top of the next row of stogies.

Jack picked it up. His name was scrawled in Uncle Danny's handwriting across the front.

Shit.

Jack opened the envelope and unfolded the letter.

Jack,

If you're sitting at my desk smoking my cigars, then I guess this feeling in my gut is right on target. Haven't been up to snuff these last few weeks. Well, damn. Don't grieve too much. I've had a great life, much longer than I thought I'd get on this earth, considering.

I hope you accept your inheritance and its conditions for two reasons. You need to settle down, establish some roots, be near your family. And I still need a favor from you. Aye, here's the rub.

I hired a woman to take over as caretaker. I need you to look after her for me. She's in some sort of danger. Sorry, I don't have any more details. This is a favor for someone I owe the last forty years of my life to. And obviously I'm unable to satisfy the debt. She has no idea the job's a setup to keep her safe, so keep that to yourself. I trust you'll take care of the situation.

I'll miss you boys. Enjoy these cigars with Quinn and Sean. Nothing's more important than family. I learned that the hard way.

Danny

P.S. There's another case of The Macallan in the basement.

The letter dropped to the leather blotter.

Son of a bitch.

Well, that certainly answered a few of Jack's questions. And raised about three zillion more.

Thunder boomed and Jack glanced out the window. Pregnant black clouds blotted out the evening sky. A door slammed. Ben called for his sister as footsteps thudded on hardwood.

Jack set the glass and unlit cigar on the desk next to the letter and headed for the hall. The boy never ran in the house. Or yelled, for that matter.

"Ben, is something wrong?"

"Yeah, I can't find Katie. She's really afraid of loud noises. This storm's gonna freak her out. Mom told me to stay with her. I—I just turned around for a second to shut the door. The wind was pushing it." The boy raked a hand through his hair.

Before Jack could speak, the lights went out. Another crash of thunder vibrated the windowpanes.

"It's not your fault, Ben. Don't worry," Jack assured him. "She came in the house with you, right?"

Ben gave a quick nod.

"Then she's here somewhere." Jack rummaged around in the hall closet in the dark and came out with two heavy-duty flashlights.

"OK." Ben took one and switched it on. "Where's Henry? He'll find her."

Jack held back a snort of laughter. The children thought Henry was Lassie reincarnated. "You look down here. Check all the closets, under the furniture, behind the drapes. I'll take upstairs. OK?"

Ben ducked into the living room. "I found Henry. He's hiding under the coffee table. His teeth are chattering. Is he afraid of thunder, too?"

"Yeah, he is. Doesn't it figure?" Jack shook his head.

On the way up, Jack leaned heavily on the banister, but he made it. He turned into the first bedroom, obviously Beth's. Shining the light under the dresser, he absorbed the details in the room as he searched. He couldn't help himself. Once a cop, always a cop. And geez, this was a moral search warrant, the perfect excuse for him to poke around in Beth's room without feeling guilty about invading her privacy.

He found a couple of empty duffel bags in the bottom of the closet. Minimal clothing and few personal effects. No Katie.

He checked the attached bath. Jack had never seen a woman's medicine cabinet that wasn't full to bursting. Yet Beth only had a couple of cosmetic items—and a box of black hair dye. He'd been right. That color wasn't natural.

There was one surprise. Over the shower curtain rod. Bras and panties hung in a sexy row of skimpy lace and satin that made Jack's mouth water. That black satin thong, the item of his most recent sordid dreams, dangled at eye level next to a tiny white number adorned with flowers on the back strings.

Holy hard-on, Batman!

There was definitely no time to stand here and wonder what kind of panties Beth was wearing right now, yet in the blink of an eye, Jack's mind conjured up a picture of Beth wearing that little white thong. The yellow flowers would nestle under those two dimples she'd have at the base of her spine. He'd run his tongue… Damn.

You are in big trouble, O'Malley.

Jack reminded himself he was looking for a scared child and moved on. He entered the next room, Katie's. Nothing under the bed. A backpack in the closet contained most of the little girl's clothes. Apparently, she wasn't ready to unpack. Sadly, it occurred to Jack she wasn't sure how long she was staying. A stuffed giraffe was tucked under the covers in the bed.

The beam of light moved across a few well-used children's paperbacks on the dresser: *Clifford the Big Red Dog, Henry and Mudge*. No wonder Katie loved Henry so much. He was a shoe-in.

Jack moved to Ben's room. The kid had fewer possessions than soldiers kept in a military barracks. Paperback editions of the entire Harry Potter collection sat on the nightstand. Wait, what was that sticking out of Ben's copy of *The Chamber of Secrets*? A photograph.

It was mostly in plain sight. The kind of thing he wouldn't need a warrant to see. It also seemed silly to worry about looking at a photo when he'd fantasized about Beth's panties just a few seconds before.

Jack held the flashlight on a picture of man and a little boy of about four or five years old, standing in front of a fire truck. Jack assumed the boy was Ben. He was standing in an enormous pair of fireman's boots that engulfed his legs all the way up his skinny thighs. A large, dark-haired man hunkered down on one knee next to the child. Both man and boy smiled for the camera. It was a happy moment, a slice of time captured forever before the family's life imploded with tragedy.

Jack swallowed the lump in his throat as a wave of sadness passed over him. He couldn't imagine losing his father, and he was forty-seven. How did a five-year-old boy deal with it? With sad determination, he replaced the photo and exited the room.

Jack limped toward the bathroom at the end of the hall. He opened the linen closet behind the door and shone the light inside. A small figure huddled on the cold tile. Katie's knees were drawn up to her chest. She hugged her legs and rocked. Looking up at Jack, she opened her mouth to scream, but she was so frightened her throat only emitted a small squeak.

Jack's heart squeezed. Gritting his teeth against the pain, he set the light on the floor and leaned down as far as he could.

"Come on out, honey, I won't hurt you." Jack kept his voice calm and soothing, like he was talking her off a ledge. "Ben's waiting downstairs for us. He's worried about you." Katie didn't respond. She rocked back and forth, staring straight ahead at the wall with an alarming, blank expression on her pale face.

"Henry is really scared of storms. I'll bet he'd feel a lot better if you sat with him."

The little girl swallowed and blinked, slowly shifting her gaze to Jack. She scooted forward a couple inches. Jack bent closer and held out his hand. Katie hesitated for one more second, then set her tiny hand in his palm. Jack curled his fingers around hers. When he started to straighten, she catapulted herself into his arms and wrapped all four limbs around him, sobbing.

Knocked off balance, Jack stumbled backward and leaned against the vanity. He held her close. "It's OK, baby. It's only a storm. Nature's fireworks. You're safe with me."

Smoothing the damp hair away from her face, he squinted down at her in the peripheral glow of the flashlight. She leaned against his chest. Her hands clenched his shirt in tight fists, and she hiccupped between ragged breaths. Christ, she couldn't weigh more than forty pounds.

With a death grip on the railing, Jack carried her down the stairs. A flash of lightning illuminated the foyer, followed by a loud clap of thunder. Katie jumped in Jack's arms. Holding her hands against her ears, she buried her face in his shirt. Hot tears soaked through his T-shirt. "Shh. It's OK. I've got you."

"Hey, Ben. I found Katie," Jack called out, trying to keep his voice casual and relaxed.

"Great. Thanks, Jack." Ben's relieved voice came from the kitchen. "I couldn't think of anywhere else to look."

"Your mother make it back yet?" Jack glanced out the French doors. Rain pounded against the glass. He carried Katie into the room, pulled a camp lantern out of the cabinet, and switched it on.

"She was closing up the barn. I hope she's OK. It's raining sideways." Ben raised a hand to his mouth and chewed on a ragged edge of nail.

The kitchen door burst open and Beth surged through, leaning on the door to force it closed. Dripping, she turned to face the group. Wide-eyed, Beth froze and stared at her daughter. Katie was still wrapped around Jack like a spider monkey. His knee threatened to explode from her extra weight, but he didn't have the heart to forcibly dislodge her. And even if he could disentangle himself from her embrace, his heart squeezed at the thought of wrenching her off of him.

Beth's hair was plastered to her head, and her jeans and T-shirt clung to her body like a second skin, outlining her slim legs and rounded breasts. What he wouldn't give to help her peel those wet clothes off, then maybe lick the raindrops from her skin.

Sigh. That wasn't going to happen. If he knew only one thing about Beth, it was that she didn't want to be touched, especially by him.

A puddle spread around her feet, and Jack bit his cheek to keep from laughing. "You're soaked. Why don't you go upstairs and get out of those wet clothes? When you come back down, I'll go out and try to start the emergency generator."

He couldn't help himself. His gaze dropped to her breasts again. Not too large or small, he noticed once again how perfectly they'd fill his palms. Beth caught his look and blushed. She dropped her gaze from his face to the floor, and Jack decided that, although his chances of ever seeing her naked were only slightly greater than winning the Pick-6, he liked her face all flushed and flustered. Ten different ways to get it that way popped into his head simultaneously. They all required her to be naked, which seemed to have become a recurring theme in Jack's imagination.

Beth cleared her throat and spoke in a firm, back-to-business voice. "I sent them up here as soon as I saw the storm coming. I didn't want them outside when it started. Good thing, too. By the time I finished closing up, it was coming down in sheets. I was soaked through in less than a minute." She didn't run out of the room or even back up a step. She didn't seem at all intimidated by his blatant leer.

Score. Maybe it wasn't such a long shot after all.

"You're dripping," Jack prompted. "We're all fine here. Please go change into something dry before you get sick." He handed her a camp lantern and tried not to laugh at the slapping sound her sodden socks made on the floor as she walked past.

OK. Now he had two problems. Not only was he obligated to protect this small family, via Uncle Danny, but they were starting to grow on him. All of them. So much for any confrontations with Beth. Now that he knew they were in danger, he couldn't take the risk that she'd leave.

Shit.

CHAPTER THIRTEEN

Beth scanned the short grocery list Mrs. Harris had given her and started down the produce aisle. She crossed off several items, and then threw a bag of Granny Smith apples into the cart. The store was empty this early in the morning, and she moved up and down the aisles at breakneck speed. She needed to get back in time to meet with the landscaper. As she turned the corner of the last row and grabbed two gallons of milk, someone bumped into her from behind.

"Excuse me," she said automatically and turned around.

"Hello, hot stuff." Will Martin loomed over her, his big body crowding her in the open refrigerator case. The moisture in Beth's throat evaporated.

"I thought that was O'Malley's pickup outside. I was hopin' to run into you."

She tried to back up, but her legs hit the ledge of the cooler behind her. Swallowing her fear, she took a deep breath. The smells of man, sweat, and animals saturated her nostrils. Beth glanced up and down the aisle, but there was no one else in sight.

"Please move out of my way." She tilted her head up to look him squarely in the eye, disguising her fear with a rigid spine. Sweat trickled down her back, turning cold in the frigid air blowing from the open dairy case.

"Don't get your panties in a twist, princess." Martin's expression turned smug. "I'm not going to drag you to the floor right here in the grocery store. I'd be glad to show you a good time somewhere else, though. You don't know what you're missin'." He stepped closer and pressed his hips into her belly. The hard ridge in his jeans ground into her stomach.

She froze. Bile rose in her throat but she swallowed it. Her heart tripped as she overcame her paralysis and raised her knee between his legs. With little room to maneuver, she barely bumped his groin, but he stepped back with a grunt. His face flushed, and veins protruded from his neck and temple.

Beth attempted to step sideways, but he shifted his weight forward again. His eyes glittered with excitement.

"Beth, are you all right?"

Beth's body almost went limp with relief at the sound of Jeff Stevens's voice.

Martin tensed, then leaned closer. Hot breath whispered down her neck. "I'll have you yet, you little cock tease. You think you're better than everybody else. But you're a slut like every other woman." His voice was raspy with anger. "You wait. I'll have you on your knees, yet, bitch."

"Take your hands off her, Will." Jeff approached with a brisk stride. Martin had at least forty pounds of bulk on Jeff, but something beyond anger glittered in her neighbor's eyes, something Beth had never seen before, something dark that made Martin back off despite his size advantage.

Martin turned and strode off, leaving her shaking in the cold draft.

Jeff hurried to her side and placed his hand on her elbow. Beth searched his eyes but saw no trace of darkness. She'd probably imagined it. Still, his touch turned her already-nauseous stomach over again.

"Everything OK here?" A portly, middle-aged man in an employees' green apron pushed a cart loaded with cases of ice cream. His eyes narrowed at Martin's back as it disappeared around the corner. "Was he bothering you, ma'am?"

With a throat too tight for words, Beth shook her head.

"I think she's OK now," Jeff answered for her. "Thanks, Ray."

Ray frowned. "Let me know if you need anything." He turned and continued down the aisle to the freezer section at the far end.

Embarrassed, Beth straightened. "I'm fine. Thank you, Jeff." She took a step back and willed her knees to stop trembling.

"It's OK. Nobody likes Will. He's a jerk." After a quick squeeze, Jeff released her arm and stood back to give her some room. Beth exhaled in relief. He nodded toward her cart. "You want some help with that?"

"No. I've got it." Beth smiled. It was weak, but it was the best she could muster at the moment.

"You going to be OK driving home?"

Beth managed a short nod. She just wanted to get out of there.

Operating on automatic pilot, and keeping an eye out for Will Martin, she went through the checkout, loaded the bags into the rear seat of the truck, and climbed in.

She sat in the quiet truck interior without starting the engine. What would have happened if Martin had caught her alone in a more private place? Would he really hurt her, or did he just enjoy frightening her? Regardless, she couldn't afford to make trouble, couldn't go to the police for help—or even to Jack for that matter. If Jack found out about this episode with Martin, he'd want her to file a report, but she didn't dare risk the scrutiny. From now on, her jaunts off the estate would be few and far between. She'd have to make whatever excuses were necessary to avoid going into town.

She was reminded once again how completely alone she was—and that she needed to reevaluate her options.

What would James do? She pictured the pay phone in the vestibule of the grocery store. He'd said it was too dangerous for her to contact him, but surely a pay phone was safe. She got out of the car and hurried back into the store, where she was relieved to find the phone intact and working. After plugging coins into the slot, she dialed James's number. The receiver emitted a high-pitched peal, then a digitized message played: "The number you have reached has been disconnected."

Disappointed, she headed back to the pickup. As she climbed into the cab, a car in the far corner of the near-empty lot caught her eye, a shiny black sedan that looked out of place on the cracked, weedy asphalt of the Stop 'N Shop parking lot. The way the sunlight glinted off the darkened glass, Beth couldn't tell if anyone was inside the vehicle.

OK. Now she was being totally paranoid. This was a farming community, but that didn't mean everyone drove a truck. The car probably belonged to the store manager, which would explain why it was parked all the way in the back.

Beth started the pickup and pulled out onto Main Street into what passed for morning rush-hour traffic in Westbury. As she passed through an intersection, she glanced in the rearview mirror. She sucked in a gasp, and her heart leaped into her throat. Six cars behind her was a shiny black car.

Will Martin? A black sedan didn't fit his image.

All Richard's men drove shiny black vehicles.

The houses and the traffic thinned as she approached the end of the town proper, a good ten miles from the estate. Playing it safe, she made three right turns and circled the block. When she eased back onto Main Street, there was no sign of the black car.

The air whooshed out of her lungs. It hadn't been following her.

Her paranoia was giving her a run for her money this morning. She supposed the altercation with Will Martin had set her nerves on edge. As she steered the truck toward the country road that led to the estate, her heart was still beating too quickly, like an over-wound metronome.

And her gaze kept straying to the rearview mirror.

– – –

Interrupted by the sound of a single knock, Beth raised her eyes from the computer screen. Mrs. Harris stepped through the doorway of the study. In jeans, a T-shirt, and sneakers she looked much younger than her sixty-plus years. "I'm off to the salon. Gotta keep the gray at bay. Be back in a couple of hours. Jack just left for physical therapy, so the house is all yours. The kids are watching TV." She turned away, then hesitated, one hand on the doorjamb, and glanced over her shoulder at Beth. "Are you OK here by yourself?"

"I'm fine. Thanks for asking." Beth smiled and pointed at the keyboard. "I have enough bookkeeping to keep me busy for the rest of the morning."

Mrs. Harris laughed. "Considering how Danny kept records, I think you have enough there to keep you going till Christmas."

"You're probably right." Beth grinned.

"Well then, I'll see you around lunchtime." With a wave, Mrs. Harris withdrew. Her quick steps in the hall rapidly faded away.

Beth listened for the slam of the back door. As soon as she heard it, she moved to the window to watch the housekeeper drive off a few minutes later. The yellow car disappeared into the late morning sunlight. Beth hurried upstairs to her room and pulled a duffel from the top of the closet. Setting the bag on the floor, she unzipped it and lifted out a small lockbox. The dials of the combination lock spun smoothly, despite the trembling of her fingers. The lock clicked, and Beth opened the door.

Sunbeams from the window glinted off the blue steel of a Sig Sauer P232. Beth stared at the nine-millimeter handgun for a long minute. A wave of nausea rolled through her stomach, and her heart ached with crushing intensity. With one forefinger, she tentatively stroked the cold metal. Guns and children did not mix. This she knew for a fact. She'd seen it with her own eyes.

Her parents were probably rolling over in their graves at this very moment.

Beth shook off the memory. She lifted the key on the chain around her neck from under her shirt and removed the trigger lock. Her brother had been dead for twenty years. But she'd do whatever it took to keep her children safe, even if that meant embracing the very instrument that had killed him. Besides, she was obsessive-compulsive about keeping the gun on her person or unloaded and locked in the safe. Richard posed a much greater threat than a handgun accident.

Straightening her shoulders, she strapped on the ankle holster and secured the gun before shoving a box of ammunition into her pocket. A third sock concealed the black nylon. She pulled her boot-cut jeans down over her leg.

Stepping into her sneakers, she took a few tentative steps. She'd never get used to the weight dragging at her leg, but awkward and uncomfortable was way better than dead. And in summer clothes, the ankle holster had been the only realistic option. Sure, that left her in long pants all the time, but a little sweat was a small price to pay for her family's safety.

James would be furious if he knew she hadn't been carrying the Sig day and night and practicing regularly. She could practically hear him chastising her: *No sense in having a gun if you don't carry it or can't use it.*

The gun wouldn't have done her much good in the grocery store this morning, but if Richard ever did find her, a bullet was the only thing that would prevent him from orphaning her children. And claiming them. Although he'd never formally adopted them, they had no other family besides their stepfather. Richard didn't like children, but his PR people would love having two orphans to trot out for the media anytime he started to slip in the polls.

So, no excuses this morning. She was alone on the estate. Time to get back to the routine designed to save her life. She jogged down the stairs, ignoring the cumbersome weight of the steel strapped to her foot.

On her way out of the house, she stopped at the threshold of the living room. "Ben, I'm going outside for a little while. You two stay in the house, OK?"

"OK, Mommy." Katie turned back to *Sponge Bob.*

Beth pointed at her ankle and raised her eyebrows. Ben nodded. His gaze flicked to her foot. Not only did Ben know about the handgun, James had taught him to handle the weapon as well, just in case.

She glanced down and mouthed, "Can you see it?"

"No. You're cool." He shook his head and went back to reading the copy of *Huckleberry Finn* he'd found in the study.

She borrowed Jack's golf cart. After a quick stop at the barn for a couple of bales of straw, she drove into the stand of pines behind the garage. Occasionally Jack showed up at the barn, but he never came back here. No reason to. Nothing but trees.

Birds and squirrels chattered over the distant babble of the creek as she stacked the bales and clipped a piece of paper to the center of the one on top to serve as a target. After loading the weapon, she inserted her earplugs. The silence was disconcerting; her pulse echoed like drumbeats.

The gun was cold and heavy in her hand. With a deep breath she assumed her stance, raised her weapon, then squeezed off a shot. The Sig jerked in her hand. The bullet hit the bale two feet to the left of the paper target. She exhaled and tried again.

As usual the first few reports made her jump. A half dozen rounds later, she relaxed and fell into a rhythm. The last six shots were dead center.

James was right. Practice made perfect.

CHAPTER FOURTEEN

While Beth brought the last horse in from the pasture for his dinner, she kept one eye on her daughter. A safe distance away, Katie sat in the grass holding a scrap of chicken in front of Henry's nose. The dog complied with her requests to sit and lie down, never once making any move toward the chicken until it was offered.

Beth snickered. Jack couldn't get the dog to do anything. Henry would sing a tune for Katie if he could.

Over the past couple of weeks, she and Ben had developed a daily routine. Beth ducked into the barn and began checking water buckets while Ben measured feed and dumped it into the tubs in each stall. Black rubber banged against wooden walls as the horses nosed for stray bits of grain. Finished with the feeding, Ben fetched a pitchfork to shovel manure from the aisle while Beth headed up into the loft for fresh hay.

She was two rungs from the top when a loud crack startled her. With a splintering sound, the wooden ladder pulled away from the wall and began to tip backwards. She shifted her weight forward and stretched her hand toward the wall, glancing down at the floor ten feet below.

Beth froze, her breath trapped in her throat. Everything remained motionless for a few seconds. Her heart pounded inside her rib cage. Then, ever so slowly, the ladder began to tip back toward the loft. She exhaled and reached for the handrail.

Almost there.

Her hand was inches from the wooden supports when the ladder split in two under her sneakers. The barn turned upside down. Pain ripped through her right arm as it caught on a piece of debris. Beth crashed down into the dirt aisle, where she landed with a solid thud on the packed earth. Dirt and blood flooded her mouth in the split second before pain exploded in her head and everything went black.

– – –

Jack sat in the study, sipping iced tea and reviewing the roofer's estimate. He knew the mansion had an acre or so of neglected roof, but he hadn't been prepared for the size of the quote.

Holy crap.

Not only was it six pages long, but, Christ, the total was more than his annual salary had been. With a resigned sigh, he pulled out a calculator and began adding figures. Just because he had the money didn't mean he wanted to give it all to the roofer. Living on a budget for forty-eight years had left its mark. He might have become a millionaire, but he'd be a tightwad forever.

After just a few weeks of living at the estate, he was starting to understand why Danny had let it get so rundown. It wasn't just the money. No shortage there. His uncle had had a knack for picking investments. Repairs and maintenance for a property of this size took a sizable chunk of time and energy.

Figures totaled, Jack set the page aside for Beth. The numbers looked OK to him, but her math and bookkeeping skills were far superior. No doubt she'd double-check the quote and generate a spreadsheet for their records in the efficient manner he'd come to expect and rely on. Jack glanced at the clock. Beth and the kids should be returning from their evening chores any minute. Ears tuned for the sounds of their entry, Jack reached for a stack of bills Beth had set aside for them to discuss this evening after the kids had gone to bed. He was looking forward to reviewing the accounts with a ridiculous amount of anticipation. No doubt she'd keep the conversation all business, but they'd still be alone. Damned if he didn't like talking to her as much as he enjoyed fantasizing about which thong she might be wearing.

A door slammed. Sneakers squeaked on hardwood.

"Jack." Ben's yell carried through the closed door of the study. "Where are you?"

"Ben?" Jack jumped out of his swivel chair and limped into the hall, nearly colliding with the boy. His heart skipped when he saw the blood smeared on Ben's hands. "What happened?"

"Mom fell. Her head's bleeding and she's unconscious." Ben's voice broke. The boy's hair stood up, wet and red from running his shaking hands through it. He wiped his trembling, bloody hands on his shorts.

"Where's Katie?" Jack followed Ben through the house, jamming his cell phone and keys into his pocket as they sped through the kitchen. The kick of adrenaline dulled the pain in his knee. He paused long enough to grab his first-aid kit from the pantry and snag his cane from its resting spot behind the door.

"She wouldn't leave Mom."

They jumped into the golf cart, and Jack jammed the pedal to the floor. The cart careened along the rutted path. At the barn door, Jack skidded to a stop in the dirt. Ben leaped out of the cart and beat him into the stable. Jack followed, cursing his weak leg. He flipped open his cell phone. The battery was dead. *Fuck.*

In the dim aisle, Henry lay next to Beth's prostrate form, whining and licking her limp hand. Next to the dog, Katie knelt in the dirt, face pale and drawn. Tears streamed down, leaving clean trails on her dirty face.

Jack dropped his cane, lowered his body onto his good knee, and wrapped one arm around Katie's shoulders. He tugged her backward. "Let me get in here, honey."

Ben helped Katie scoot backward a few feet.

"Beth? Can you hear me?" Beth lay on her side against the wall. Blood oozed out of a gash on her forehead and another just above her elbow. Her T-shirt was soaked deep red. Jack pressed two fingers against Beth's throat. Her skin, always pale, was nearly gray, but her pulse felt strong and steady. Although both cuts had obviously bled copiously at first, the bleeding had slowed to a trickle.

He opened the first-aid kit and tore open the white paper envelopes of several large square gauze pads. At the sound of paper tearing, Beth's eyelids quivered. She moaned softly. Her eyelids fluttered, then opened. He looked down into her unfocused eyes, brushed a stray lock of blood-soaked hair off her forehead, then pressed a folded, clean piece of gauze firmly against the cut.

"What happened?" Beth's eyes blinked hard as she squinted at Jack's face.

"You fell. Don't move." Jack reached for more gauze. "Do you know where you are? Can you tell me what hurts?" He wrapped the wound on her arm in gauze and secured it with first-aid tape.

Beth squirmed. "I'm all right. Let me get up."

Jack placed a firm hand on her shoulder. "Take it easy. We need to get you to the hospital. I have to go back to the house to call an ambulance."

"No, no ambulance. I can walk." Beth pushed the blanket aside and tried moving her legs.

Jack pinned her legs to the ground with one hand across her ankles.

"Hold still. You fell pretty far. You could have spinal injuries. Let the paramedics move you."

"No!" She successfully pulled herself to a sitting position and turned her head from side to side. "My neck is fine. See, I can move everything."

Jack felt his blood pressure spike. His voice rose. "For Christ's sake, would you stop moving?"

Ignoring him, Beth bent her legs. "I don't think anything's broken."

With a glance at the children, Jack inhaled and lowered his voice. "Cut it out. OK, no ambulance, but do not try to get up." He put a hand on her shoulder to hold her down.

"You two stay here with her while I bring the car around. Be right back." Jack patted Katie on the shoulder as he moved past her. "Ben, don't let her move. I mean it. Sit on her if you have to." He looked directly at Beth and pointed at her for emphasis.

A few minutes later, Jack drove the SUV right into the barn, as close to Beth as he could manage. "Take your time. Lean on me."

If he'd had had two good legs, he'd have scooped her up and carried her to the car, but the best he could do was wrap an arm around her waist and keep her on her feet.

He wasn't exactly knight in shining armor material.

Luckily, the ride to the hospital was short, and the number of ski resorts in the area meant it had an excellent emergency room. Tiny though it was, Westbury Community Hospital served as the Regional Trauma Center.

Jack parked under the carport at the emergency entrance and helped Beth through the automatic sliding doors. The kids followed like baby ducks. They passed a man filling out forms on a clipboard, his ice-pack-encased foot elevated on a plastic chair. A sleeping woman and a teenage girl waited in another row. The teen didn't even look up from her rapid-fire texting as they passed her.

"You two wait here. I'll be back." Jack motioned the children toward an empty row of chairs. Even with the support of the cane, his knee throbbed as he half carried Beth up to the desk. The blue-scrubbed nurse at the desk took one look at the blood-soaked bandages and rounded the counter to fetch a wheelchair.

"We'll put her in room one."

Jack eased Beth into the faux leather seat and read the nurse's nametag. While Jack helped Beth onto the examination table, he asked, "Is Dr. Wilson working tonight, Jean?"

"Yes, he is. He should be here in a minute." Another nurse entered the room, her white soles squeaking on the linoleum.

"You need to come with me and fill out some paperwork." Nurse Jean tapped Jack on the shoulder and motioned for him to follow her. "Betty will take good care of her. Here's Dr. Wilson."

Jack stepped into the hallway to greet his cousin, Quinn, who pulled him into a shoulder-slapping hug. "What's wrong?"

"Hey, Quinn, I'm sure glad to see you." Jack described Beth's accident, and Quinn ducked into the examination room.

Jack gathered a stack of forms and a clipboard from the desk. As soon as his butt hit the hard plastic chair, Katie curled into his body. On his other side, Ben bit his nails, or what was left of them. Jack answered as many of the questions as he could. He was not surprised when Ben claimed to not know his mother's birth date. "Do you know if you have medical insurance, Ben?"

Ben shook his head. "Are they gonna make her leave? We don't have any money."

"It's OK. They'll take care of your mom. They always do, even if you can't pay. Doctors are the good guys. Besides, it's my barn and my responsibility."

Ben continued to gnaw on his fingertips.

Jack put his hand on Ben's knee. "Don't worry, Ben, I'll take care of it. Dr. Wilson is my cousin. He's a really good doctor and a nice person. I promise he'll take good care of your mom."

Jack made a mental note to look into some medical insurance for his employees.

With the forms as complete as they were going to get, Jack leaned back against the wall and reviewed Beth's accident in his head.

Damn. This was all his fault.

Beth hadn't mentioned the barn needed any repairs, but the estate was his responsibility now. He should have made sure the building was safe. The roof needed to be replaced. It wasn't a huge stretch to assume the barn had additional structural defects.

He rubbed his braced knee, which ached from the night's exertion. There was no way he'd get up a ladder to see if the loft had any other major problems. Tomorrow he'd call a carpenter. No more excuses. It was time he took care of business, including his new employees, instead of whining about his knee and being cheap about repairs. This estate was turning into a full-time job, and he'd better accept that fact before any more damage was done.

– – –

The acrid smells of antiseptic and disinfectant assaulted Beth's nose, and her stomach rolled with nausea. She swallowed and breathed through her mouth.

The doctor looked familiar, but she couldn't place him. He was in his late forties, with a touch of gray sprinkled through his sandy-blond hair. Wearing jeans, a polo shirt, and sneakers on his lanky frame, he lifted the stack of bloody bandages off Beth's head and examined the cut.

"Not too bad. I'm Doctor Wilson, but you can call me Quinn, since I'm Jack's cousin and all. If I hadn't fallen asleep, we'd have met the day you arrived at the estate."

Oh, right. Quinn had been out cold on the living room sofa that day. No wonder his face rang a bell.

"Dizzy or nauseous?"

"I'm all right."

Quinn gently probed around the cut with gloved fingers.

Beth flinched.

"Sorry." The doctor shined a penlight into her eyes. "Jack said you were unconscious for at least five to ten minutes. Have you had any concussions in the past few years?"

"Yeah, a couple."

"A couple? How long ago?" The doctor's face revealed nothing as he continued to examine her.

"About a year and a half. I was in a car accident." Beth shifted uncomfortably on the table. Lying took a lot more energy than she had at the moment.

"That accounts for one."

"I fell down the stairs last year."

Quinn moved his hands down to her stomach and lifted her shirt a few inches. As he gently pushed on her ribs around a darkening bruise, he zeroed in on the thick line of scar tissue that ran across her rib cage. "How did you get that?"

"In the car accident."

Quinn's eyebrows shot up, but he didn't ask about it again. Which was a good thing, because she was way too damned tired to spin a believable story. She swallowed the lump in her throat and shifted her eyes away from Quinn's, counting the tiles in the exam room ceiling.

"OK. X-rays first, stitches second. Then we'll talk again."

Beth opened her mouth to protest but he'd disappeared.

CHAPTER FIFTEEN

Richard Baker crossed the thick grass and approached his father. The former senator, Stafford Baker, leaned on the fence, watching a broodmare and her foal in the early twilight. The mare's elegant lines were indicative of careful breeding. Her colt's parentage was evident already in the slope of his shoulder and prance in his step. This baby would be a fine addition to their racing stock.

Stafford glanced sideways at him. "Johnson has a lead on Elizabeth's whereabouts."

Richard rested his forearms on the rail and bit his tongue for a few seconds, not wanting to reveal his excitement at the news.

"I'm sorry I talked you into marrying her." Stafford placed a hand on his shoulder. The apology was a surprise. His father didn't often admit to making mistakes. "But you needed a wife to get elected. People were starting to talk, linking your name to celebrities, whores—and worse."

Richard nodded. If his father only knew. A few celebrity scandals were nothing compared to the truth.

Stafford removed his hand and thumped a tightly clenched fist on the top fence rail. "I thought Elizabeth would be easy to control, but I misjudged her."

"We both did." Richard had learned all about keeping women in their place from dear old Dad. Elizabeth had seemed so vulnerable. Grieving widow, no family, young children to provide excellent leverage if necessary. He'd assumed she'd be malleable. Her backbone had been an unpleasant surprise.

The bay mare approached. He patted the big animal's neck, and then scratched the colt behind the ears when it stuck its bony head through the fence rails to nibble on his trousers.

"Where is she?" Richard kept his eyes on the horse, barely containing the thrill that coursed through his blood. The urge to hurt his wife grew with every beat of his heart, flowing through his veins, fueling his dark desire the way gasoline powered an engine. It was all he could think about since he'd made the decision to do the deed himself.

"Westbury, Pennsylvania. It's just past the Poconos. My men had already narrowed it down to there or one other Podunk town, but when someone made a call to James Dieter's number from a pay phone in Westbury, that clinched it. We have photo confirmation." His father turned toward him. "You need to let Johnson handle this. It's his job. We keep people like him on the payroll for a reason."

Richard met his father's hard stare. The old man's eyes were the same bluish gray as a shark's and just as cold. "I'll take care of Elizabeth. Your men have already failed several times. I have another situation that requires Johnson's expertise."

The vein in his father's temple throbbed just once before he responded. "I'll have Johnson contact you. He'll take care of whatever you need." Stafford turned back to the horses.

Did he suspect? Richard often wondered. Good old Dad would never ask for the details of his only son's transgressions. The Bakers came from a long line of powerful men. Their wealth and sphere of political influence swelled with each generation. Their appetites were insatiable; their need for control, absolute. In such an atmosphere, it was just as easy to be tainted from within the family as from the outside. Keeping one's hands clean could be a chore.

Stafford's jaw tightened. "I assure you that Johnson is more than capable of multitasking. This time I'll make sure he does the job himself. No subcontracting. There can be no question that her death is anything other than a tragic accident. The wheels are already in motion. You stay in Washington, far away from Elizabeth."

Richard almost always followed his father's advice, but this time, well, that just wasn't going to happen. His father's employee needed to dispense with the blackmailer first. Richard would make that clear, and he'd provide a little extra incentive for Johnson to back off Elizabeth. Stafford might be the head of the family right now, but Richard was the future. Johnson would shift his allegiance. No question.

His calendar was full for the next few days with appearances he couldn't get out of without attracting attention, but after that Richard would arrange a few days off to relax at his Philadelphia home, which happened to be just ninety minutes from the Poconos—and his lovely wife.

CHAPTER SIXTEEN

Jack shifted in the hard seat. His shoulders extended far beyond the back of the chair, and the curved plastic dug into his back. He didn't want to move, though. Katie slept against his shoulder. Ben slumped in the chair on Jack's other side. Given the awkward tilt of Ben's head, the boy would have a stiff neck later.

Jack's gaze was drawn to the industrial clock on the wall. It had been nearly two hours. Where was Quinn? Could Beth's injuries be more serious than he'd thought? He shouldn't have given in and moved her. What was wrong with him? He knew better. He should have pinned her to the ground and called that ambulance.

His mental flogging was in full swing when Quinn appeared in the waiting room doorway and motioned for Jack to join him in the hall. Jack extricated his shoulder from beneath Katie's head and slid out of the chair. His cane was trapped on the other side of Katie's chair. His cousin frowned as Jack limped toward him without it.

Jack kept his voice low. "How is she?"

"Lucky. Half dozen stitches in her head, another eight in her arm, and a concussion, plus numerous bruises and abrasions, but miraculously, no broken bones. She'll be really sore for a week or two, but after that she should be fine, provided she gets some rest." Quinn removed his glasses and scrubbed a hand down his face. "I'd like to keep her overnight, do a CAT scan in the morning, but she won't stay. I can't make her. She already signed a release." Quinn hesitated. "How much do you know about her?"

"Not much. Why?"

"Just a feeling." Quinn frowned and was quiet for a moment. "I shouldn't really give you any medical information—you're not her family, but I think you need to know just in case I'm right." He paused and glanced quickly up and down the empty hall. "She's evasive about the origins of some previous injuries. Does she have a husband or boyfriend?"

"Not that I know of. She says she's a widow." Jack looked over his shoulder through the doorway behind him to make sure Ben and Katie were still sleeping. "None of them will talk about their past, but they're afraid of something. I don't want to push too hard for information. I get the feeling they'd take off. They need help." Jack told his cousin about their uncle's letter. "So, let's keep this low-key, OK?"

Quinn sighed. "OK, but you are going to have to watch her carefully for the next couple of days. You've had a concussion or two. You know the drill. Call me tomorrow and let me know how she is."

Jack returned to the waiting room and lowered himself into the chair next to Ben. Katie was still sleeping, curled in a tiny ball on Ben's other side. Her face was far more peaceful in sleep than the haunted expression she wore when awake.

Jack looked at the tall, lanky youth slumped in the chair beside him. Ben's eyes were closed, but Jack knew he wasn't asleep by his uneven breathing.

"Is she gonna be all right?" The boy's voice shook.

"Yeah, she should be fine. She'll be ready to go home soon."

"I can take care of the horses and stuff until she's better. I know how," Ben offered.

"I'm sure you do, Ben. Don't worry about anything like that. We'll all pitch in for the next couple of weeks." Jack paused. "You know, Ben, your mom always seems so nervous. She's too thin. She needs to take better care of herself. I'm worried about her. I'd like to help you guys."

The boy silently contemplated the worn tread on his sneaker. With a tug of guilt, Jack pushed harder, sensing Ben was near the breaking point. The strain of the night's events had overloaded the boy's already stressed system.

"Ben, I was a policeman for a long time, but I can't help if I don't know what happened to you guys. You can't run from your problems forever. They tend to catch up with you eventually. That's no way to live. Let me help."

"He hit her." A single tear slipped out of Ben's closed eyes. "While they were dating, he was always so polite. Mom said he was the perfect gentleman. After, she stayed because he said he would hurt us if she didn't do what he told her. One night, they had a really big fight. Mom came and got us out of bed. She wouldn't talk about it, but she was bleeding and he was out cold on the floor. We left right then. He's been trying to find us ever since. Uncle James hid us for a while, but we had to leave his house because it got too dangerous."

Ben wiped a hand across his face and sniffed. He sat up a little straighter, like a burden had been lifted from his shoulders. "Are you going to tell her I told you? 'Cause she said we could never talk about it, but I don't think she planned on getting hurt like this. I like it here. We don't have anywhere else to go." Ben grabbed Jack's arm in a panicked grip. "You can't let him find us."

"It's OK, Ben. You're not alone anymore. I like having you guys around." Jack put his arm around Ben's shoulders. To his surprise, the boy didn't draw away, but leaned into him instead. Ben's body relaxed, and Jack's throat clogged for a minute.

Damn straight the asshole wasn't going to hurt them again.

"Did he ever hurt you or Katie?" Jack asked quietly, knowing he had to do it but not sure he wanted to hear the answer.

"No. But I don't think he likes kids very much."

Thank God for small favors.

"Can you tell me who he is?" He doubted Ben would answer, but it was worth a shot.

Ben shook his head. "I can't. I already broke my promise. He's a really important man." The boy looked as if he were going to cry again. His jaw was clenched and his hands balled up into fists. "I should have protected her. I should've done something."

"Ben, anything you could have done probably would have made things worse. It was best to let your mom handle it."

Ben glanced at Jack. "Please don't tell her I told you. She'll get real upset. She might make us leave. I shouldn't have said anything."

"You were right to tell me, Ben." Jack gave the boy another one-armed hug. He didn't want to push him too much. "When your mom is better, I'll talk to her. Maybe I can get her to trust me, too."

– – –

Afraid that Beth would try to get up by herself during the night, Jack grabbed a pillow and blanket and settled himself in the overstuffed chair in the corner of her room. Quinn had suggested he wake her every few hours anyway. And shit, he'd slept sitting in the front seat of a car plenty of times on stakeouts. With Beth sleeping soundly, he dozed off as soon as his head hit the back of the chair.

The rustle of bedding woke him. Jack opened his eyes and scanned the dark room, settling his gaze on the bed. Beth moved restlessly under the covers, whimpering. He glanced at the bedside clock. Several hours had passed. It was time to rouse her anyway.

He lurched to his feet and sat on the edge of the mattress. Moonlight streamed from the window across Beth's face, casting her skin ghostly white. Tears leaked from her closed eyes.

"Beth. It's Jack. Wake up. You're dreaming." He placed his hand gently on her forearm.

Her eyes snapped open. Her body jerked upright and flew backwards as if jolted with an electric shock. She huddled against the headboard like a wounded wild animal. Under the thin T-shirt, still spotted with dried blood, her chest heaved.

Jesus H.

Although he was tempted to back away and leave her to come around on her own, Jack held his position—and his breath. This was a make-or-break moment. She'd either accept or reject his help in the next couple of seconds. The fear that she'd push him away coiled tightly in his chest. "Beth, you're safe. You're having a nightmare."

Her haunted eyes blinked. She scanned the room and focused on him. Recognition dawned in her eyes, then humiliation. Slowly she sank down into a sitting position with her knees drawn up to her chest. She pressed the side of her face against her legs and closed her eyes, as if unable to endure his scrutiny.

Jack commiserated. No one wanted an audience for an emotional breakdown. As she fought for composure, he wiped any trace of sympathy from his face. Not an easy task.

Beth hadn't moved, but pain shadowed her face. Jack guessed she was too exhausted to cover it up. The shadows under her eyes were dark as bruises, as if she hadn't slept in a year. Then again, maybe she hadn't. Not if she had nightmares like this one.

She drew in an audible, ragged breath, and Jack wished he'd been able to make her stay in the hospital overnight. He'd feel a lot better about the situation if she'd had that CAT scan.

Her shoulders trembled. A protective instinct surged through Jack's body.

The sudden desire to hold her in his arms was overwhelming. It wasn't sexual. Oh, who was he kidding, there was definitely a sexual component, but this was more than that. His arms ached with the desire to comfort her as she cowered, small and alone, against the headboard.

He needed to hold her.

Jack's heart hammered as if he were walking on a frozen pond, waiting for it to break under his feet as he turned and slid backward, toward Beth. "Must have been some nightmare. A concussion can really mess you up. I've had my share."

Beth froze as he eased toward her. Their hips were nearly touching when he stopped. Stretching his legs out on the bed in front of him, he leaned back against the pillows and waited for a response. When she didn't pull away, he slid his arm gently around her shoulders and drew her to his chest. She stiffened for a moment reflexively, but a few seconds later, she gave in with a sigh and sagged against him. Warmth surged through Jack's chest. Her hair smelled like antiseptic instead of berries, but he inhaled anyway. Underneath the hospital smell was her scent, and Jack drew it in as affirmation that she was here, safe, in his arms.

Her breathing slowed as she relaxed back into sleep and physical exhaustion won out over nerves. A shiver passed through her body. Careful of the bandage on her arm, Jack lifted the blanket over her shoulders and closed his eyes. The adrenaline that had kept him operating at full tilt during the crisis had dissipated, sapping all of his energy.

As her sleep deepened, she pressed closer, as if her body sought more contact with his than her brain would allow when it was awake. Her heart thumped against his chest.

Jack lay in the dark, savoring the feel of her soft body clinging to his until sleep claimed him as well.

– – –

Jack blinked at the predawn light filtering through the blinds. Beth's body was warm and relaxed against his. Her head rested on his chest. Her breasts pressed against his ribs. He could get used to waking up like this. But how would Beth feel about the vulnerability she'd shown last night? Or the fact that she'd slept in his arms all night long? Given her aversion to physical contact, he doubted she'd be comfortable with the situation.

Slowly, and with some regret, he slid out from under her and gently eased her onto the mattress. The light fell across her face, highlighting her bruises against her pale skin. An ache formed in Jack's chest. She looked like she'd been beaten. She didn't stir as he rose and crept from the room.

Downstairs, he grabbed a quick shower. Ben was already in the kitchen when Jack headed for the coffee pot.

"I'll feed the horses," Ben volunteered.

Jack considered Beth's accident. He wasn't going to let anything happen to Ben. "Wait for me. I'll go with you."

Ten minutes later, the sun was barely above the trees as Jack stood in the barn aisle and stared at the ladder debris. Broken bits of woods of various sizes were scattered in a ten-foot arc. He would call a carpenter this morning, but he couldn't leave this mess in the aisle. Leaning on his cane, he bent down and started tossing pieces of wood into a wheelbarrow.

Ben slid the last stall door shut, latched it, and returned the scoop to the feed room. In the stalls around them, buckets banged against wood as the horses ate. "I gave them their grain, but I don't know how I'll get hay out of the loft."

"We'll get the extension ladder out of the garage as soon as I get this cleared away." Jack picked up a board. Bent, rusty nails protruded from the end.

"Can I help?"

"You could find me a rake." Jack could not let Ben near this junk. God only knew when the kids last had a tetanus shot booster, and they'd spent more than enough time in the ER last night.

Ben jogged off on his quest. Jack picked up a split ladder rung and moved to toss it into the pile when a mark on the edge caught his attention.

What the hell?

The narrow cut looked fresh and clean, and cut straight across the grain, not like it had broken by accident but as if someone had cut through it with a saw. Had to be a coincidence. The wood was old and worn. Chances were it had simply fallen apart. The only other possibility was that someone had done this intentionally, to try to hurt Beth. Jack's gut clenched at the image of Beth's battered body. He could still feel her curled up against him, soft and vulnerable in the dark.

He glanced up at the loft, roughly twelve feet above his head, then looked down to reexamine the broken wood in his hands. Beth could have broken her neck in the fall, but sabotaging a ladder wasn't an efficient way to try to kill a person. The chances of the attempt being successful were too slim.

No. This had to be an accident.

But as Jack gathered the remaining debris in the wheelbarrow and carted it back to the garage, the back of his neck began to itch.

A suspicious accident was an excellent way to flush someone out of hiding.

CHAPTER SEVENTEEN

Beth blinked. Daylight stabbed her eyeballs. She squinted at the bedside clock and winced. She hadn't slept till noon since she was a teenager. Guilt edged into her thoughts. Were the kids OK? Although she knew in her gut that Jack would look after them, habitual panic crept over her. They had to be scared.

She needed to get her butt out of bed. Seeing her up and moving would alleviate their fears. She also had to get down to the barn and retrieve her gun before Jack found it. Ben had stashed it the night before while Jack went for the car. Ben could handle the Sig, but the sight of the gun in his hands always brought Beth's deepest fears bubbling to the surface.

She sat up slowly. Her head throbbed, and her elbow was stiff and swollen. She grimaced. Pain shot through her cheek. Her body ached like she'd been beaten—she happened to know just what that felt like. On the bright side, being upright did not generate dizziness or nausea. Not bad, considering how far she'd fallen.

Physical assessment complete, her hand drifted to the indentation of Jack's head and shoulders on the mattress. She lifted the pillow and held it to her face. Closing her eyes, she let his masculine scent waft over her. For a second, she longed to feel his body next to hers, solid and warm, fooling her brain into thinking that everything would be all right. Her body tensed. One innocent night together and his absence left her bereft.

She'd let him get too close.

There was nothing she could do about it today. With her injuries, she wasn't going anywhere anytime soon. The estate was the safest place for the children. James had said so. And he was the only person she truly trusted. Not for the first time, she thought she should have told him her whole, humiliating story. He wouldn't have doubted her. But what could one elderly man do? James didn't have money or any kind of power.

But Jack did. Jack could help them.

Should she tell him everything? Not only did Jack have the financial resources, he'd been a cop. A homicide detective. He'd seen things far worse than domestic abuse and attempted murder. Surely he'd believe her. Wouldn't he?

That was the real problem. She just didn't know for sure. Her story was pretty far-fetched. In her current physically vulnerable state, the risk was too great.

She dangled her legs off the mattress for a few seconds before pushing herself to her feet. Her knees wobbled but held as she shuffled into the bathroom. One glance in the mirror and her eyes filled. She'd been hurt before, but Richard had been smart enough to keep his fists away from her face. A few broken ribs hadn't been a problem, but a congressman's wife couldn't have a black eye.

The bright lights emphasized the bruise on her temple. Her eye was black. Between the bruising, her pallor, and the bandage on her forehead, she looked like a walking corpse, something out of *Night of the Living Dead*.

She eyed the concealer and pressed powder in the medicine cabinet. Not going to happen. There wasn't enough makeup in Hollywood to make her look alive. Plus, the skin on her face was too tender. The best she was going to manage this morning was clean. And that was going to hurt.

Beth took a deep breath, turned the tap to warm, and washed the dried blood from her face and hair. Stripping off her blood-stained clothes, she scrubbed the hospital smell from her skin. A few minutes later she eased into a pair of sweats and an oversized T-shirt.

Even with a clear head, Beth took a firm hold on the banister as she descended the curved stairs. Her knees were still shaky, her body ridiculously fatigued from washing up.

Shock lit up Jack's face as she stepped into the kitchen.

"What are you doing out of bed?" He leaped to his feet, limped across the kitchen, and cupped her uninjured elbow. "Why didn't you call for me? You shouldn't have come down the stairs by yourself."

Beth barely registered the words. Instead her attention focused on the warmth of his palm on her arm. Heat flowed from his skin to hers. His aftershave drifted down, and Beth resisted the urge to bury her face in his neck for a deep sniff. If she did, he'd wrap his arms around her and pull her against his long, hard body. She already knew what it felt like to be embraced by his strength, and she leaned toward him like a plant growing toward the sun.

Fire gathered in her belly. She froze. She was in deep trouble. Over her head, sitting on the bottom of the ocean deep. She *should* have been embarrassed about her behavior the night before. But her whacked-out body chose to flood with pleasure at the physical contact instead, as if it knew where it belonged—in his arms.

Clearing her throat she managed to reply, "I'm fine, really."

He led her to a chair and eased her down into it. His hand slid up her arm to squeeze her shoulder for a second. The tension in his fingers transmitted the concern he didn't voice.

Beth lifted her eyes to his. There was something else there in addition to worry. Desire? No way. Impossible. Not the way she looked this morning.

Her thoughts returned to the way his arms had felt around her cold body the night before: strong, reassuring, protective. His presence had kept her nightmares at bay. She hadn't slept that deeply in years. Her heart told her this man would not betray her.

Her heart?

She jerked her gaze away. The quick movement of her eyeballs sent pain flashing through her temples.

What was wrong with her? The knock on the head must have killed too many brain cells to process rational thought. She'd had two serious relationships in her life. One had ended in death, leaving her with a broken heart she'd never get over. The second man she'd trusted had beaten the hell out of her, then imprisoned and tried to kill her. She could not rely on her instincts. Her heart was too easily deceived. Her heart was a total chump.

Jack's forehead wrinkled as he registered her withdrawal. Disappointment crossed his face. She could only hope he'd attribute last night's weakness to pain and disorientation rather than the deep attraction she felt for him.

His hand slid off her shoulder, leaving her cold in its absence. He took a step back and winced as he reached for the counter for support. "What would you like to eat?"

Beth's stomach churned, either from the headache or emotional turmoil. Or both. "I'm not really hungry."

"Head hurt?" he asked, brows furrowed.

At her nod, he moved to the counter and slid a piece of bread into the toaster. "Let's see if you can get a piece of toast down. Then I'll get you some aspirin."

With an elbow on the table, she rested her forehead in her hand—anything to keep her eyes off Jack. She didn't trust herself to remain aloof when her body responded to him without consulting with her brain.

A bark drew her gaze to the door. Henry stood on the patio. The second Jack let him in, he trotted to Beth's chair, rested his massive head in her lap, and whined. She stroked his head.

"Where are the kids?" She steeled her spine and turned to Jack. She needn't have worried. He'd erased all traces of desire from his face.

"Mrs. Harris took them down to the pool." He opened the fridge and poured a glass of juice. "Henry was with them. I wonder what brought him back? He must have been hot."

Jack set the toast and juice on the table, along with a bottle of aspirin.

As Beth began to eat, Henry lowered his body to the floor and rested his head on her bare feet with a sigh. Although her foot fell asleep, Beth left the dog's head right where it was as she drank her juice and swallowed two tablets.

"If you need something stronger for pain, I can call Quinn. Let me know."

Beth's stomach turned. "No. Nothing stronger. I don't like to take medication."

Jack shrugged. "OK. The option's there if you change your mind."

"I won't."

Jack cleared her dishes from the table and placed a first-aid kit on the counter. "Your bandages need to be changed." He unfolded a yellow carbon copy of her discharge instructions. After settling reading glasses on his nose, he reviewed Quinn's notes before unraveling the gauze from her elbow. She steeled herself for his touch, but the brush of his fingers on her skin still sent tremors up her arm.

He paused. "I'm sorry. Did I hurt you?"

Beth shook her head but remained silent. What could she say? *I know I look and feel like a corpse right now, plus I'm a complete emotional wreck, but I'd still like to jump your bones?* Hardly seemed appropriate.

Jack continued, gently blotting her stitches with antiseptic and applying antibiotic cream before bandaging the wound. Holding her chin still with one hand, he repeated the process with the cut on her temple. While he worked, his thumb gently stroked her jaw. The effect was nearly hypnotic, and Beth felt her body relax.

Mrs. Harris's muffled voice came through the French doors, followed by a high-pitched little girl laugh.

Jack released her chin and sat back. Beth exhaled as space opened up between their bodies. Jack placed a hand on her forearm. Her breath caught as he looked straight into her eyes. "You'll tell me if you feel worse, right? Any dizziness, nausea, or confusion? Since you insisted on leaving the hospital without that CAT scan last night, we have nothing else to go on but your symptoms. So I need to be able to trust you on this." He nodded toward the French doors. Mrs. Harris and the kids were stepping onto the patio. "For their sake."

With a silent prayer that she'd heal quickly, she nodded. "OK."

He released her arm, but not before she caught a glimmer of something new in his eyes. Could his feelings for her run deeper than mere desire? A tiny bud of fear bloomed inside her. If that were the case, could she handle it? Would she ever be able to handle a real relationship again, or was she just too damaged? And if she couldn't deal, what would that do to Jack?

She closed her eyes. What would she do after she'd recovered? If she stayed here much longer, there'd be no denying the powerful bond developing between them.

CHAPTER EIGHTEEN

The thick fog cleared, rolling away over the hills like smoke in the wind. The green and dripping forest came into focus. The woods were silent except for the babbling of water over rock and the intermittent plop of moisture from the canopy. Mist floated along the muddy bank of a small stream.

In the shallows near the edge, a woman's naked body lay face-down, caught in the exposed roots of an overhanging tree. From the waist down, she was submerged beneath the knee-deep water. One slim hand rested upon a bluish rock, as if she were reaching for dry ground. Long dark hair swirled in a patch of rotten leaves and algae. Insects buzzed, feasting on the grayish-green skin. On the gentle current, a leaf floated off the curve of a shoulder, revealing the small butterfly tattoo that decorated the bloated skin.

The shrill neigh of a horse woke James.

He bolted upright from a deep sleep.

His lungs heaved. Soaked with perspiration, his white undershirt clung to his skin like a clammy hand. Heart slamming inside his chest, he glanced around the hotel room. The only sound was the faint hum of the ceiling fan. No horse. No woods. No creek.

More importantly—no dead body.

He wiped a shaky hand across his face. Swinging his feet off the bed, he reached for the bottle of water on the nightstand and took a long swallow. He gave himself two minutes, just enough time for his pulse to return to normal without losing the connection. Then he gritted his teeth and pulled the image back into his mind. James concentrated on the details to blot out the stomach-clenching horror.

Beth doesn't have a tattoo. It's not her.

Relief clogged his throat as the image dissipated. He exhaled hard and finished the bottle of water.

From the back the dead woman bore a superficial resemblance to Beth. Caucasian, slim bone structure, long brown hair. But the tattoo was the key. He'd seen Beth in plenty of tank tops. He'd have noticed a purple butterfly on the back of her shoulder.

But then, why was he getting a vision of a dead woman? It didn't make sense. One, he didn't normally see people who were already dead. His visions normally tapped into the violence that caused their deaths. Once they were gone, for him that was it. Two, he'd never dreamed about a stranger before. Who was she? She must be connected to him somehow. Without an image of her face, and given the condition of the body, he'd never know.

Hell, it could have just been a damned dream. It'd never happened before, but what the fuck? Shit happened. People dreamed of things that didn't have horrific consequences all the time. Other people. Normal people.

Resigned to the bizarre nature of his life, James headed for a hot shower. A few minutes later, after ordering coffee and breakfast through room service, he fired up his laptop and began to scroll through the hundreds of images he'd shot of Congressman Baker.

Instinct told him he'd missed something.

He hit the slideshow button, sat back, and watched the pictures flash onto the screen one by one. The photos of Baker's speech at the DC park popped up last. James sat up straighter. It was here. He knew it. What was he missing?

He set the album from that day to run in a continuous loop and cleared his head, letting the images roll over him. Room service delivered his breakfast. He was through his omelet and half a pot of coffee before he spotted it.

There. James hit the stop button. His face pulled into a grin. Now he knew the bastard's secret.

He hadn't caught it because he'd been looking at the wrong person.

Now all he had to do was verify his suspicion.

CHAPTER NINETEEN

"Did you hear about the accident over at the O'Malley place?"

Over the clink of silverware on plates, the name caught his attention. He paused, a fork full of eggs halfway to his mouth. Focusing on the conversation in the booth across the aisle, he resumed eating. Two women, both in their fifties, sipped coffee while they waited for their order. He'd seen them both before around town but couldn't recall their names. Only young, beautiful women caught his attention.

The skinnier woman continued, "My sister was at the hospital last night with her daughter. Shannon sprained her wrist at gymnastics. They saw Danny O'Malley's nephew, the one who inherited everything, in the ER with some woman who works for him."

His heart rate accelerated. He swallowed but didn't even taste the omelet.

"His name is John or Jack, I think." Chubs fanned her face with a menu. "As my daughter would say, he's a hottie."

He clenched his jaw as the old bats discussed O'Malley's physical attributes. He stabbed a piece of sausage and sliced it through with one stroke of the knife.

Get on with it, bitch!

Skinny sighed. "Not that it matters. According to my sister, he's got a thing for this woman. Vicky could tell just by the way he treated her. Anyway, seems she fell out of the barn loft…"

He listened until the women moved onto another topic.

Such was life in a small town. Everybody knows everything about everyone—or so they thought. He'd lived here all his life, and no one would ever suspect what he'd done. Or how many times he'd done it.

Calmed by the memories, he finished his hash browns and buttered a slice of toast.

Beth's injuries presented a problem. If the old bitch was right, he doubted Beth would be off the estate much in the next week or so. He was too smart to try to grab her there. As an ex-cop, O'Malley'd be armed. And suspicious.

Disappointment crushed him. He'd been so excited. Beth didn't go out much, but he could count on her two early-morning trips into town to run errands each week, usually Tuesday and Friday.

Today was Wednesday. His playroom was all ready. He'd been hoping, planning on snatching her this week, or next at the latest. How hard would it be to wait another two or three weeks? His fingers tightened on his fork.

No way could he wait that long. He'd need a substitute to tide him over until Beth was ready.

But who? How should he choose? After Amelia, he'd never be satisfied with a whore again. He needed a worthy opponent. Should he whip out his dartboard again? Or maybe find another way to liven up the game?

The waitress drifted past his table, stopping to fill his coffee cup and ask him if he needed anything.

"No thanks, Mary Ann," he answered.

She smiled and ripped his check off her pad. Mary Ann was dark-haired and petite, with a wide smile and a trim figure.

He stood and reached into his pocket for his wallet, tossing a few bills on the table for a tip. Business was slow this late on a weekday morning, and there wasn't a hostess on duty. In the diner's tiled vestibule, Mary Ann rang him up at the cash register.

He'd known her casually for a long time. Why hadn't he noticed how pretty she was before? Not beautiful, just wholesome and fresh-faced. He handed her a twenty. "You look nice this morning."

Dropping her head shyly, she blushed and handed over his change. "You have a good day."

"I will. Thanks." He exited the diner with a new spring in his step.

Mary Ann was lovely.

He wondered how loudly she could scream.

CHAPTER TWENTY

"It'll be fun." Jack rose from the table, crossed the sunny kitchen, and emptied the coffee pot into his mug. It was only his second cup this morning, so Beth must have consumed three-quarters of the pot already. He glanced at the digital clock on the microwave's black keypad. Seven a.m. She'd already fed the horses. He glanced at the kitchen sink. No sign she'd fed herself. No surprise.

Beth pressed the fingertips of one hand to her forehead and rubbed them in a circle. Again. "It's not that I don't think it'll be fun. But they're your family. I don't want to intrude."

"Headache?"

Beth's hand froze. "Just a little. It's OK."

Jack didn't comment. She was the world's worst liar. If her skin got any paler or the circles under her eyes any darker, she'd be able to pass for a vampire. She'd been working on the bookkeeping late every night and rising early to care for the horses. Pushing herself was taking its toll, especially since it had only been five days since she'd fallen. Pain shadowed her face, and she'd lost weight from a frame that couldn't spare an ounce.

Although Jack had framed his invitation to Quinn's house as a social affair, in truth he wanted his cousin to check on Beth's recovery. Nothing short of duct tape and chloroform would get her back to the hospital, but someone needed to take a look at her, if only for Jack's peace of mind. She ignored his suggestions to slow down and rest. "It's only a barbecue. It'd be good for Ben and Katie to be with other kids."

"I don't know, Jack." Beth bit her lower lip, a gesture he tried like hell not to find sexy. Not working, despite her battered state.

"Come on, Beth." He persisted, counting on the fact that she was too tired to argue with him. "They don't bite. Well, not anymore. Mark went through a biting stage when he was little. He mostly bit Steven, though, who deserved it. So, I'm not sure it counts. Besides, the kids deserve to have some fun, don't they?"

After Ben's revelation at the hospital, Jack understood why she was reluctant to take the children out in public, but they'd be safe at his cousin's house. Of course, he couldn't use that argument, because he wasn't supposed to know they were in danger.

Tangled webs and all the shit that went along with them were giving *him* a headache.

As he expected, she relented. Jack felt a twinge of guilt, which he shook off. He was doing the right thing. So why did he feel like such a prick?

That afternoon, Jack turned the SUV into the long driveway of Quinn's yellow and white farmhouse. A mix of clover, grass, and weeds flanked the gravel on both sides. Parking behind Quinn's minivan, he went to the rear of the vehicle to release Henry while Beth and the kids climbed out. Ben handed him the cane that he'd stowed in the back seat. Baskets and pots of bright flowers hung on the porch. Two bikes had been left near the base of the wide steps, and a pair of small, muddy cleats stood drying on the porch.

Jack stole a glance at Beth as she closed the car door. Instead of the jeans she normally lived in, her slim body was draped in a khaki skirt and fitted polo. Now that he thought about it, he'd never seen her in anything other than jeans, which was odd, considering the heat. He wasn't complaining. Most of her jeans were so old and worn they cupped her ass like hands, but this snug skirt gave him a new appreciation for her bare, toned legs.

With Beth and the children close behind him, Jack pushed open the squeaky screen door and led the way toward the kitchen in the back of the house. Henry bolted down the hallway. Something metal crashed to the floor.

"Ouch! Get down, Henry. Good boy. Go on outside and see the kids."

As Jack entered the sunny room, his cousins' wives were pushing the big dog out the kitchen door. Henry resisted, sitting back on his haunches like a mule until he heard Quinn's boys yelling out in the yard. Then the dog shot through the doorway with a happy bark.

"If you taught your dog not to steal food from the counters, I wouldn't have to give him the boot." Quinn's wife, Claire, greeted Jack with a kiss, then smoothed her short blond hair away from her face.

Jack introduced Beth and the kids to Claire and Amanda, Sean's wife.

"Hi, Beth. It's nice to meet you. Ben, the boys are out back. Katie, Sam and Ally are playing in the living room. I'll take you in there if you want." Either Claire had universal Mommy appeal or Katie was coming out of her shell. The child took Claire's hand and followed her down the hall without hesitation.

"Do you want to sit down?" Amanda's eyes lingered on Beth's face, and Jack cringed. Amanda's face, along with the rest of her, belonged on a magazine cover, which emphasized Beth's fresh-from-the-boxing-ring appearance.

Beth gave her head a quick shake. "No, I'm OK. It looks worse than it feels."

Christ, he hoped so.

Sean stepped through the back door, slapped Jack on the shoulder, and greeted Beth with "Man, that's gotta hurt. Can I get you a beer?" Leave it to Sean to not only point out the elephant in the corner but to trot the fucker out for inspection. Subtlety wasn't his cousin's forte.

"No beer for the lady with the concussion, you idiot." Quinn came through the back door and smacked his brother on the back of his head. Sean was large and lethal, but he was still the younger brother. "Iced tea, lemonade, soda, yes. Alcohol, no." Quinn shook his head. "Hi, Beth. How's the head?"

"It's fine. Thanks." Each time she said it, her voice grew weaker. She raised her chin to answer, squinting at the late-afternoon sun slanting through the windows.

Leaning on his cane, Jack took her by the arm with his free hand and led her out to the patio. "Come on outside. The boys are playing ball." He deposited her in a cushioned chair then returned to the kitchen for two glasses of lemonade. Returning, he handed one to Beth. Her face was turned to the field where Ben was playing catch with Steven and Mark.

Jack moved away as Quinn stepped outside, started up the gas grill, and approached Beth. "Did you take anything for that headache today?"

"No."

Quinn sighed. "Did you get that prescription filled?"

"No. I don't like to take drugs."

"Nauseous?" Quinn sat down in the chair next to Beth.

She shrank back a hair. "A little."

"Sleeping?" Quinn dug a penlight out of his pocket and checked her eyes.

"No. She doesn't sleep very much," Jack called out from the other side of the patio, where he was using his cane to fill in a small hole Henry had dug in the mulched flowerbed. Beth flashed an angry glare in his direction.

Quinn went back into the house and returned a minute later. He handed her a small tablet. "This is for nausea. Your choice." At her doubtful stare, he added dryly, "It's not crack or heroin, promise."

She squinted up at him for a few seconds before taking the pill and washing it down with lemonade.

"I'll send you home with some samples. There's no reason to feel awful when you don't have to. And remind me to take out those stitches before you leave." Quinn turned toward the boys. "Steven's working on his batting." He raised his voice and called out over the field, "Let me get the burgers on. Then I'll throw you some balls, Steven."

"I can toss him some, Dr. Wilson," Ben offered, trotting over to the makeshift mound. Steven grabbed a bat. Mark jogged out a dozen yards behind Ben.

Sean emerged from the house and handed Quinn a platter of food. "I'll catch." He grabbed a mitt and walked over to Steven, squatting down a safe distance behind him.

Ben threw an easy pitch right across the plate. Steven swung, missed. The ball hit Sean's mitt dead center with a solid thump.

Sean raised an eyebrow, threw the ball back to Ben. Another perfect, easy pitch sailed dead center over the plate. *Thump*. Sean glanced over at Jack, who shrugged his shoulders. After correcting Steven's stance and raising the boy's elbow a few inches, Sean tossed the ball back to Ben, who continued to throw until Steven hit a grounder.

"Can you throw a fastball, Ben?" Sean asked in a deceptively nonchalant tone. At the grill, Quinn's head swiveled toward the boys like a hawk sighting a mouse.

"Sure." Ben put a little more effort into his windup and let the ball fly. It sailed across the plate and hit Sean's mitt with a loud smacking sound.

Quinn's mouth dropped open. "Oh, man."

Jack glanced at Beth, but he didn't think she'd heard. Her eyelids drooped, and her head lolled back on the chair's high back. Once again, the complete exhaustion on her face troubled Jack, but at least she was finally getting some rest. He turned back to the boys and crossed the yard to get a better view.

Quinn closed the grill. "I'll throw you a few, Ben. Mark, you and Steven field."

Quinn took the mound. Ben swung, making solid contact and sending the ball sailing far out into the pasture.

"Sorry, Dr. Wilson. I'll go get it." Ben jogged off into the pasture, followed by Steven, Mark, and Henry, who raced ahead of the boys to steal the baseball. Quinn and Sean started back toward the patio.

"Henry, give it back!" Steven yelled as Henry dodged his attempt to take the ball.

Jack looked over at Beth, sound asleep. He frowned at the awkward tilt of her head.

"Earth to Jack." Quinn tapped him on the shoulder. "Did you know he could play like that?"

Steven dragged Henry to the back door and shoved him into the house.

"I had no idea." Jack motioned toward Beth. "What did you give her, Quinn? She's out cold."

"Just something for the nausea. She looked like shit warmed over. Drowsiness is a side effect."

Jack shook his head. "You probably should've mentioned that."

"No worries. She'll feel better when she wakes up." Quinn shrugged and waved him off. "Now, back to Ben and my vision of him on my Little League team in the spring. When's his birthday? He's twelve, right? Please tell me he doesn't turn thirteen until after January first."

Sean got a beer from the cooler and joined Jack and Quinn.

Jack shook his head. "I don't know." He glanced back at Beth, still sleeping, then looked out into the pasture where the three boys had returned to playing catch. He lowered his voice so only his cousins could hear and summarized his suspicions and his conversation with Ben.

"You need help, you call me." Sean's blue eyes went flat.

Jack had already counted on Sean's help. Not only did Sean's home security company install top-notch systems, but his cousin had unsavory associates with access to records that weren't legally available to the general public.

"For starters, let's talk about bringing the estate's alarm into this century." Jack leaned closer to Sean and lowered his voice. "Then I want you to do a little research for me. Completely under the radar."

His cousin nodded. "Tell me what you have."

"Not here." Jack's gaze shot to Beth, stirring to life on the patio. He shook his head. "I'll call you tomorrow."

— — —

Beth sat up and rubbed her eyes. Her head felt like it was filled with rubber cement. What the hell had Quinn given her?

"Good, you're awake. Dinner's almost ready." A few feet away Amanda set down a huge tray of condiments on the picnic table. Behind her, Claire carried a bowl of salad and a tall glass.

"I'm sorry. I didn't mean to fall asleep." Beth would have blushed if her nerve endings weren't semicomatose.

"Not your fault. My husband drugged you." Claire smiled as she handed her an iced tea. "He should be apologizing to you. Quinn can be presumptuous. He always thinks he knows what's best. Unfortunately for his super-sized ego, he's usually right. Some caffeine should perk you up a bit. You've got a few minutes yet until the burgers are ready."

Claire and Amanda returned to the house to retrieve more food.

Jack stood with his cousins on the other side of the yard, watching the boys play catch in the field. He caught Beth's eye and walked over to sit in the chair next to her. He set his cane aside and stretched out his damaged leg. His uninjured knee touched hers. Beth, still woozy, stared at the hard length of Jack's thigh.

"You OK?" He must have thought she was zoning out because he rested a hand on her forearm, and Beth felt something inside go warm and pliant. The drug suppressed her anxiety and inhibitions, and all she could think about was Jack's body so close to hers. Close enough to touch. Her hormones needed a leash. The familiar and enticing scent of Jack's aftershave drifted to her nose, and Beth felt the undeniable ache for him deep in her belly. *Yikes.*

She moved her knee away from his and nodded. "Yes, but I don't like sedatives."

"Ben's a great baseball player. Hell of an arm." Jack changed the subject with a frown as she tugged her arm out from under his hand.

Distracted, Beth sucked down some iced tea, willing the caffeine to jump-start her brain cells. "I know. It's genetic. He used to play on the travel team. His father played in the minors." She bit her lip as that bit of personal information popped out of her mouth. Thankfully, Jack didn't pursue that thread of the conversation, but it reinforced the reason she didn't drink alcohol, not even a single glass of wine. She couldn't afford to let her guard down.

"Don't tell Quinn. He's already drooling."

"Dinner's ready!" Claire shouted inside the house, then again outside.

The screen door opened. Katie and two little blond-haired girls emerged with Henry at their heels. The big shepherd wore a yellow bonnet, tied in a fat bow under his chin.

"Uncle Jack! Look, we painted his nails." One of the blondes dragged the hundred-pound dog over to Jack by the collar. Bright pink polish coated the dog's nails.

Jack hung his head toward his seven-year-old niece. "Sam, you're killing me here."

Sam grinned. Henry wagged his tail and licked her face.

"Christ! Let me get my camera." Quinn wiped the tears from his eyes and ran into the house. "You're never gonna live this one down, Jack."

Sean laughed so hard he almost fell off his chair. Sam released Henry and climbed into her father's lap. Her younger sister, Ally, claimed his other knee. "What's so funny, Daddy?"

Even angry with Quinn, Beth couldn't contain a snicker.

Henry looked hopefully at the platter of hamburgers on the table and drooled. Katie sidled up between Beth and Jack. Then, to Beth's surprise, the little girl leaned on Jack's shoulder.

"Want to sit with me?" Jack whispered. When she nodded her head, he lifted her into his lap and wrapped both arms around her. She rested her head against his chest.

In the next chair, Beth's heart ached. Katie didn't even remember her father, nor had she ever had anyone to fill that hole in her life.

After nightfall, they drove back in Jack's truck. Katie fell asleep in the back seat. Ben yawned, and Henry snored. Instead of driving around to the garage, Jack parked at the head of the circular drive. Beth got out of the car and opened the back door to pick up Katie, but Jack was already there.

"I've got her." He lifted her up onto his shoulder and carried her into the house.

"But your leg…"

"She doesn't weigh anything, Beth." He held Katie in place with one hand. He left his cane just inside the front door and leaned on the banister.

Beth followed them up the steps. Katie looked small and helpless draped over Jack's big body. In the child's bedroom, he set her on the bed and started to remove her pink sneakers.

Beth's breath hitched at the site of Jack performing such an intimate, parental chore. "I'll take it from here."

Swallowing any reaction to her rebuff, Jack stepped back as Beth took his place at Katie's side. "OK. Good night." As he turned to leave, Henry pushed past his legs and settled on the floor, resting his black muzzle on his huge, pink-tipped paws.

"Jack?" Beth didn't look at him as she tucked Katie into bed. "Thanks. They had a good time today."

The kids had chased lightning bugs, eaten too much ice cream, and done all the things normal kids did on a hot summer night. Beth had gotten through it, too. After the drowsiness had passed, her head hadn't ached. She'd even eaten a hamburger.

"I'm glad." Jack paused in the doorway. "I know you're mad at Quinn, but he sent some of those pills home for you. You might want to consider taking one before you go to bed. I'll leave them in the top kitchen cabinet with the aspirin." Before she could respond, Jack turned and left the room.

Loneliness crushed her chest. Her next deep breath threatened to split her open. She closed her eyes and exhaled. The pressure didn't abate.

What she really wanted to do was follow him and climb in his lap like Katie had earlier. But that same thought also terrified her.

Beth brushed the hair from her daughter's forehead. Jack had slipped through their defenses. How could her kids endure yet another separation if—no, when—it became necessary? Eventually they would have to leave. This would be over only when Richard was dead. He'd probably sent hired help to kill her. She and Richard wouldn't ever end up face to face. And she could never go after him herself. Shooting someone in self-defense was one thing. Premeditated murder was quite another.

CHAPTER TWENTY-ONE

Beth sat on the living room sofa and flipped through a landscaping magazine on her lap, feet curled under her body. She stopped to make a few notes on pruning overgrown rhododendrons. A purple jungle suffocated one side of the house. A dull ache throbbed behind her eyes, and she closed the magazine. Enough eyeball strain for the moment. On the floor in front of the couch, Ben and Katie worked on a puzzle they'd found in an upstairs closet. Stretched out beside them, Henry snored. The overcast late-morning light filtered through the blinds, projecting stripes across the thick Oriental rug.

It was the quiet sort of day that would have been unremarkable a few years ago. But now she appreciated the peace. After a month at the estate, she felt at home.

Her eyes drifted closed. She regretted taking a second pill before climbing into bed. Quinn's medicine had worked wonders on her nausea last night but had left her with a foggy hangover. The kids' voices muted as she dozed.

The squeak of sneakers on hardwood jolted her. Her eyelids snapped open.

"Oh, geez. I woke you. I'm sorry." Guilt crossed Jack's face as he stepped through the door, his lean body clad in gym shorts and a chest-hugging T-shirt. "I'm headed to physical therapy."

"OK." Even in her drowsy state—or maybe because she was chemically relaxed—Beth drank in his muscular biceps and torso, the hard chest she'd clung to that one night. Her fingers itched to touch his bare skin. Desire sparked in her belly. She swallowed and averted her eyes.

Jack's brows knitted as he studied her face, as if trying to understand her discomfort.

Fat chance.

"Are you sure? I can cancel. I don't really want to leave you here alone," Jack said.

"I'll be fine. Mrs. Harris'll be back in an hour or two." Time alone was exactly what she needed, along with a cold shower and a strong dose of reality to take her mind off his truly fine physique. The fact that his personality was just as attractive didn't help.

Jack shook his head. "Still…"

"Go," Beth interrupted. "You're making such good progress. Please don't do anything to hold back your recovery. I can't possibly hurt myself sitting on the sofa."

"OK. I have my cell if you need anything. The rehab center's only fifteen minutes from here." Jack nodded to Ben. "You have my number, right, Ben?"

"Yes, sir."

Seemingly satisfied, Jack ducked out of the room. His uneven footsteps faded down the hall. The front door opened and closed.

Beth walked to the window to watch him navigate the walk and climb into his SUV. The limp was still pronounced, but his stride had gained strength. He might not be able to return to the police force, but he still had a life ahead of him.

Jack's truck disappeared down the tree-lined driveway. Beth moved away from the window.

Beth turned to Ben and gave him a pointed look. "I'm going outside for a while. You and Katie stay in the house, OK?" She picked up the remote and clicked on the TV for background noise. A *Hannah Montana* rerun popped onto the screen. "And don't let Henry out."

Katie glanced up and smiled. "OK, Mommy." Her daughter's attention flickered between the puzzle and the television.

Ben scowled. He knew exactly what she was planning to do. "But you told Jack you weren't going to do anything."

"I know, honey. Sometimes grown-ups have to do things they don't want to do."

And it totally sucks.

Despite her son's frown, Beth retrieved her gun, ammunition, and ear protection from the bedroom and walked out behind the garage. Since the incident with Will Martin in the grocery store, she'd kept the Sig strapped to her ankle whenever she went outside. She stuck to wearing her extra long and baggy jeans but lived in fear Jack would notice if she wore the gun around the house. He seemed to notice everything.

The gun's weight was a constant reminder of her vulnerability. It kept her from pretending she had a normal life. She took a minute to calm down, center herself, focus. She buried her turbulent emotions. According to James, the cooler the head, the better the shot.

She inhaled the clean, country air through her nose.

A bird chirped in the tree to her left. Light wind blew a few dry pine needles to the ground. Tree limbs above her head swayed. A small animal rustled a nearby bush.

She exhaled through her mouth.

With both hands she raised the gun to shoulder level, and then spread her feet to shoulder width. Her injured arm trembled. Gritting her teeth, she steadied it and pictured Richard's face, contorted with perverse pleasure as he raised a fist over her. She sighted and fired at the hay bale. The gun jerked in her hand, sending sharp jolts of pain to her elbow.

But she'd hit the target dead center.

She squared up to do it again.

– – –

Jack parked in front of the garage and walked over to Sean's Yukon. "Thanks for coming out."

Sean climbed out and stood next to the open door. "No problem. Finished up that last job early anyway."

"Yeah, well. Since my physical therapist canceled, I thought we might get a jump on testing the existing alarm." Jack scratched his chin. "I'd like to add quite a few features." He still held onto his theory that Beth's accident in the barn was caused by old and rotten wood, but the remote possibility that someone had managed to sneak onto the estate to hurt her gnawed at his gut.

"Who knows? Danny never used it. Wouldn't let me touch a single wire. We'd probably be better off ripping the whole system out and starting from scratch." Sean tossed his keys onto the seat of his truck.

"Maybe, but I don't want to go without right now, even for a few days."

Sean raised an eyebrow. "I'll see what I can do."

The report of a gunshot rang across the forest. Jack and Sean ducked behind Yukon's door.

"That was close!" Jack peered through the side window.

"I'm pretty sure it came from that direction." Sean pointed over the garage. "Probably just a kid. Or somebody target shooting."

Jack pulled out his cell phone.

Sean stared. "What are you doing?"

"Calling Mike."

"You really want to bother the chief of police to arrest some kid and his old man shooting a possum or coyote? This isn't the city, Jack. Up here people shoot guns for perfectly legitimate reasons. Hell, everybody in Westbury has at least one gun."

He had a point. Jack snapped his cell closed.

"Besides, we take care of our own up here." Sean leaned into the vehicle and pulled out a nine-millimeter Glock. In case the shooter's reasons weren't so legitimate, Jack supposed.

"Come on. We'll check it out." Sean ran and Jack limped around the side of the garage. Sean paused and peered around the corner. He gave a low whistle. "Oh, man."

Another shot rang out. This time very close.

Jack smacked his cousin's shoulder and whispered, "What?"

Sean dropped to one knee so Jack could see over him. Beth stood with her back to them, pointing a handgun at a hay bale target twenty-five or thirty feet away. She fired. Straw shuddered. Small bits poofed into the air.

"That is so hot." Sean's voice startled Jack. They needn't worry about Beth hearing them. Heavy-duty earplugs stuck out of her ears.

"What is wrong with you?" Jack glanced at his cousin.

"Don't know. I'm a happily married man, but a gorgeous woman handling a gun like that always gives me a chubby." Sean sighed. "She's a hell of a shot."

His cousin's assessment of Beth's shooting was correct. She fired the weapon several more times, amassing a neat cluster of bullet holes in the target. But obliterating a bale of hay wasn't even close to the same thing as shooting at a live, moving object.

He applauded her skill, even if it didn't mean she'd be able to actually shoot a person should the need arise. But should he let her know he'd seen her practicing? Would it freak her out? Everything else did.

Jack pulled Sean behind the cover of the building.

His cousin protested, "I wanted to watch."

Jack shook his head as they started back toward their cars. "I don't want her to know I know she has a gun. Christ, that doesn't even make sense."

"I get it. She might not take it well." Sean huffed. "Doesn't mean I have to like it."

They rounded the long, low building and approached their vehicles.

"She doesn't trust me." And wasn't that the kicker? He didn't have physical prowess to offer a woman anymore, which left him with emotional connection—and he was failing on that front, too. Shit out of luck again. Relationships weren't something he had much experience with, having purposefully sought out women who weren't interested in long-term commitments. His last relationship, with an assistant district attorney, had been of the friends-with-benefits variety.

Sex without baggage had seemed like a good idea at the time. With Jack's unusual work hours, finding time to date at all had been difficult. The older he got, the less he tried. Besides, marriage and police work didn't mix well. Most of the guys on the force had at least one messy divorce under their belts.

"She has good reason not to trust anyone." Sean paused outside his truck. "What are you going to do?"

Jack glanced at the time display on his cell phone. His therapy appointment, if it had gone as scheduled, would have ended in thirty minutes. "Go to the diner and have lunch, then come back and pretend I didn't see anything. Hungry?"

"That's ridiculous." Sean rolled his eyes. "But I'm in if you're buying."

Fifteen minutes later Jack snapped his menu closed and tucked it behind the napkin dispenser in a booth at the Westbury diner. "I'll have a club sandwich and coffee. Thanks."

The pretty brunette turned to Sean, who hadn't needed a menu. Except for his stint in the Army, Sean had lived in Westbury most of his life, unlike Jack, who'd only been able to stay with Uncle Danny during summer vacations.

"I'll have the Greek salad and iced tea. Thanks, Mary Ann. How's Robert?"

She scratched his order onto her palm-sized tablet. "He's good."

"Tell him I said hi."

"Will do." Mary Ann hustled their order toward the kitchen. The diner wasn't full, and she appeared to be the only waitress on duty. Not unusual. The manager, Carl Johnson, was known for overworking the staff.

Jack scanned the room. At the next table, Ray Gallagher, the manager of the grocery store, sat with his wife and their three elementary school-aged boys, who were fighting over a crayon. Jeff Stevens sat at the counter, working through a pile of fries as he read the paper. With a pang of annoyance, Jack saw William Martin in a booth across the room with a thick-muscled older man.

Jack caught Sean's eye and nodded toward the burly pair. "Who's that with Will Martin?"

Only Sean's eyes moved. "His dad, Frank. Owns Martin's Feed Store."

Mary Ann hurried over with Sean's iced tea and the coffee pot, flipping and filling Jack's cup before heading over to check on the Gallaghers.

"Frank's OK. Knows his son's an ass. Feels guilty about it." Sean added a packet of sweetener to his glass and stirred.

Jack dumped a tiny tub of half and half into his coffee. "Why's that?"

"Wife split when Will was little. Frank spent the next decade shit-faced."

"Mother ever come back?" Jack glanced over at the Martins' table. Empty plates indicated they'd finished their meal. Martin was swiveling his head around, probably looking for the check.

"No. Don't know if Frank ever heard from her again."

Jack almost felt bad for Will. Almost.

Keeping her distance from Will, Mary Ann stopped next to Frank, ripped one pale green sheet from her notepad, and slapped the paper down on the table. Not that Will was likely to bother Mary Ann. Her husband was a former professional hockey player and was the size of a small building.

Martin stood, letting his father pick up the check. Not a surprise. The older man walked toward the register at the front of the restaurant. Will followed, leering at Mary Ann as she passed him in the narrow aisle.

Instead of backing down, Mary Ann held the steaming coffee pot between them and emitted a disgusted sound. She raised her eyebrows at Will. "Want me to tell Robert you said hi?"

Will's mouth tightened as he turned to follow his father toward the lobby.

Jack and Sean exchanged grins.

A few minutes later Mary Ann brought their lunch, and they dug in.

Jack dipped a fry in ketchup. "You get a chance to look into that thing like I asked?"

Sean nodded and paused, a forkful of lettuce halfway to his mouth. "I've got someone on it. Shouldn't be long. Not exactly classified information."

"Your man'll keep quiet about it?"

"Don't worry. He's as discreet as they come," Sean assured him.

When they'd finished, Jack picked up the check and paid at the register. He followed Sean through the glass door.

"Jack, do you have a second?" Jeff Stevens hurried out behind them.

"Hey." Jeff nodded at Sean.

Sean held out a hand. "Thanks for looking after Danny's horses for us."

"Anytime. No big deal." Jeff shifted his weight and focused on Jack. "It's about something I saw a week or so ago." Jeff lowered his voice and told them about the scene he'd witnessed in the dairy aisle between Will Martin and Beth. "I don't know what he did, and I couldn't hear him, but he was standing way too close. She couldn't get away, and she looked awfully upset. I thought you'd want to know."

Jack's lips tightened. "Thanks, Jeff. I appreciate it."

Jeff nodded and unlocked a dark blue sedan.

Anger swelled in Jack's chest as Jeff drove away. "Well, now I'm pissed."

"We could kill him. No one'd ever find out."

He was pretty sure Sean was kidding.

His cousin nodded toward the parking lot and raised a hand in a short wave. "Look, there's Mike. Let's ask him what the deal is with our resident lecher."

Police Chief Mike O'Connell pulled his cruiser into the space next to Jack's SUV and got out of the car.

"What's up?" Mike lifted off his hat and tossed it into the passenger seat through the open window. His red hair caught the sun and blazed bright orange. The navy uniform, unbuttoned at the throat, strained at the buttons across the former collegiate wrestler's massive chest.

"First of all, you gotta lay off the weights, man." Sean shook his hand. "Your neck is MIA."

Mike snorted. "You want to keep that weak-ass body, you go right ahead."

Jack grinned. At six-four, Sean had a few inches on his old schoolmate, but Mike outweighed him by at least thirty pounds of pure muscle. "If you ladies are done comparing your figures, I was going to ask Mike an important question. What do you know about Will Martin, from the feed store?"

Mike wiped a hand across his brow. "Christ. What's that asshole done now?"

"Intimidated my caretaker. Crowds her. Won't take no for an answer, if you know what I mean."

"Martin's a bully, that's for sure." The police radio crackled, and Mike stopped to listen to the dispatcher on his car radio for a second before continuing. "I've had a few discussions with him about his behavior with women. Bump-and-grabs in a crowd. Lewd suggestions. That sort of thing. We've had a few verbal complaints, but so far no one will press charges against him. He knows how to pick a victim." Mike sighed and pinched the bridge of his nose. "I'll go have a talk with him. Let him know I'm aware of the situation. If she's willing to file a complaint, call me. I'd love to haul his smart ass in."

"Thanks, Mike. I will." Jack already knew she wouldn't.

Mike returned to his car. Jack and Sean headed back to the estate, where all was quiet. Jack left Sean checking wires and swearing while he went looking for Beth.

He found her in the kitchen, coffee pot in hand. Stowing his cane by the back door, he limped into the room.

Fatigue lined her face as she poured some of the steaming brew into a mug. "I can barely keep my eyes open. Do you want a cup?"

At his nod, she poured coffee into a second mug and handed it to him.

He gestured toward the wooden table. "Sit down. I want to talk to you about something."

She slid into the nearest chair. Jack sat across the table where she couldn't avoid his eyes. The spoon she held to add sugar to her coffee shook.

Despite the kick of guilt, Jack persisted. "Jeff Stevens told me an interesting story today about Will Martin bothering you in the grocery store a while back. Why didn't you mention it?" Jack looked at her over the rim of his cup.

Beth swallowed and stared into her mug. "He didn't actually do anything. That's why."

"According to Jeff, Martin pinned you up against the dairy case and said something to you that upset you," Jack prodded. "What did he say, Beth?"

"He made some vulgar comments," Beth answered vaguely.

"Like what?"

The trembling in her hands increased. She set her coffee down. "Jack, I really don't want to repeat it."

"Did he threaten you?" Jack took her silence as an affirmative response. He fought to keep his voice level. "Martin pushes you up against a wall and makes obscene threats, and you don't tell me about it? Come on, Beth. That's not smart. I talked to the chief of police, and he said Martin's done this sort of thing before to other women." Jack reached across the table and squeezed her hand. "You could press charges."

He wasn't surprised when she shook her head.

Jack sighed. "If he comes within a hundred feet of you, I want to know about it."

She nodded, but doubt and disappointment crept into Jack's chest as she pulled her hand out from under his, rejecting him and his help yet again.

CHAPTER TWENTY-TWO

Black numbers swam across the monitor. Beth blinked and rubbed her eyes. The figures were clear for a few seconds before blurring again. She glanced at the digital clock at the bottom of the screen. Nearly midnight. Definitely enough accounting for one night. Jack had gone to bed an hour before.

She saved her spreadsheet and closed the software. The Web browser was still open on the screen, beckoning like a crooked finger. Her hands hovered over the keyboard. Why hadn't she thought to Google James before tonight? Maybe because her life was one long string of crises.

She typed his name into the search bar and tapped enter. After the confrontation with Jack earlier in the day, she needed a backup plan. She needed to talk to James. He'd been adamant that Daniel O'Malley's estate was the right place to go, but so much had happened since then. Would James have wanted her to stay if he knew about Danny's death? And what would he say about Jack's ex-cop status? James wasn't too keen on authority.

And, dammit, why was his phone disconnected?

She scrolled through the search results. Nothing relevant. With a deep breath she pulled up the Web page of the *Richmond Gazette*, then searched through the archives for James's name in the days after she'd left. Bingo.

Beth felt the blood rush from her head. She grasped the worn leather arm of the chair.

No.

Two days after she'd come to Westbury, James's bar had burned down. He was missing. The body of Anthony Cardone had been found in the rubble. He'd been killed by a knife wound to the back. The fire was classified as arson.

Cardone was a repeat violent offender who'd been in prison for robbery and assault. Two years before, Cardone had been charged with murder. The charges had been dropped when crucial evidence disappeared. Authorities were still searching for James Dieter. Due to Cardone's criminal history and the fact that the till had been emptied, the police suspected a robbery attempt gone wrong. An investigation was underway, but so far, the police didn't have any leads.

If Cardone had tried to rob the bar, where was James?

There must have been more than one man. Could the other criminals have turned on Cardone for some reason? Killed him and left him to burn?

The police were either clueless or hiding the real story. The way she saw it, James had been kidnapped and then most likely killed because of her. Thanks to her stupidity in marrying Richard, the only person even close to being family was dead.

Tears welled up in her eyes. She wiped them away and drew in a shaky breath. Her chest constricted with sorrow.

She was all alone now.

Despair edged into her mind. She pushed it away. There was no use lamenting her past when her children's lives depended on her. She'd make it through somehow.

She scanned the article one more time before she stabbed the power button on the tower next to her feet. Windows would bitch at her in the morning for not closing the browser properly, but she didn't care.

With no desire to face her dark bedroom with only her thoughts for company, she opted for a distraction and a change of scenery. Sleep was out of the question. Tucking the thick volume of *The Practical Guide to Estate Taxation* under her arm, she headed for the living room. Not exactly light bedtime reading, but if she was going to be awake most of the night, she might as well do something useful.

She settled on the sofa, curled her feet under her body, and opened the thick volume.

– – –

She opened the French doors and stepped out onto the veranda. The suite overlooked a beach fringed with lush tropical greenery. Beyond, the Pacific Ocean stretched into the horizon. The sky blushed with a pale pink sunset. Closing her eyes, she inhaled the sea air.

Nerves that had settled after yesterday's formal wedding were renewed as she faced the prospect of her honeymoon. Last night she'd squashed the small seed of disappointment when Richard had fallen asleep on the couch in their suite, but it had been late. The reception had gone on until nearly two in the morning. Still, the fact remained that he hadn't wanted her enough to stay awake. And this morning they'd awakened at dawn to endure the fourteen-hour trip from Philadelphia to Maui.

She was exhausted, but also exhilarated. She'd had sex once since Brian died, about three years ago, with a man she'd met at a friend's wedding. He'd been very kind and hadn't freaked out when she'd burst into tears afterward. But he hadn't called again and she'd been relieved.

Inside the suite, she heard her new husband speaking to the porter. With a smile, she turned back into the luxurious living room as he peeled off a few bills and handed them over. Clad in elegantly tailored casual slacks, a polo shirt, and sport coat, soon-to-be congressman Richard Baker was a beautiful man. A thrill skipped up her spine as she pictured him naked, all those smooth muscles gleaming.

He closed the door behind the porter and tossed his wallet onto the mahogany writing desk. "We should unpack."

"Can't it wait?" Crossing the room, she slid her arms around his neck. "We finally have some time alone."

He lifted her arms by the wrists and unwound them with a small frown. "I made a nine o'clock dinner reservation."

"We could stay in." She flattened her palms on his broad chest, rising up onto her toes to press her lips to his. His mouth didn't respond.

This was getting downright bizarre. While they were dating, she thought his insistence that they wait to have sex until after they were married was charming, even practical considering the intense public scrutiny he endured as a political candidate. But now it seemed like the real truth was that he just didn't want to sleep with her. But that didn't make sense. He'd married her, hadn't he?

She ran her fingers along his muscled biceps and forearms, sliding them down to grip his hips and pull them against hers. He was soft against her belly. Oh no. Was he impotent? Or maybe just tired and tense? Whatever it was, they could deal with it together. And even if sex wasn't a major factor in their relationship, she could live with that. She'd married him more for companionship than passion anyway. She'd had the fairy tale once. Surely fate only allowed one per person. She'd been lucky to have those precious years.

She didn't want to love another man the way she'd loved Brian. She'd never survive another loss that soul-splitting deep. Friendship would have to be enough this time around.

But still, some benefits to go with that friendship would be nice. Maybe Richard just needed a little more stimulation.

She moved her hand around to the front of his trousers and stroked him through the fabric. Still nothing.

"I should have known you were a slut." His frown deepened as disgust flashed across his face. He took hold of her hands. "Just another dirty whore."

She pulled back in shock, an oh-no-what-have-I-done feeling lodging deep in her belly. Obviously his lack of interest went much deeper than simple erectile dysfunction. She chose her words carefully. "Richard, we're married now. There's nothing wrong with a man and wife making love."

"Well, if that's what you want." The fingers of one hand encircled both her wrists and yanked them above her head. His free hand grasped the front of her silk blouse and tore it down the middle. He reached inside and squeezed her breast hard.

"Richard, stop. That hurts." She tried to pull her hands free, but he held them fast. "Let me go or I'll scream."

"No, you won't. Remember, my parents have your children." His chest heaved, and excitement flashed in his eyes as the threat loomed between them. "From now on, you'll do exactly what I say."

She froze, lightheaded with disbelief and horror as he shoved her backward. The back of her head bounced off the wall. Pain ricocheted through her skull. Her shoulders hit the sheet rock, knocking the breath from her lungs. He pinned her against the wall with his body, still soft against her stomach.

– – –

"Beth. Wake up. It's Jack." The deep voice sliced through her pain and terror as she fought her way back to the surface.

"Come on, Beth. It's a nightmare."

She gasped for air in a chest still constricted by the weight of a larger body. Lungs heaving, Beth opened her eyes.

Jack sat on an ottoman in front of her, fists clenched on his thighs as if he didn't know what to do with them.

She lay unmoving. Her heart rammed against her rib cage like it was trying to break free. Perspiration coated her skin and soaked through her gray cotton T-shirt. She raised her eyes.

Jack was staring, and the pity in his eyes made her look away. Rain pattered against the black living room window.

Taking a deep breath, she sat up and swung her feet to the floor. A chill passed over her clammy skin and she shivered. Jack shifted next to her on the sofa and touched her arm. Instinctively, she flinched from his touch. Her fear and shock from the dream were still so fresh that it felt as if the fight with Richard had just happened. Jack let his hand drop.

"I'm sorry, Jack."

"It's OK." He pulled a blanket from the back of the couch and draped it over her shoulders. Then before she could react, he moved one arm around her shoulders and scooped under her knees with the other, drawing her onto his lap. Her body stiffened. Jack tucked her head under his chin. As her muscles relaxed, she rested against his chest and listened to the thud of his heart. He was warm and solid. Gradually her trembling ceased.

When she'd recovered enough to speak, she pulled her head back. "I'm sorry."

"Shh." Lowering his head, he gently put his lips to hers. They were warm and dry. Heat spread through her body. The kiss was tender and gentle, and she was startled at how cold she felt when his mouth left hers. Jack lifted his head, searching her face for a reaction.

She felt no fear, no recoil through her body. In fact, it took her a few seconds to realize that his hands were slowly running up and down her back. Instead of flinching or pulling away, she arched under his touch like a cat. The hard bulge under her thigh left no question as to whether Jack was attracted to her. She felt safe sitting on his lap, even with his arousal evident against the backs of her legs, or ironically, because of it. Her body curled against the warmth of his flesh.

Jack's hand slipped around her waist to caress her back through the worn cotton of her T-shirt. She closed her eyes. Her entire world was reduced to the skin on her back. Nerve endings stood at attention, tingling as his fingers stroked. Each square inch of skin yearned for his touch. His lips brushed her ear on their way down the side of her neck.

"Beth." He breathed her name and took her mouth again. More demanding this time, his tongue urged her lips to part and swept into her mouth. Hot and possessive, it claimed her, licking deep into her mouth. She welcomed it. As her mouth opened to the invasion, her thighs loosened, wanting to open for the rest of him. Her body responded to his urgency, arching toward him, encouraging him to take more. Desire drugged her, flowed over her, hummed through her veins like an electric current. Heat bloomed beneath the surface of her skin. Her brain went numb. She couldn't think. She could only *feel*.

His tongue slipped from her mouth to move hungrily over her jaw and neck. Teeth scraped her collarbone. The strong hand that had slipped down to clench her hip trembled ever so slightly, as if he teetered on the brink of losing control. His hand slid around, and when he cupped between her legs through the fabric of her shorts, pleasure shot from her center straight through to the base of her skull.

Jack lifted his head as her body bowed, pressing harder against his palm. A strangled sound emanated from his throat. His brown eyes, hooded with desire, went dark.

His lack of restraint spurred her on. She needed to touch him, to render him equally helpless. Her hands sought and found his chest, slipped under his shirt, and splayed across the firm muscles of his chest. Blood pulsed thickly through her veins in time with the beat of Jack's heart. A moan escaped her mouth as she explored his hard body, and Jack's muscles tensed under her hand. His hips surged under her legs.

He breathed into her ear. "I want to feel your skin, Beth. Can I touch your skin?"

Her answer was a moan, and his hand slipped beneath the hem of her T-shirt. He groaned, chest heaving between gasps. "My God. You're soft. So soft."

He drew his fingertips across her rib cage to caress her stomach. His palm pressed against her belly. His long fingers splayed across her small frame from hipbone to hipbone. He began to stroke upward, over her ribs and toward her aching breasts.

Stopping short, freezing when his fingers encountered the thick scar on her side.

The mood cracked like thin ice, plunging her back into ice-cold reality.

Richard's face and James's fate flashed into Beth's mind.

"Jack. Don't." She pushed his hand away and jerked her legs off his lap, falling to the floor with a thud onto her tailbone. White pain shot up her spine.

My God, what was she thinking? She hadn't been thinking. She'd been feeling. For the first time in years, she'd let her tight rein of control slip. But she couldn't allow anyone to get close. Richard would find them again. With his unlimited resources, it was only a matter of time. And when that happened, her only option would be to find a new hiding place. The less Jack knew about her the better—for everyone.

She glanced sideways. Next to her, Jack's face flushed and his chest heaved like he'd just sprinted a full mile. All because of his desire for her. Feminine power threatened to renew her lust, but he didn't deserve to be treated the way she'd treated him. What was between them could never be. She couldn't take what he offered. No matter how much she wanted to.

She tried to say she was sorry, but her throat choked off the words. She was filled with a brand-new sense of loss, a shock considering she'd thought she didn't have any feelings left to risk. She'd thought Richard had depleted her, but apparently her ability to experience pain was infinite. Unable to speak, she simply shook her head. Who was she kidding? "Sorry" could never be enough to explain what had just transpired between them.

Disappointment and frustration darkened Jack's face. His jaw clenched. "Beth, you can trust me."

How the hell could she explain to Jack that trusting him wasn't the issue? She couldn't. She buried her face in her hands. He wouldn't mean to put her at risk. He'd think he was doing what was best, but any action on his part would bring disaster. Richard only had to get word of one inquiry, and he'd have men tracking her like sharks on a chum trail.

Jack rubbed between her shoulder blades. "I want to help. Let me."

"I can't." She felt too much for him to let him get involved. If she had anywhere else to go, she'd leave before he was hurt, before his kindness and her emotions got the better of her. But she was stuck in limbo. She'd put her kids at risk if she left the estate. But if she told him everything, how long, as a former cop, could he resist taking action?

Despite all this, she felt her resolve eroding. She couldn't stay in the room with him any longer, or she'd cave to the yearnings of her heart and body.

Without a word of explanation, she scrambled to her feet and walked out of the room. Jack didn't follow her, and she didn't allow herself so much as a glance back as she headed up the stairs.

She checked on the kids before taking a quick shower, slipping into an oversized T-shirt and climbing into bed. She hardly expected to fall asleep, but it was worth a shot. Lying in the dark, she contemplated her options. Stay or go? Tell Jack or keep him in the dark? Her chest ached with the magnitude of her questions. No matter how many times she tried to assess the situation, the answers eluded her.

– – –

Frustration rose in Jack's chest as Beth bolted from the room. She'd been on the brink of letting him in; then he'd mauled her like an over-sexed teen. Shit. Why couldn't he have stopped at holding her? What the hell was wrong with him? His instincts were screaming that she was in big trouble. And that he should do something useful about it, not try to get her into his bed.

How badly had he bungled things this time? At this rate, would he *ever* get her to confide in him?

And what was up with that scar? The way she'd reacted to his touch told him the story behind it wouldn't be pleasant.

Through the open door, the grandfather clock in the hall chimed three times. He sighed. At least he'd gotten a couple hours' sleep before the throbbing in his knee woke him. He'd heard Beth thrashing around on his way to the kitchen for some aspirin. His heart had clenched as he envisioned her trapped in her mysterious but obviously terrifying nightmare.

Jack drew a deep breath into his lungs. His heart beat staccato against his ribs. There was no way he'd be able to relax enough to fall back to sleep tonight. Not after that disturbing interlude. His nerves were on edge, his dick was hard as stone, and yeah, his feelings were hurt.

The veteran detective was sulking because a frightened woman wouldn't spill her guts to him after he'd tried to paw her clothes off.

He was such an idiot. This was why he'd never opened himself up to a serious relationship. Emotions complicated everything. His feelings for Beth made him question everything she did until he wanted to bang his head against the wall.

She'd been traumatized. Someone was after her. Of course she didn't trust him. The fact that she didn't trust anyone didn't make it any easier to accept.

For a moment he contemplated going after her to apologize for acting like an animal. He could have sworn, when he was kissing her and touching her, that she was just as into it as he was. Could he have misinterpreted her reactions that much? Her hand had been on his chest, *under* his shirt. His skin quivered as he recalled the caress of her fingers on his bare flesh, the pressure of her mound against his palm. Sure hadn't felt like she'd been pushing him away. His erection twitched against his zipper.

He was in no condition to talk to her tonight. He'd leave her alone. Apologize in the morning. He'd wrought enough damage for one evening.

Jack flexed his knee. The joint cracked, but the pain had receded to a dull ache.

On the bright side, Beth's scarred psyche had taken his mind off his pain until the aspirin had kicked in. He limped into the hall and turned into the study, heading straight for the credenza. He poured two fingers of scotch into a tumbler, then sat down, reached under the desk, and depressed the power switch on the computer tower.

The screen blinked to life and a message box popped up. Windows hadn't been shut down properly. He had two choices: restore the current session or start a new one. Hmm. Beth was using this computer right before she'd retreated to the living room to read that appalling tome on tax law. Jack clicked the restore button. He'd take any opportunity to see what Beth was up to. Was it an invasion of privacy? Maybe. But hell, it was his computer.

As the computer whirred, he sipped his drink, letting the smooth oak flavor sit on his tongue before swallowing. The whisky slid down his throat and warmed his belly. His gaze lit on the humidor on the corner of the huge desk. He lifted the lid, letting the aroma of tobacco escape. Wait. Shit. He had kids living with him. He couldn't smoke in the house. With a resigned sigh, he lowered the top.

The exciting life of a millionaire bachelor. Not.

The tower chugged for a few seconds before the browser window appeared on the screen, revealing an archive page for the *Richmond Gazette*. Jack read the article about the fire that destroyed a local tavern, the body found in the rubble, and the subsequent disappearance of the proprietor, James Dieter. The piece was dated just a couple of days after Beth arrived.

Ben had told him that before they came to stay at the estate, they'd lived with their "Uncle James." It had to be the same man. But what had happened to him? And who had killed Anthony Cardone? Jack didn't believe for a minute the journalist's asinine theory that the arson had been an attempt to cover up a robbery gone wrong.

James Dieter was in his early seventies. Jack stared at the head shot alongside the column, taken the previous summer when Dieter had won the senior division of a local triathlon. The blue eyes that peered out from under Dieter's white buzz cut were sharp. Aging hadn't softened the hard lines of his lean, tanned face. Still, it was unlikely that a senior citizen had knifed a professional thug in the back. Had someone rescued him and helped him get away? If so, then Dieter was on the run, too.

Another possibility was that there had been more than one "robber" and that Cardone's associates had turned on him. Again, Dieter could have gotten away, but it wasn't likely. If these guys had been after Beth, they likely took Dieter in case the old guy knew where Beth was hiding. Several weeks had passed since the fire. Dieter was probably dead. Had he known where Beth was? And had he told his abductors?

Jack's chest tightened as he pictured Beth reading about her uncle, alone and upset. Beth was intelligent enough to come to the same conclusions as he had. Hence the nightmare.

Well, he remained determined to help them, despite her lack of cooperation. Just made his job more difficult. If someone had gone to the trouble to kidnap James Dieter and burn down his bar in order to get to Beth, then she was in even more danger than he'd realized. And the possibility that Dieter had divulged her location just upped the risk to DEFCON two.

Jack glanced at the still-black window. As soon as dawn broke, he was calling Sean about the new security system. Sean had put in an order for all the necessary parts and had blocked off several days the following week for his company to do the installation. A week suddenly seemed like a very long time.

Sean should also have the information on Beth's past for him. With all the information Jack had put together, his cousin hadn't thought that uncovering Beth's real identity would be very diffi-cult. How many ex–minor league baseball players turned firemen could have died in auto accidents in 2003?

Wes might have found the information faster, but Jack didn't want to involve the department. Too many eyes, and paperwork left trails.

Jack glanced at the corner of the computer screen. Two hours till dawn. He closed Windows and shut down the computer. Then he selected one of his uncle's—no wait, his—favorite Dominican cigars and snipped off the end with a cutter. Tucking a lighter in his pocket, he picked up his scotch and left the study. A minute later he slipped through the French doors. Pulling the dripping cover from a patio chair, he settled into the deep cushion and propped his aching leg up on the table.

He set his drink on the bronzed metal table and lit his cigar. The darkness was alive with chirping crickets, and the soft babble of the creek carried on the breeze across the back lawn. No honk-ing horns interrupted his thoughts. No sirens floated on the night air. He sipped his drink and puffed his cigar. The flavors blended on his tongue and rose into his sinuses.

He rested his head on the back of the chair and glanced up at the sky. Caught in the soft breeze, gray clouds gave way to moonlight. Despite his frustration, the tension melted from his muscles. Jack scanned the expansive lawn, the intricate stonework of the patio, and the old but comfortable furniture. It was all a far cry from the tiny balcony off his shabby apartment, which had been home to a single white plastic chair, an ancient rusted hibachi, and a dead plant.

An owl hooted from the woods beyond the yard and outbuildings. He closed his eyes and pictured the yard as it had looked in the summers of his youth. Rows of flowers had lined the beds in front of neatly trimmed shrubs. The lawn had been a deep, Irish green. Down by the garage his uncle had maintained a precisely measured horseshoe pit. Canoes, kayaks, and fishing gear had filled the boathouse. Dawn often found Jack and Quinn paddling through the mist over the glassy lake. Sean, five years younger, tagged along when he got old enough.

Despite the fact that Danny never married or had children of his own, he kept the estate ready for his nephews. Jack had spent every summer of his childhood with his uncle.

The decision flooded over him with the memories. He would bring it all back. Every blade of grass, every colorful bloom would be restored to its former glory. His nieces and nephews deserved to have the same memories.

In the darkness, he raised his glass in silent toast to his uncle, who was much more astute than Jack ever knew.

Here's to you, Uncle Danny. Thanks.

CHAPTER TWENTY-THREE

In the final weeks of summer, darkness fell earlier every day, as if the season itself were tired and in a hurry to be over. The soft evening light that lasted until nine o'clock in June faded before eight as September approached. By ten o'clock, night had fallen in earnest. Mary Ann steered her ancient Corolla through the last stoplight in town and turned onto the country road toward home. Her arches protested the extra half shift the manager had forced her to work after he'd fired the other waitress on duty for dropping a loaded tray. Carl hadn't been nicknamed "The Prick" by accident. He'd earned it. Carl didn't usually bother Mary Ann though, as her husband intimidated her boss at every opportunity.

Thoughts of Robert and home perked her up. She couldn't wait to take a hot bath. Her husband would pour her a glass of wine and rub her feet. Maybe they'd work on making that baby tonight if she didn't fall asleep first.

Ten minutes from home, Pink's latest faded into Nickelback's "If Today Was Your Last Day." Mary Ann turned up the radio and was singing along when the steering wheel began to pull in her hands. She rolled down her window a few inches to hear a familiar *whump, whump, whump.*

Damn. She did not need this right now.

She pulled over to the shoulder of the dark road and got out of her old Toyota, circling around the front of the car to examine the front right tire. Giving in to a fleeting childish temper tantrum, she planted a solid kick on the flat rubber. She pulled her cell out of her pocket and held her breath as she illuminated the display. Reception was spotty on this stretch of road. Shoot. No bars. So much for her network.

The damp night air chilled her skin, raising goose bumps. Insect noises echoed from the surrounding woods. An owl screeched, and Mary Ann jumped. There wasn't anything dangerous to humans out there in the forest, but still…Better get this done and get home. If she didn't show up in the next thirty minutes, Robert would come looking for her. His protectiveness was legendary.

She circled around to the rear of the vehicle and opened the trunk. After lifting the rubbery carpet out of the way, she reached for the tire iron.

A car engine approached. She straightened and turned toward the sound. Headlights sped closer along the country lane, pulled to the side, and stopped behind her car. Mary Ann held up her hand and squinted against the glare. A figure exited the car, unidentifiable in silhouette against the bright light. The shadow walked toward her. She exhaled in relief when she saw the familiar face.

"Hey, there, Mary Ann. Can I give you a hand?"

– – –

Philadelphia was a beautiful city. Sure, like any other urban center, it had its problems, but this seat of American democracy was infused with history. Visitors could walk through the rooms where the founding fathers debated and wrote the Declaration of Independence and the Constitution. From the aged red brick colonial buildings in Old City to the racing sculls at Boathouse Row, Philadelphia's legacy shone like a patriotic beacon.

James would have enjoyed a few days to view the historic sights. Philadelphia reminded him of why he'd gone to war all those years ago, and what had been at stake. He'd been sent to Vietnam to preserve democracy. All those antiwar protesters could kiss his hairy old ass. Forty years might have passed, but the way he'd been treated when he'd returned still burned him. Bunch of commies.

But what really stuck in his throat was men like Baker, who used their position in government for their own gain and shit on people in the process. James took such acts of selfishness as a personal betrayal. He'd shed blood for this country. He'd watched countless men die protecting its ideals. No one should get away with corrupting it.

So, the sightseeing would have to wait. James had a mission. This visit would be all business.

He made his way to the affluent Main Line region northwest of the city after dark. Congressman Baker's house was in the old money part of town, where homes all sold in the millions. James cruised down the tree-lined street at a leisurely pace, looking for an inconspicuous place to park his rented sedan. He drove past the congressman's address without stopping. Mature and stately, the big stone house sat back from the road. Tasteful landscaping lights illuminated the shrubs and flowers lining the facade, which was partially hidden from view by a few massive oaks.

James left the car by a small park down the road, then walked back. He'd brought a cane, and added a stoop to his shoulders and a shuffle to his stride. He did his best to look frail, though the street was dark enough that his appearance didn't matter much. Nobody really looked at old people.

Ten minutes later he gloved up, crouched behind a shrub, and picked the pathetic lock on Baker's back door. Behind him a patch of woods provided excellent privacy. For an expensive home, the security system was a joke. James bypassed the alarm and entered the commercial quality kitchen in under ninety seconds.

Not bad for an old fart.

According to Baker's agenda, the congressman would be in Washington until tomorrow afternoon. Then he was taking a long weekend at home. Based on James's surveillance, he knew the housekeeper arrived around noon and stayed until eight, whether Baker was in residence or not. The gardener showed up at six a.m. So the place was fair game all night.

Here in the back of the house, James risked a quick sweep of his penlight to get the lay of the land. Acres of granite, marble, and stainless steel made the room feel about as inviting as a mausoleum. No need to fine-tooth the kitchen. Baker probably didn't spend much time in there.

James ambled through the antique-filled living room, which looked more like a museum than a house. He bet nobody had ever put their feet up on the glossy Federal style coffee table or leaned back on that stiff leather settee and cracked a beer. A few photos of Beth were perched on the grand piano. Beautiful as always, but she didn't look particularly happy in any of them. Newlywed bliss must have faded before the champagne toast. There were only two pictures of the kids.

He moved on to search the rest of the house. Baker was more likely to hide something interesting in the private rooms. A wall safe in the master bedroom yielded a few pieces of jewelry, no doubt the real deal, that James considered pocketing just for the hell of it. But a theft would tip Baker off that someone had been in his house, which would defeat the purpose of tonight's maneuvers. The study held another safe. His gloved fingers worked their magic. Nothing exciting inside, just a pile of legal documents and a few grand in cash. Not enough to cause any real suspicion. For a guy with this kind of coin, a few thou was pocket change. Couldn't take the money either. With a resigned sigh, James left the stacks of bills inside the safe.

But the basement proved to be a real treasure trove. James missed Baker's cache on the first pass. But a second, slower perusal uncovered a well-concealed space underneath the stairs that held a collection of unmarked DVDs. Interesting. He slid two into his pocket for future viewing and swept the rest of the room once more before calling it a night.

He strolled back to his car, stooping his shoulders and walking with a practiced hitch in his gait. No one paid any attention.

Later, back in his elegant room at the Bellevue Hotel, he opened his laptop and slipped in one of the discs. The opening credits read "*Romeo and Julian.*"

He'd just confirmed his theory about Baker's secret; now if only he could prove it.

With a click on the X, he closed the media player.

Beth must have discovered that her husband preferred other men. Must have been a hell of a surprise. He thought of her skittish behavior. Or maybe not. Powerful men with secrets were dangerous. Regardless, James needed some real proof. A couple of gay porn DVDs in the congressman's basement didn't prove anything. Hell, Baker would just claim they belonged to the gardener. And if the Mexican immigrant wanted to keep his green card, he'd dance out of the imaginary closet in yellow chiffon if his employer asked him to.

No, he needed real evidence of the congressman's sexual preference. He wanted Baker by the short hairs. If James's suspicions were right, that look he'd seen between Baker and his aide hadn't been one of the boss-employee variety. Now, if the congressman was taking a long weekend off, what were the chances his boy toy might accompany him? Pretty damned good.

Going up against the congressman was dangerous business, but James didn't care. He was old. Beth had her whole life ahead of her, and he'd do everything in his power to make sure she got to live it. If it was his time, so be it. As the saying went, he'd rather go out with a bang than a whimper, anyway. If that happened, he'd just have to make sure he took the congressman with him.

He needed to catch up with Beth soon. The visions were gaining clarity every day, but it still felt like he had some time. Hopefully enough time to get what he needed. He'd spend the weekend right here, with a telephoto lens aimed at the congressman's window.

– – –

Branigan Road stretched in both directions, empty and black, slicing through the thick forest. He waited until Mary Ann turned her back to him to point out which tire had gone flat. Like he didn't know. She was still dressed in her waitress uniform. The sneakers weren't exactly a turn-on, but the white skirt that ended just above her knees gave him a nice view of her smooth, tanned legs. And the subservient images the uniform inspired more than made up for the shoes. In an instant, he was as hard as the metal bar he slid from his pocket.

With a quiver of excitement, he brought the bar down on her head, catching her body as she pitched forward. She sagged in his arms. He ducked under her and pulled her torso over his shoulder. She was smaller than Amelia had been, and he had no trouble balancing her weight. A few seconds later, she was curled on the tarp in his trunk like she was taking a nap. Aside from the blood dripping down her temple, she looked quite peaceful.

This was the dangerous part of the abduction—which naturally made it the most exciting as well. If anyone happened by at this moment, the game would be up. Mary Ann's unconscious body in his trunk would be tough to explain. Of course, he was prepared to kill anyone who stumbled on him at this vulnerable moment, but then he'd have to move on. His evening would be totally ruined.

Mary Ann groaned. He licked his lips in anticipation.

Patience. There were details that needed to be addressed before he could indulge.

He glanced up and down the dark road. No cars in sight. He drew a hypodermic from his kit and measured out enough Ace to keep her out of it for a while, at least until he got her home and set up his work area. He kept the dose light. He didn't want to kill her accidentally. He wanted to kill her on purpose. As a final safety measure, he looped duct tape around her wrists and ankles. There was nothing worse than opening the trunk and having a pissed-off woman launch herself at him. Been there, done that.

Leaning over, he scooped the blood from her face with a small spatula, then placed it in a Ziploc bag with a couple of long, dark hairs plucked directly from Mary Ann's head. He closed the trunk. Crickets chirped from the surrounding forest as he went around to the front of his car and slipped into the driver's seat. His luck couldn't have been better. When he'd jammed the nail into her tire, he'd gambled the tire wouldn't go flat in the parking lot. On the other hand, it could have held until she got home to Robert. There was no way he'd take the chance of that monster seeing him anywhere near his wife. Robert could and would break him into little pieces.

But fate had blessed him, and the tire had made it just to the outskirts of town. In fact, this section of road was perfect. Absolutely perfect.

He patted the baggie in his chest pocket. He had one more small matter to take care of before he could truly enjoy his time with Mary Ann. One more detail to ensure no one would suspect him. Then she was all his.

He started the engine and pulled out onto the road, humming the theme to *Gilligan's Island* under his breath.

CHAPTER TWENTY-FOUR

Beth pushed her cart into the checkout lane at Wal-Mart and began pulling items out of the blue plastic cart. A bathing suit for each child, socks, two pairs of clearance jeans, and a paperback for Ben hit the conveyor belt, along with a small package of Polly Pocket dolls for Katie, just like the ones she and Jack's nieces had played with at Quinn's. An indulgence for sure, but Beth had just cashed her first paycheck. An extra three dollars wasn't going to break the bank. The smile the purchase brought to her daughter's face was worth every penny.

Katie refused to allow the cashier to put her package in a bag and clutched the box against her chest as they walked across the steaming parking lot. Overhead the midday sun cut through a hazy sky.

They stowed the bags behind the driver's seat of the estate's extended cab pickup, which Jack had insisted she drive when he learned the air conditioner in her station wagon didn't work. She'd protested, but as they climbed into the stifling cab, she was grateful.

She'd avoided Jack all morning, along with the discussion he would want to have about last night. She should regret what had passed between them, but she couldn't. He'd shown her that passion was still possible. In fact, it had almost been a reality. But they had no future together. Jack was a good man, and hurting him wasn't right. What happened last night couldn't happen again.

She and Ben rolled down their windows to let some of the heat escape as she turned the key. The truck was only a few years old and started on the first try. They were going to get spoiled.

She snorted. It hadn't been that long ago that she'd been driving a Mercedes. And look how that had turned out for her.

She could use Jack's truck for now, but what would she do if her station wagon died on her? A new car would eat up her entire emergency fund, and she had no way to replenish it. She had a little money in the bank from before her marriage, but there was no way she could access her savings. Richard would be monitoring her bank accounts, and he'd find her in a heartbeat.

"Is your seat belt fastened?" Beth glanced in the rearview mirror at her daughter.

"Yes, Mommy." In her booster seat in the center of the second row, Katie held her unopened box tightly, as if it were filled with precious gems instead of three-inch dolls. "I'm hungry."

Beth checked the dashboard clock and met her daughter's gaze in the mirror. "We'll be home in a bit. Would you like a grilled cheese for lunch today?"

Katie smiled and nodded.

Ben leaned over and changed the radio station as Beth pulled out of the parking lot onto the main road, then merged onto the interstate. Metrostation blared from the speakers, and Ben's head began to bob like a dashboard dog. Beth reached down and lowered the volume to slightly below deafening. Ben shot her a grin, and she smiled back at him. The ordinariness of the exchange felt alien and almost blissfully normal at the same time.

A few miles later, she exited onto the narrow, mountainous road that led toward Westbury. Cool air began to rush from the vents, and she sighed in relief as it washed over her sweat-dampened face.

She slowed the truck as they approached a sharp bend in the road. Vertically-sheered-off rock extended up the left side of the road and plummeted on the right. She glanced in her rearview mirror and gasped when she glimpsed a shiny black sedan bearing down on them. Beth stepped on the gas, but the car continued to gain ground until it was just a few feet behind them. She couldn't go any faster, not with the curve just ahead.

Suddenly, the pickup jerked forward. The sedan had slammed into the truck's rear bumper.

"Mom!"

Beth had no time to respond to Ben's shout. She clenched the steering wheel and focused on keeping the truck centered on the narrow road. Metal crunched, and the truck lurched forward again as the sedan rear-ended it a second time. The wheel jerked in her hands, and the truck hurtled toward the guardrail and the fifty-foot drop on the other side.

Beth pulled the wheel hard to the left, crossing into the oncoming lane. Tires squealed. Katie screamed. With a loud metallic scrape, the truck lurched sideways against the rock wall. Beth fought to keep the vehicle straight as the sedan whipped by in a black blur. Before Beth could catch her breath, a horn blew. She swerved back into the proper lane, barely avoiding a head-on collision.

The wheel wobbled under her hands. The truck's engine sputtered.

After they cleared the bend, the road widened and Beth pulled over. Her chest constricted, and nausea rose into the back of her throat. She exhaled the breath she'd been unconsciously holding. Hands shaking, chest heaving, she looked both her children over.

Ben's knuckles were white and his face, pale. In the backseat, her daughter cried. Beth's pounding heart ached for her. She took a deep, steadying breath.

"It's all right, baby." As soon as she was certain her legs would hold her up, she'd get the kids out of the car.

Katie's voice shook. "What happened, Mommy?"

Beth cleared her throat and attempted to control her voice. It came out smooth enough, but a little higher than normal. "Just an accident. We're all fine. Nobody got hurt and that's all that matters." Except that Jack's truck was trashed. She looked through the windshield. The hood was buckled on one side, and steam hissed out from underneath. The damage to the side had to be worse than what she could see from the driver's seat, and she didn't even want to think about the back of the truck. She turned the car off.

"Accident?" Ben's brows were knitted, but he said nothing else in front of his sister.

Before Beth could answer, a white Toyota pulled up behind them. An elderly woman got out and walked up to Beth's window. "Is everyone all right, dear?" At Beth's nod, the woman continued, "I saw the whole thing. Probably some drunk. I called the police on my cell." She held out one blue-veined hand for Beth to shake. "I'm Ellen Wheelan. Let's get you all out of there."

It took fifteen minutes for a police car to drive up. Beth left the children in Ellen's car, where the older woman had insisted they take refuge from the blistering heat. Despite the humidity, Beth was shivering.

Meeting her in front of Jack's pickup, Lieutenant Winters introduced himself and asked for her documents.

She wiped her palms on her jeans before she handed them over, hoping her nervous appearance would be attributed to the accident. The gun strapped to her ankle seemed to have increased in weight and size since the policeman arrived. Thankfully, the officer seemed distracted and only gave her license a cursory glance as he wrote the numbers down.

"I'm sorry it took so long, ma'am." He glanced down at the truck's registration and raised a brow. "How do you know Mr. O'Malley?"

"I'm the estate's caretaker."

He took her statement and that of Mrs. Wheelan, filled out several forms, and snapped pictures of the scene and the truck. A low whistle came from his pursed lips as he scanned the damage to Jack's truck. "Could take Earl hours to get here with the flatbed, ma'am, and I'm not comfortable leaving you all here. If it's OK with you, I'll drop you at Mr. O'Malley's."

– – –

On Branigan Road, Jack pulled his Explorer onto the grass behind a line of official vehicles and a local news van. Yellow crime scene tape defined a large area around a four-door blue Corolla parked on the gravel shoulder. A state police CSI unit sat twenty yards or so behind the Toyota. Technicians buzzed around the vehicle.

A large group of people had gathered at the edge of the woods. Search volunteers. Jack's stomach clenched. He spotted Police Chief Mike O'Connell at the head of the crowd, talking and gesturing. Jack scanned the faces, recognizing some of the volunteers.

His cane sank into the ground as he walked over and stood a few feet behind the police chief.

Mike divided the volunteers into four groups, assigned areas on an aerial map, and handed out walkie-talkies. He gave the usual *if-you-find-anything-don't-touch-it* speech. On the side, Todd Foster restrained a pair of baying bloodhounds. Mary Ann's husband, Robert Spencer, white-knuckled something pale pink and fuzzy. A sweater?

Jack swallowed the lump in his throat and immediately wished he'd had the chance to apologize to Beth this morning. But he couldn't blame her for avoiding him.

Robert passed the item to Todd with shaking hands. At a signal from a crime-scene tech, Todd led the dogs to the Toyota and gave them a whiff of the sweater. Some initial baying and excitement right around the vehicle petered out as the animals failed to pick up a scent. Todd widened the circle, spiraling outward. On the grassy area between the road and the trees, Robert vibrated with anger and desperation, his empty hands curled into bowling-ball-sized fists, his red-rimmed eyes bleak and frantic. Jack took in his pasty skin and disheveled appearance. Instinct told him Robert didn't have anything to do with his wife's disappearance, although Mike would have to investigate him. Significant other always headed the list in a disappearance—or murder.

Unless the police already had another suspect in mind.

Mike dispersed the groups into the woods, then approached Jack. "Thanks for coming, Jack. I could really use your expertise here."

Jack glanced around at the small army of local and county uniforms. "Anytime. What do you have so far?"

"Robert called me at eleven thirty last night. Mary Ann was due home around ten thirty or so. She'd worked an extra half shift at the diner because the manager, Carl Johnson, fired the other waitress. Mary Ann clocked out at ten oh five. When she didn't show up at home by eleven, Robert went looking for her. He drove the route she took home from work and found her car here." Mike nodded toward the Toyota. "Right front tire's flat. No sign of Mary Ann."

The chief paused. "Except for a few drops of blood, her purse, and her cell phone on the ground next to the car."

Jack glanced over at the forest, where Todd was walking his dogs along the tree line. His placid, uninterested dogs. Jack's stomach curled into a fist; acid rose into his throat. He lowered his voice. "Mary Ann didn't walk away from here."

Mike's gaze was also on the dogs. "I know."

"Search is probably pointless."

"I know that, too." Mike shoved a hand through his hair. "But they have to do something."

Judging from the abundance of personnel already in place for a woman missing barely fourteen hours, Mike had obviously come to the same conclusion as Jack. There was only one possibility that would garner this much attention this quickly. The police were operating under the assumption that Mary Ann had been abducted by the Riverside Killer. No one was ready to say the words until there was more evidence, though, especially since there was a news crew lurking about. The media loved a serial killer.

The chief took a deep breath and let it out in a rush. "You don't think I'm crazy pulling out all the stops this early?"

"No." Jack shook his head. "Setup's close enough to justify it. Victim profile fits."

"When I worked in the city, we wouldn't even have filled out a form for two days."

"This isn't the city. Unless she sprouted wings, either someone picked her up or someone grabbed her. With the blood, I'd bet on force."

"God, I was hoping you'd disagree with me." Mike shoved a hand through his hair in frustration.

"Sorry. What's your gut tell you?"

Mike huffed. "It's not happy. What are the chances that the Riverside Killer just happened to be driving along this completely empty stretch of road this late at night at the same exact time as Mary Ann?"

"He's been working his way north."

"Yeah, but I spoke with the FBI profiler. The Killer has always operated in depressed urban areas or along interstates, places where he's likely to encounter lone women. He doesn't stalk, he ambushes. He's never abducted anyone off a road as out of the way as this one. The scene fits, except for the location. According to the profiler, this is not his typical hunting ground."

Jack didn't answer; he just sighed. "Which means it's either a copycat, an unrelated crime, or..."

"The Killer's one of us," Mike finished his sentence. "He passed Mary Ann and couldn't pass up the opportunity."

"Feds on their way?"

"Yeah. Any way I could talk you into sitting in on that? I haven't worked on anything bigger than a domestic disturbance or an overdose in ten years." Mike swallowed and stared at the Toyota, which was being winched onto a flatbed. "Can't screw this up."

Neither one of them was going to say it, but if they were right, the chances of seeing Mary Ann alive were slim no matter what they did. If she'd been grabbed by the Riverside Killer, he didn't hold onto his victims for more than a day or so. He'd already had her for—Jack checked his watch—almost fifteen hours.

Mike's second in command, Pete Winters, pulled up in his patrol car. "Jack, can I talk to you for a minute?" The lieutenant stepped out of his car and hitched up his belt. Pete wasn't exactly fat, just short and square with a bulldog face to match. "I just dropped your caretaker and her kids off at your place. Someone ran them off the road and damaged your truck."

Jack snapped to attention. "Are they all right?"

Pete nodded. "Just a little shook up. She barely missed a head-on, though. Got real lucky." The officer's eyes scanned the figures of a search group combing the edge of forest. "I'll get Earl out there later to get your vehicle."

"Don't worry about it. The truck's not important right now." Jack shook his stubby hand. "Thanks, Pete. I appreciate you taking them home." Jack turned back to the chief. "Mike, I gotta check on them."

Mike waved him off. "Go. Make sure they're OK. I'll talk to you later."

Jack was already moving toward his truck. "Call me when you have a definite time for the meeting."

"Will do."

Jack's stomach rolled as he floored the gas pedal. His lungs felt like they couldn't inflate all the way. Pete had said they were fine, but until he saw them with his own eyes…

He turned onto the private road a little too fast. The SUV fishtailed. Straightening the vehicle, Jack eased off the accelerator and took a deep, shaky breath.

Calm down. You're going to scare the crap out of them.

Two minutes later, he parked at the head of the circular drive and bolted up the walk. He tried the knob, but the door was locked. Smart but unusual. Had Beth already heard about Mary Ann's disappearance?

Jack went around to the back of the house and walked into the kitchen. Ben was at the kitchen table. Katie sat on the floor next to Henry, one arm draped over the dog's back. The little girl's eyes were puffy, but she didn't look upset now. In front of the stove, Beth flipped a sandwich in a frying pan. The kitchen smelled like grilled cheese.

"What happened? Is everybody OK?"

Katie jumped to her feet and latched onto Jack's leg. She murmured into his thigh, "Mom wrecked your truck."

Jack leaned down and picked her up. She wrapped all four limbs around him, and for a few seconds, he just held on. Closing his eyes, he inhaled the floral scent of No More Tangles in her hair.

He leaned back and scanned her for any sign she'd been in a car accident. Nothing. Relief flooded through his body, making him light-headed. "That's OK. The truck's not important. As long as nobody got hurt." He set her back down on her feet and leaned a shoulder against the wall.

Katie stared up at him. "We got to ride in a police car."

"Was it exciting?"

"Not really. It was stinky inside. Mom made us wash our hands really good when we got home."

Jack's mouth twitched. The child almost made him forget the horrors of the day for a few seconds. They could have been killed. All three of them. The depth of his feelings for this small family hit him like a sucker punch to the solar plexus. He pressed a fist to the burning sensation rising from his abdomen.

Beth slid two sandwiches onto plates. She hadn't said a word and avoided making eye contact. Was she still upset about last night?

Jack caught Ben's eye and nodded toward the doorway. "Why don't you two take your lunches into the living room and watch cartoons?"

Katie snatched her plate before her mother could veto Jack and invoke the no-television-in-the-afternoon rule. She turned to call for Henry, but the dog was already following her—and her sandwich.

Ben, however, didn't budge from the table. He had a stubborn set to his jaw that mimicked his mother's.

Beth slid his plate onto the table then returned to the stove to wipe up the counter. As soon as the door swung shut behind her daughter, Beth spoke without facing Jack. "I'm sorry about the truck. You can take the cost of repairs out of my pay." She picked a cup of coffee up off the counter and wrapped both hands around the mug as if she were trying to warm them.

"I don't give a damn about the truck, Beth. You could have been hurt." And by *hurt* he meant killed. Jack raised his eyebrows at Ben, silently asking his opinion.

Ben was more than happy to oblige. "The guy did it on purpose. He hit us more than once and didn't stop to see if we were OK or anything."

"We have no way of knowing that for sure." Beth pulled out a chair and sat down, deflating as she rubbed a hand across her face. Her voice sounded tired, and she didn't sound like she believed her own argument.

"Did you get a description of the car?" Jack asked both of them, pulling out a chair and sitting across from Beth. Let her try to avoid eye contact when he was sitting two feet away.

She shook her head. "Not enough to be of any use. It was a black sedan. I don't know what make or model, and I didn't catch a single digit of the license plate number. The windows were tinted."

"Ben, could you go and check on Katie?" Jack asked.

Ben shot him an injured look but he went.

"First of all, are you sure none of you needs to go to the ER?" Jack knew Beth wouldn't hesitate to take the kids to a doctor but that she'd ignore her own injuries.

"We're OK. Not even a scratch." She met his gaze squarely. No visible bruises. Her eyes looked clear, except for a defeated fatigue that seemed to have aged her ten years since breakfast.

"OK then, second piece of business. Mary Ann Spencer disappeared last night on her way home from working her shift at the diner."

Beth's eyes opened wide, and she drew in a sharp breath. Jack's hand itched to reach across the table and grab hers, but after last night, he knew better. He could, however, make that right.

"I'm sorry about last night, Beth. I shouldn't have kissed you. It won't happen again."

She didn't respond, but sadness flashed in her eyes. Jack wondered if it was because of the kiss or because he wasn't going to be kissing her again. Clearly, she wasn't going to tell him how she felt.

"Tomorrow I'm going to get you a cell phone. Until we know what happened here and the truck is fixed, if you need to leave the estate, please let me take you. I don't want you getting stranded in that wagon."

"She just disappeared? No clues?" She didn't argue with him, but she didn't agree to his request either. Should he push?

"Nothing." Jack suddenly had a vision of Mary Ann's blood on the street, and his paranoia grew. Someone had tried to kill Beth today. "I was at the scene. They're searching. Called out the dogs and everything, but it doesn't look good."

"Who would do such a thing?"

Jack let her question go unanswered.

"You don't need to stay here with us, Jack, if you'd rather be helping with the search. We're OK."

"I'm not very useful in that capacity anymore." Jack glanced down at his leg. "But I promised the police chief I'd be available to meet with the FBI later."

"Are you sure?" Beth stared down into her coffee. Why was she so anxious to get rid of him? What was she planning?

Jack nodded. "I don't think they're going to find her today." There was no way he was leaving her alone, not when whomever she was hiding from may have found her. "Beth, promise me—"

"I hear Katie." Beth jumped up and rushed toward the door.

Jack let her go, but he wasn't fooled. She hadn't promised to stay with him.

– – –

A knock signaled Sean's arrival. Jack opened the French doors. His cousin stepped into the kitchen, briefcase in hand.

Mrs. Harris looked up from loading the dishwasher. "You need something to eat, Sean? There's some roast beef left over from dinner."

His cousin shook his head. "No, thanks, ma'am. I already ate."

Jack put his hand on Sean's shoulder and steered him toward the swinging door. "We'll be in the study going over the new security system."

"No smoking in there, boys." Mrs. Harris gave them her *don't-screw-with-me* look. "There're children in the house."

Jack suppressed a grin. "Yes, ma'am."

"And spare your livers. Go easy on the scotch."

Even though Jack hadn't smoked in the study, the room still reeked of premium cigars. Four decades of indulgence wasn't going to fade overnight. He could have the place thoroughly

cleaned, he supposed, but Jack found the odor familiar and com-
forting.

"Sorry, would have been here earlier, but I stopped by the station to see Mike." And on that note, Sean stopped at the credenza
to pour two fingers of scotch into a glass. He tipped the bottle
toward Jack.

"Just a short one," Jack answered. "I was there when he cleared
her husband, Robert. He get anything else yet?" Robert Spencer's
brother had been with him the whole night. Jack had also sat
through the meeting with the FBI, but hadn't learned anything
more about the Riverside Killer than what Wes had already told
him. Mike was running a full-scale investigation in case Mary
Ann hadn't been taken by the serial killer, but no one had much
hope she was still alive.

"He brought Carl Johnson and Will Martin in for questioning." Sean passed Jack a crystal tumbler with a generous "short"
shot of single malt.

Jack's eyebrows shot up. "Really? Based on what?"

"If Carl hadn't asked her to work late, Mary Ann would've
been home at six." Sean raised his glass.

Jack tipped his glass and took a small swallow. The liquid
slipped down his throat in a warm and welcome rush. "Yeah, but
wasn't he still at the diner when she got off shift?"

Sean shook his head. "Night manager came on at ten. Carl left
right after Mary Ann. Went home alone. No alibi."

"If he's innocent, sucks to be him," Jack said.

"He's a prick anyway." Sean shrugged. "Mike knows the connection's tenuous, but he's got to cover his bases. And he'll grasp
at any available straw to find Mary Ann."

"What about Will?" Jack sipped his drink. Scotch went down
way too easily these days.

"Seems someone told Robert about that incident at the diner last week. You remember? Mary Ann threatened to tell Robert that Martin was buggin' her."

Jack nodded. "I remember. Seems thin, though."

"Not to Robert."

"Good point. How'd Will take it?"

Sean shook his head. "Don't know. Mike and the FBI guy took him back. I didn't stick around to see how it played out. Figured it was going to take a while."

"What do you think about Will and Carl being on the short list?" Jack asked.

Sean shrugged. "Will's got a history, but he's not smart or subtle enough to be the actual Riverside Killer. Don't know Carl all that well. I'd say he fits the profile better. He's quiet, lives alone, and thrives on the misery of others. But grabbing his own employee would make him the dumbest serial killer in history."

Unfortunately Jack agreed with him. "Either one of them could be copycatting the Killer, though."

"True. Or it could be some other white male between twenty and forty who lives alone or otherwise fits the general serial killer profile." Sean finished his drink.

"I really hate to think someone around here took Mary Ann."

"I know, but the FBI profiler's betting on a local. Branigan Road is too remote for a random criminal."

"Who else is on Mike's short list?" Jack asked.

"Besides every single white male in the township?" Sean snorted. "Because of their ready access to Ace, which they know the killer used from the autopsies on the earlier victims, he's added Doc White, the large animal vet; Dr. Ritter, the small animal vet; and a handful of horse breeders and trainers, including your neighbor, Jeff Stevens."

"Don't know Dr. Ritter, but Doc White seems a bit old."

"Strong as an ox, though," Sean pointed out.

Jack pictured his neighbor. Jeff couldn't be more than five-foot-seven and was on the lean side. "Think Jeff would be strong enough?"

"He handles thousand-pound animals all day."

"Good point," Jack conceded.

His cousin opened his briefcase and took out two folders. He tossed the first onto Jack's desk. "That's the updates I'm recommending to the security system. Motion sensors, cameras, intercom, everything we talked about and more. We'll run a phone line and place a camera or two down at the barn as well. My men'll be here first thing in the morning to start the installation."

Jack set his glass down. He already suspected what was in the second folder.

"And this is everything you ever wanted to know about your new caretaker, who by the way, fate has royally pissed on."

Jack stared at the folder. Beth's real identity was right in front of him. So why was he hesitant to open the file? Because even though she'd lied to him and presented him with false identification, it still felt like an invasion of her privacy. Which was stupid. He had every right to know whom he'd hired. And, more importantly, how could he help her if he was in the dark about her situation?

"After you read that, you'll see why I've added a few additional features to the alarm system. She's in deep shit right up to her pretty neck."

CHAPTER TWENTY-FIVE

Jack's hand hovered over the folder.

"For Christ's sake, will you just open it?"

Jack reached out and flipped back the cover, ignoring his cousin's outburst. He knew Sean's report would be comprehensive, but he still wasn't prepared for the photo of Beth that stared back at him from the front page of a missing person report. Jack's gaze moved from the head shot to the text below. Her name was—holy shit—Elizabeth Baker.

Jack's brain froze for a few seconds as he tried to recall what he'd heard in the news about her disappearance. The congressman hadn't lived in his jurisdiction, but Jack had known about the case. He suddenly remembered that Congressman Baker's missing wife was crazy—or so they'd been told. Sometime before her disappearance she'd tried to buy a one-way ticket on the Ambien Express.

Jack picked up the report to read the details. Elizabeth Andersen Baker disappeared from her Main Line Philadelphia home last fall. Congressman Richard Baker had gone to visit his father in Washington the previous evening for advice on a legislative issue and had stayed the night. When he'd returned home the next morning, his new family was gone. Mrs. Baker's car was missing. The police were called a half hour later.

Usually the police preferred to wait forty-eight hours before filling out a missing persons report for an adult, but since Elizabeth Baker had been recently hospitalized with severe depression after her suicide attempt, she was thought to be a danger to herself and the children. She hadn't taken her medication with her. The police began searching for Mrs. Baker right after the report was filed. Jack suspected that the fact she was a congressman's wife also had something to do with the white-glove, concierge-level service Baker had received from law enforcement.

Elizabeth had had at least a twelve-hour head start. In the month following her vanishing act, there'd been hundreds of unsubstantiated sightings of Mrs. Baker, but the police hadn't confirmed a single one.

Mrs. Baker had no family. During summer vacation her freshman year at college, her ten-year-old brother had been killed by a friend in a handgun accident. Her father had been a gun collector and had neglected to lock his gun safe. Her dad had then used a second pistol to decorate his study with a Rorschach pattern of his own brain matter the next day. Elizabeth had found him. Her mother had died of cancer the following year.

After flipping through boring college transcripts and legal documents pertaining to Beth's first marriage and the births of her children, Jack skimmed over the accident report of Brian Andersen's death. The information matched what Beth had told him. He looked up at Sean. "I assume you read all this?"

"I skimmed through it, yeah." Sean moved to the sideboard and uncapped the bottle of whisky.

"What do you think?" Jack reached for the glass of scotch he'd forgotten.

Sean poured a short shot. "I think there are two possibilities here. Beth's depressed and delusional, or Baker's lying."

"Yeah."

His cousin cut through the bullshit to the heart of the situation with surgical precision. "On one hand, her life's been filled with enough tragedy to warrant depression. But you have to ask yourself why she would suddenly decide to pack it in so many years later. She'd been an accountant, doing the single mother thing for, like, five years before she even met Baker."

Jack finished Sean's thought. "So why would her depression get worse if her life had gotten better?"

"Exactly." Sean crossed his arms and leaned on the credenza.

"Plus, Beth is fanatical about not taking medication. Didn't even want to take anything for her concussion. I've never even seen her drink a glass of wine." Jack scratched his chin. "Which means that Congressman Baker is lying through his perfect teeth."

Sean snorted. "Probably picked her because of all the tragedy in her life. Plus she has no immediate family. She was nice and vulnerable. Baker thought she'd be easy to manipulate."

Anger tightened Jack's chest.

His cousin crossed his arms over his chest and gestured with his glass. "You have to ask yourself, why would a man with a depressed, possibly suicidal wife leave her all alone overnight? Worse, he left two children in her sole care. Two children he claims to love as if they were his own."

"Good point," Jack agreed. "It's not like he couldn't afford to hire live-in help."

"When the police asked him that, he said that as a politician, he hated to give up what little privacy the family had." Sean's eye roll transmitted his opinion on the congressman's statement.

"I guess that makes sense in a normal family." Jack shook his head. "But not in this case. No one with any sense would leave a mentally unstable woman alone with two children. He's either lying or guilty of criminal neglect."

"Unless she isn't mentally unstable," Sean added. "She seems sane enough to me. Any chance her paranoia is all in her head?"

"Definitely not. Imaginary threats don't drive black sedans." Jack filled Sean in on Beth's accident.

Sean's fist thudded on the desk. "Accident my ass. Baker's after her."

"The congressman has something to hide." Jack met Sean's gaze. "Something he doesn't want his wife to talk about."

– – –

Later, after Sean had left, Jack pulled out the articles on the Bakers his cousin had included in the file, having made up his mind that the congressman's story was total bullshit well before he'd talked to Jack about it.

Jack lifted a photo from the file. There she was in a full-color glossy with the congressman at some charity event during their engagement. Baker's hand rested intimately on the small of her back. She looked different with her light brown hair, which was shorter, highlighted, and cut in a polished, modern style. In the picture she was ten or fifteen pounds heavier, which changed the whole shape of her face. No wonder Jack hadn't recognized her. The biggest difference, though, was in her expression. Her eyes did not hold the haunted look Jack was accustomed to seeing. She looked happy, healthy, and beautiful.

Jack looked at another picture, taken shortly after their wedding. The happy smile was now forced and tight. She stood a little farther away from her new husband than she did in the engagement picture, just out of his reach. She was thinner, and her eyes were not quite as bright.

The next picture was taken several months later. The change in her appearance was startling. Her weight had fallen dramatically. She looked tired and sick. Dark circles had formed beneath her eyes. She was a different woman, like she'd been struck with cancer or some other serious illness. Depression had been the official diagnosis, but Jack wondered how much physical and psychological abuse Beth had suffered during those long months of her marriage.

Jack then pulled out the information on Congressman Richard Baker. Ivy League education, captain of the debate team, lawyer turned politician, Baker had been elected to Congress shortly after marrying Elizabeth. An attractive new wife and two ready-made kids were evidently assets to a politician. The Bakers were an old money family, complete with a gigantic house in the Hamptons, racehorses, and a yacht. There was a picture of Richard and his father in the winner's circle with one of their horses after the Brandywine Derby.

Jack flipped through the pictures of the congressman. Richard Baker was athletic looking and blond, with a country club tan. His hair was Ken-like in its perfection, his clothes classically styled, and his smile sincere. Baker didn't seem to mind having his face in the paper, and he was always willing to give an interview, even when he claimed to be distressed about his missing wife.

Jack had seen enough victims and their family members to recognize the signs that intense grief and worry left on a person. Some people reacted with anger, while others harbored their misery within themselves, but the despair was always visible in their eyes. Long periods of not eating or sleeping left a person worn and beaten. They neglected personal hygiene, bit their nails to the quick. Genuine grief inevitably took its toll and manifested itself as a physical illness.

The congressman, however, didn't look upset in any of the pictures. His expression appeared grave and concerned, maybe, but his clothes and hair were still mannequin perfect. He hadn't lost any weight worrying about his missing family, and Jack didn't see any shadows beneath his eyes. This guy probably hadn't missed a manicure, let alone an hour of beauty sleep.

If Baker *had* hired the goon in the black sedan, Beth and the kids were in even more serious jeopardy than he'd realized. The Bakers had money and connections, many in the legal system, and probably some outside the law as well. He knew well enough that money and power could manipulate the law as easily as fresh Play Doh. In this case, money and power did not give up after one failed murder attempt.

Rising, Jack closed the file and stored it in the wall safe. He didn't want Beth to know he had this information yet. He still hoped she would trust him enough to tell him everything, but at least he now had some information that might enable him to protect her.

Now he just had to find out why. Why did Baker want his wife dead?

Flipping off the light in the study, Jack turned into the hall with the intention of dropping the two dirty tumblers in the kitchen before heading to his room. The faint sound of a zipper drew his attention to the stairs. With one hand on the banister and the other on his cane, he limped up the steps. Following the sounds of light footsteps, he turned left at the top of the stairs. A light glowed from around Beth's door, which was slightly ajar.

Jack peered through the gap and gasped.

A large wheeled suitcase lay open on the bed, neatly folded clothes stacked inside.

Beth was packing.

CHAPTER TWENTY-SIX

Beth folded a pair of jeans and set them in the suitcase. Though the morning's events had chilled the blood in her veins, she couldn't help but turn them over and over again in her mind. Only one thing was crystal: her *accident* that afternoon had been anything but.

Richard's men had found them.

They needed to leave. Tonight.

The kids were going to be devastated. Though they'd only lived here for a short time, they loved the mountains. They were attached to Jack, too. Her throat constricted at the thought of leaving him. Strengthening her resolve, she opened her closet and began pulling out the few items that hung inside. She couldn't afford to think about Jack. She had children to protect.

She'd let the kids sleep a few more hours, let whoever might be watching think they'd settled in for the night. Then they'd take off a few hours before dawn. It was their best chance at slipping away. Their only chance, really. If they waited any longer, that man in the black sedan would be out there, somewhere, waiting for them.

Her hands began to shake so hard that she could no longer fold her clothes. She stuffed the rest of the pile into the suitcase in a large ball.

"Beth?"

Lost in her panicked thoughts, she whirled.

Jack stood in the doorway. "What are you doing?"

Her heart clenched at the mixture of shock and fear in his deep brown eyes. If he knew the truth, he wouldn't want her anyway. She'd lied to him from the very beginning. Words began to bubble out of her mouth. "I'm packing. Don't you see? He's found us. We have to leave. Now. I can't believe I've pulled you into this mess. He'll kill you, too." Aware of the children sleeping in adjacent rooms, she kept her voice to a panicked whisper. She turned away and closed the suitcase, unable to watch the turmoil of emotion on his face. Her hands were shaking so hard she couldn't zip the bag. "It's not safe here anymore, not after today."

She felt Jack cross the room and stop behind her, his body inches from hers. His hands hovered above her shoulders. She wanted to lean against him and absorb his strength. But she couldn't. It would be one more deception.

"You can't leave. If you're right, he'll follow you. You'll be completely unprotected. Think of the kids. They're much safer here. Let me help you. Please."

"Jack, you don't want to get any more involved in this, with us. It's too dangerous. I've lied to you. I've been lying the whole time." The pressure in her chest threatened to cleave her in two.

He spoke softly into her ear. "Please don't go. Sean and his men will be here in the morning to turn this place into Fort Knox. Getting to you here isn't going to be easy. Let me help. You can't keep running. I don't want you to leave, Beth."

Though he wasn't touching her, the heat from his body warmed her back. His breath caressed her neck. She was so focused on his strong, solid body that it barely registered that he seemed to know more than she'd told him.

He was right, though. Running wasn't the ultimate answer, but knowing Richard's hired killer could be this close filled her with mind-numbing terror. She shivered, took a deep breath, and turned to face Jack.

His face had gone pale and his mouth, tight. His eyes were filled with much more than concern. The prospect of risking her heart one more time was nearly as frightening as Richard. It'd already been shattered twice before. She wouldn't survive another loss.

"You can trust me." Jack accurately read the indecision of her face. "Please. Please don't leave."

"There are things you don't know about me." She searched his eyes for any hint of anger or disappointment. "It's all been a lie. Everything I've told you."

"There's nothing you can tell me that would keep me from helping you." Jack took her hands in his. "I've known you were lying since the very beginning. I wouldn't have been much of a cop if I hadn't figured *that* out. Doesn't change the way I feel."

His eyes held no trace of doubt. It was all or nothing now. There would be no turning back from this decision. But if he was going to accept her, help her, risk his own life for her, then he had to know the truth. The whole truth. Every dirty detail.

"My name is Elizabeth Baker, and I'm married to Richard Baker, Congressman Richard Baker, and I don't know what to do. You're right. I can't run forever." For once, her eyes sought direct contact with his. "I need help."

To her amazement, there was neither shock nor condemnation in his eyes, just relief. He gave her hands a gentle squeeze. "I need you to tell me everything."

Beth nodded, relief making her light-headed.

Jack glanced back at the hallway. "Let's go downstairs where we can talk."

– – –

Jack chose the study because he could shut the doors. Not wanting space or furniture between them, he ignored the desk.

Beth paced the length of the small room.

Jack moved to the credenza, poured her a splash of scotch, and then guided her to the loveseat against the wall. He pressed the glass into her hand. "First of all, I already knew who you are. Sean figured it out."

Surprise and suspicion flared in her eyes. "How long have you known?"

"About a half hour."

Relief passed over her face. "Oh." Her fingers clutched the glass, but she didn't drink.

He thought of the thick file in the safe and brushed off the guilt. He'd done what he'd thought was best. No going back now. "I've read the official story behind your disappearance. Now you need to tell me what really happened."

Her eyes shifted to the window as if she were contemplating jumping through the glass. She sighed. Her body deflated, and her gaze dropped to the floor.

"The last night, the night we left, Richard was in his study. A package had come for him, special delivery. I assumed it was important, and he would want it right away. I tried not to make him angry." She paused and took a minuscule sip of scotch while Jack digested that small, telling statement. Translation: she'd done her best to avoid having the shit kicked out of her. Anger swelled in Jack's chest and roared in his ears. He tamped it down and struggled to listen.

"I knocked on the door. The latch hadn't caught and the door swung open. Richard was watching a movie on his flat screen. He was so absorbed he didn't hear me come in. I just stood there. I couldn't believe what I was seeing on the TV. It was two men. Two naked men. They were, um…" Beth shook her head and took a healthy swig of scotch. She waved a hand in the air. "You know…"

Holy cannoli. "Didn't Baker get elected on a platform of family values? Didn't he promise to push for a federal ban on same-sex marriage?" Jack asked.

Beth nodded. "It was the center of his whole campaign and the key to most of the contributions he received, but there's more." She took a shaky breath and drained her glass without coughing or sputtering. "The film wasn't professional quality, more like a home movie. At first I couldn't see the man's face, but then he turned and I saw…Richard. He was on the DVD with a much younger man I didn't recognize."

Smelled like a setup for blackmail. Jack doubted the congressman would have recorded his own transgression.

"I must have made a noise, because Richard's head snapped around, and he saw me in the doorway. The way he looked at me, I knew he was going to kill me. There was no way he'd let me live after I'd seen…that. Even in the moment, I remember thinking it explained a lot of his behavior, like why he couldn't…um…perform…with me."

That information was the best news Jack had had in weeks.

Unable to sit still any longer, Beth shot to her feet and resumed her pacing. "I ran down the hall. He chased me. He had a letter opener in his hand. Managed to cut me once on the side."

Jack flinched as he remembered the thick scar that snaked across her ribs. Two inches lower and they wouldn't be having this conversation. She'd be dead. Jack gradually absorbed this new information. Her husband had attacked her with a knife. He hadn't lost his temper and beat her in fury. His act wasn't physical punishment for a transgression—but an intent to kill her.

Baker would stop at nothing to silence Beth forever. With vast resources behind him, he could pursue her for as long as it took.

Then Jack, the decorated cop, believer in justice, supporter of the legal system, had a vision. He wanted to kill Baker. Not just kill him, but punish him. Jack could see the knife in his hand, slicing and dicing the congressman like a Japanese hibachi chef. A cut for every time he raised a fist to Beth. Jack's inner caveman wanted revenge.

Jack's eyes shifted back to her as she continued her story. He blinked the image from his head and concentrated on what she was saying. The details were important.

"I got as far as the kitchen. Grabbed the big metal flashlight we kept on the wall for emergencies. When he lunged at me, I hit him over the head, and not just once. I hit him a couple of times to make sure he was really out cold. Then I tied him up with duct tape so he couldn't follow me. I figured if I was lucky, no one would find him until the staff arrived in the morning. I emptied his wallet, grabbed all my jewelry, a few changes of clothes for me and the kids. We were out of there in fifteen minutes. There was no use calling the police. They'd just believe whatever Richard told them. They always did." She blurted all this out in one breath and raised the empty glass. "Could I have a little bit more?"

He poured a half shot of whisky into her glass. At her body weight, single malt could pack a serious punch, especially for someone who never drank. She took the glass with both hands and tossed it back like a sailor.

Jack lifted the empty glass from her grasp and set it on the desk. Without thinking, he pulled her to his chest and wrapped his arms around her. She leaned into him and inhaled in ragged breaths. Several minutes passed before her trembling ceased.

"Did you really try to kill yourself?"

"No!" Beth pushed away from his chest, anger flashing in her eyes. "Shortly after we were married, I told him I was leaving. He said if I did, I'd never see my kids again. He must have slipped something in my food or tea. I don't remember anything except waking up in the hospital. I was tied to a bed in the psychiatric ward. When I told the doctor I hadn't taken anything, he said I was delusional and increased the medication. Once a suicide attempt was on record, taking my kids away would be a piece of cake for Richard and his father."

She spoke into his chest. "When we left, we went straight to my uncle's house in Virginia." A deep sigh shuddered through her body. "He took care of everything. He got rid of my car. Got us new identities. Kept us out of sight. For a while I thought I'd be wanted for assault or attempted murder or something, but that never happened."

"Baker was probably too concerned about his image to go public with the fact that his little wife bested him." Jack leaned back and cupped his hand under Beth's chin. Moving slowly, he drew her up to his face until his lips brushed gently against hers. Then he kissed her temple. "I won't let him hurt you again." The words came out as a whisper against her hair.

"I know." Her hands slid around his neck, and he returned to her mouth. When her lips parted under his, that tenuous, tight wire of control snapped. He crushed her soft body against him. A vision of Baker manhandling her flashed through his head, and he suddenly released her. "I'm sorry."

Her eyes snapped open; her chest heaved. She blinked in confusion. "About what?"

"I don't want to hurt you. Not after Baker—" Jack swallowed, scanning her eyes for any sign of fear or disgust, any indication she didn't want him to touch her. He saw only desire.

"I have never been afraid of you, Jack. I was only afraid you'd try to find out who I was and Richard would get wind of it." She stepped closer and pressed her body against his. Beneath her soft breasts, her heartbeats fluttered against his chest. "I need you."

Those were the words he'd been wanting to hear. He buried his face in the curve of her neck. She was warm and soft and smelled like strawberries.

"There's only one problem. I'm still married."

"Not for long," Jack said.

Their mouths met. Her soft lips yielded instantly under his, and he swept his tongue between them.

CHAPTER TWENTY-SEVEN

Beth leaned into him and closed her eyes as he took her mouth. His woodsy aftershave lingered on his skin and mixed with the musky scent of his arousal. His muscular body was wonderfully hard against hers. Her legs weakened as desire coiled in her belly.

She felt his passion erupting as he devoured her mouth. His hands roamed her body hungrily, cupping her ass and pulling her closer to the hard length that pressed against her belly. He drew his head back and held her against his chest again, his hot breath on her neck making her shiver, but she wasn't cold. He slid his palms along her body until they rested against her collarbones, the thumbs rubbing the tender hollow at the base of her neck.

"Tell me if you want me to stop." His rough hand trembled with desire as it reached up to stroke her cheek.

"Please don't stop." Her body ached to get closer to his. As close as it could get.

Jack sounded more nervous than she was. He gently cupped her jaw, and she leaned her head into his palm. "Your trust in me is humbling, Beth."

She pulled her head back and met his gaze. "It's OK, Jack. I'm not afraid of you. I didn't think I'd ever want another man, but here you are."

"Yeah, here I am." He leaned down and kissed her again. His hands slid down her sides and gripped her hips, molding her body to fit his again. She felt him rock hard against her stomach.

He trailed his lips down the side of her neck. Her skin tingled, and warmth pooled in her belly as her body awakened. After months of being numb, she was suddenly aware of every square inch of skin on her body as it yearned for his touch. Long-dormant feelings burst forth as she came alive under his hands. Her skin lived and breathed for the stroke of his fingers, the whisper of his hot breath against her damp skin.

He ran his mouth along her jaw and nipped lightly on her earlobe, sending tremors racing down her spine.

He lifted his head. "Not in here." Jack took her hand and led her from the study, down the hall to his bedroom, closing and locking the door behind them.

A king-sized sleigh bed dominated the room. Or at least it seemed to.

Jack sat down on the edge of the bed, pulling her close, so she was standing between his legs. He raised his chin and looked up at her, his face flushed, eyes hooded with desire, waiting for her to take the next step. Beth reached down and pulled his shirt over his head so she could touch his broad, bare chest. She spread her fingers around the hard muscles of his shoulders and felt the heat rise off of his body. He gasped as her fingertip brushed over a nipple. His eyes dilated as her hands stroked the hard planes of his chest and stomach.

Following her lead, he slid his hands under her shirt and slowly skimmed up the smooth skin on her back. Her body arched toward him in response. Impatient to feel his hard flesh against her own skin, Beth unbuttoned her shirt. Jack's mouth followed her fingers as they trailed down the center of her chest. He peeled the shirt off her shoulders, moving his lips across her collarbone, along the hollow of her neck. Her pulse throbbed thickly against his lips as his mouth slid down her chest.

A low groan escaped from her lips as his tongue lingered just above the lace of her bra, then slid inside to flick over her nipple. The bolt of pleasure shot straight down to her toes.

"Take it off," he breathed against her damp skin. "Please."

She unsnapped her bra and let the straps slip down her arms. Jack froze for a few seconds, his gaze locked on her breasts, before he lowered his head and licked a nipple with the tip of his tongue until it tightened into a taut, sensitive peak. He lifted his mouth and blew across the wet tip. Beth's hips rolled, and dampness pooled between her legs.

Jack turned and lavished the same attention on her other breast, mumbling into her flesh, "More skin. Now."

"Wait." Beth pulled away, lifted her pant leg, and unstrapped the Sig from her ankle and set it on the nightstand. "I didn't tell you about this, either."

Strange. Jack didn't look surprised to see a gun. "That's OK. I feel better knowing you have it. Now come back here." He drew her back to the bedside, hooked his thumbs into the waistband of her jeans, and slid the fabric slowly down over her hips. When she stepped out of the pants clad only in that black thong, Jack exhaled sharply. Beth blushed as he stared at the juncture between her thighs.

"You take my breath away." He reached forward and slid his forefinger into the thong's elastic at her hip. He tugged her closer. "I haven't had to think about self-control for thirty years. God help me."

His finger slid lower, following the band of the thong until he reached her softest flesh. He moved the silk aside and touched her with feather-light strokes that drew her hips forward with an instinctive surge.

"No fair. You're still dressed."

"That's an easy fix." He flashed her a wicked grin.

She reached out to unsnap and unzip his fly. He lifted his body as she shoved his pants down and pulled them off with much less finesse than he'd exhibited. Finally, his erection sprang free, desperate for her touch. She curled her hand around the hot length of his sex. His hips rocked. He was simultaneously hard as steel and soft as satin.

"If you keep touching me like that, this is going to end before it gets started." Moaning deep in his throat, he stilled her hand with his. He slid one finger slowly inside of her and emitted what sounded almost like a growl from deep in his chest. She tensed for a second, then relaxed as he continued to caress her, breathing words of encouragement in her ear. His thumb circled her tiny bud of nerve endings.

Beth moved against him to increase the pressure. It wasn't enough. Not nearly enough.

Jack froze suddenly. Frustration crossed his face. "Beth. I can't believe I'm saying this, but we should stop. I don't have any protection."

Her hips stopped moving, but she met his questioning gaze with a sad smile. "It's OK. I can't have any more children."

He hesitated only for a second, and Beth was surprised to see an expression that just might have been disappointment flicker across his face. Then those nimble fingers went back to work and made her forget what she'd been sad about. He made her forget her own name.

Her knees buckled as long-forgotten sensations flooded her.

"I need more," she gasped, looking directly into his eyes. Then she moved over him and took him inside her, sliding all the way down until his shaft was buried deep within her body.

They both exhaled at the same time. Jack didn't move, but inside her, his erection throbbed.

"Phew," he breathed out in relief. Beth laughed softly.

"You know, this is a bad time to laugh at a man," he joked breathlessly into her ear. "Doesn't do much for his performance."

"I'll keep that in mind." She paused for a moment, letting her body adjust to his presence, the sweet pressure of invasion, savoring the feel of having him inside her. Jack held still, although the strain was visible in his clenched jaw and the corded veins that protruded from his neck. He gave her complete control, allowing her to set the pace as she began to move, slowly at first, agonizingly slow, drawing out those first surges of pleasure, until the sensations themselves gradually assumed command.

Gasping and damp, her body took over.

"Beth." He curled forward and gasped in her ear. He slid his hand between their bodies, the tip of his thumb seeking, finding, stroking her swollen flesh. She arched backward, her nails digging into his back, driving him deeper. Her entire body clenched. Pleasure pulsed deep in her belly and exploded outward through her limbs. Jack reached for her hips, thrusting fully into her before his body shuddered and went limp.

Jack collapsed backward and pulled her down with him onto the bed. His heart hammered in her ear as her head rested against his chest in the dark. Relief and satisfaction flooded her limp, damp body.

– – –

His hands settled on her back, slowly stroking the smooth skin from her shoulders to the curve of her buttocks.

"Wow," she whispered, her body still draped across his.

"Yeah. Wow." He kissed her head. He was certainly in no rush to get up. "Are you OK?" He figured he'd be ready to move again in a day or two.

"Yes, I'm more than OK. I'm wonderful." She sounded relieved. "It's been a long time since I felt this good."

Yet here she was, naked in his bed, relaxed, limp thighs draped loosely over his hips. She rolled off his chest, and he pulled her to him, savoring the feel of her silky skin against his body. He held her close for a few minutes, allowing their breathing to return to normal.

"I haven't been that wound up since I was seventeen and had this hot cheerleader I'd fantasized about in the back seat of my Chevy Nova. Took me all summer to get her there. The entire interlude took less than a minute. And I'm being generous with the time frame. Of course, at seventeen, I was ready to go again another minute later." He tucked her head under his chin. "Now that we got that awkward first time out of the way, I'm going to take my time and taste every inch of your body."

When she didn't respond, Jack turned his head and looked down at her. Her eyes were closed, her breaths deep and even in sleep. Nothing like an intense orgasm to relax a person. At least he hoped it had been as earth-shattering for her as it had been for him. He'd felt like his heart had exploded.

He watched her sink deeper into sleep. She looked younger, the signs of strain temporarily smoothed from her face in a rare moment of peace. He had never seen her this calm. His eyes ran over the length of her naked body, appreciating the contrast of her smooth, slender limbs entangled with his big, hairy ones.

Jack's heart flipped in his chest. If she hadn't needed the sleep so badly, he'd have woken her up for another round. He wanted her again already. There was a God, and Jack was obviously on his good side at the moment.

She sighed and rolled onto her side. Moonlight filtered in through the blinds and illuminated her skin. Jack inhaled slowly between his teeth as he looked closely at the skin on her stomach. A vivid reminder of her suffering, the scar stood out, raised and pink in the soft white skin. Jack ran his finger lightly over the mark. His chest tightened when he thought of how close she'd come to dying that night.

Protectiveness settled over him like a thick fog, dampening all other emotions. Nestling closer, he pulled the covers up over her shoulders and closed his eyes, trying to blot out the violent images coursing through his mind and to concentrate instead on the physical pleasure he'd been able to give her. God knew she had already experienced enough pain.

Jack didn't care how important the man was. He would personally kill the congressman and bury him in a deep hole before he ever let him near her again.

– – –

Beth awoke early the next morning, briefly surprised at the warm body pressed against her in bed. She glanced out the window across the room. The sky was pale gray, and the first orange streaks of dawn were just angling over the horizon. Not wanting the children to see her sneaking out of Jack's room, she had intended to rise and return to her own bed long before dawn. Instead she'd slept heavily without dreaming for the entire night. Amazed at how good she felt, she rolled over to face Jack. He was already awake, lying on his side and watching her. He slid his hand around her hip and cupped her butt to pull her against his hard, naked body. He kissed her deeply.

"Good morning." His voice was deep and raspy. An early-morning arousal pressed against her stomach as his hand stroked her body. She felt a deep pull low in her belly as his mouth wandered down her neck, her body already anticipating pleasure.

"I should go. Before the kids get up." Speaking coherently took some effort. His mouth was very distracting, sliding along her collarbone toward that sensitive place he'd discovered between her neck and shoulder. Strong hands slid over her supple skin, kneading the muscles on each side of her spine.

"It's early. They won't be up for an hour or two, at least." His tongue moved slowly down to her shoulder. Her skin bloomed with heat, and an ache of desire grew deep within her. Her body remembered how good it felt to have him moving inside her last night. Her hips surged toward him without any input from her brain.

"Oh, I don't know. I...think..."

"Stop thinking." His lips closed over her nipple, pulling gently. Her body arched like a drawn bow. Grinning wickedly, he made good on his promise from the previous night. His lips roamed across her ribs, brushed the soft underside of her breast. His hot breath traveled across the sensitive skin of her belly. She squirmed as his lips trailed lower. She reached for him, only to have him move away from her.

"Just relax. Enjoy." He pushed the sheet firmly away, moved his mouth down her rib cage. "I'm dying to taste you."

Sliding still lower, he licked the tender hollow next to her hipbone. Taking his time, letting the anticipation build, he tasted the length of her legs, brushed his mouth along her calves, lingered on the spot behind her knee, found patches of skin that she'd never even been aware of before he touched them. Her body writhed, wanting more as his lips moved up along the inside of her quivering thighs. With a groan of his own, he obliged her with one long stroke of his tongue right up through her center. He lifted his head and stared into her eyes. He licked his lips, and a hungry moan reverberated from deep inside him.

Circling his arms under her thighs, he spread her legs wider and lowered his mouth to her again. Her heart raced and hammered in her ears. Her hips jerked and rocked. Waves of pleasure rolled through her body as he laved her with his lips and tongue. Her hands clenched the sheets. Every muscle in her body contracted. She couldn't breathe. Then the release washed over her, flowing through her body from the inside out, making her ache to have him inside her.

He moved over her—and stopped. Pain creased his face. "Sorry. Bad position."

He rolled to his side, pulling her leg over his hip and piercing her to the hilt with one hard thrust.

She wrapped her arms around him and watched his face contort with his struggle for control. He threaded his fingers with hers as they found the rhythm together. Their bodies, slippery with sweat, slid against each other effortlessly, lost in the gradually building pleasure. His lips covered hers in a deep kiss as she reached the crest, muffling her cries with his mouth. He exploded within her in a final deep thrust and collapsed on top of her with a breathless moan.

He pressed his forehead to hers. His heart slammed against her rib cage as his body gave a final shudder. Bodies limp and tangled, she looked up into his deep, brown eyes, wishing they could stay in bed all day. He certainly knew how to drive all rational thought from her mind. She knew the kids would come looking for her soon.

"I should probably sneak upstairs and shower." A wave of relief rushed through her. Before last night, she'd thought she'd never make love again. She'd been afraid she'd never give herself the chance.

Not only did she do it, she enjoyed it. More than she had even thought possible.

Their legs were still intertwined. She was not yet ready to break the physical bond between them. She realized how much she had missed this intimate, primal connection, the feel of her man's hard body against hers, the synchronized beating of two hearts. For the first time in as long as she could remember, her body was warm inside and out, her muscles loose and slack. She felt like all the tension had been driven from her body.

"I could help you." He nuzzled her neck, moved his lips against her jaw. "I may have missed a few spots."

She smiled. "Then I wouldn't get downstairs before lunch." Her voice was reluctant, but firm.

"Probably not." With a sigh of regret, he released her and rolled onto his back. Putting his arm behind his head, he watched her walk around the room naked, gathering her clothes. She felt his gaze on her and glanced over her shoulder at him. Her heart skipped a beat at the hunger that still shone in his eyes.

She pulled on her jeans and shirt, stuffed her bra in her pocket, and leaned over to kiss him softly before quietly opening the door a crack and checking the hallway. She slipped out and crossed the hall silently. Both of the kids' doors were still closed when she tiptoed upstairs, but she heard the rustling of bedding from Ben's room indicating he'd be up soon. A wave of guilt passed over her, but she pushed it aside. What had happened between her and

Jack was beautiful, and she refused to feel any shame for taking one night for herself. Beth turned on the shower and looked at herself in the mirror while she waited for the water to heat.

She looked younger this morning, and she felt incredible. She'd slept, all night. Well, almost all night. She smiled to herself. Stepping beneath the hot spray, she let the scalding water flow over her body, wishing for a long moment that she had taken Jack up on his offer. His hands were magic on her flesh, and she couldn't think about his mouth without a wave of heat blooming through her center. Her thighs tightened and her skin tingled just thinking about his activities this morning.

She lathered her body and washed her hair. Maybe she would buy some scented shower gel. She felt like smelling nice. For the first time in years, she felt sensual. Her problems seemed so far away, less potent all of a sudden. He had seen all her scars, the secrets of her violent past had been stripped naked, and he still wanted her.

Twenty minutes later Beth entered the kitchen. The kids were eating cereal at the table. She gave them each a kiss on the head. A glance out the French doors revealed Sean and his men unloading equipment from a utility van. She greeted Mrs. Harris and accepted a cup of coffee.

She carried her coffee to the study, knocked on the closed door, and opened it to peer through the crack. Holding the cordless phone against his ear, Jack waved her in. She pulled the door closed behind her. As she rounded the desk, Jack pulled her to his side, wrapping one arm around her hips and pulling her down onto his lap. Desire flared in his eyes. Unbelievable. He'd made love to her less than an hour before.

"Hey, Wes. This is Jack. Give me a call back. It's important." He punched the end button on the phone and set it on the desk.

"Wes is my former partner. I'm going to ask him to come up here. I'd like you to tell him everything. He can help us."

Panic lodged in her throat. Talking to Jack was one thing. Spilling her guts to a strange cop was quite another. "I don't know if I want to do that."

Jack stroked her arm. "It's OK. I trust Wes completely. You can, too."

Her chest felt tight; her lungs constricted.

Jack frowned. "Hey, take it easy. If you can't do it, we'll think of something else."

Keeping her eyes on his face, she drew in a deep breath and let it out slowly. Jack wouldn't force her. It was her decision.

Her eyes locked with his. Neither of them had made any admissions of love, but she knew her own heart. And she finally decided to trust it.

"I can do it."

CHAPTER TWENTY-EIGHT

Jack pulled open the front door just as Wes reached for the doorbell. Henry had announced his former partner's arrival as soon as the Crown Vic turned into the drive.

"How are you doing, Henry?" Wes stepped over the threshold. He thumped on Henry's side as the dog circled his legs like a gigantic tabby cat. "Hey, Jack. Sorry it took me so long to get up here."

"It's only been a few days." Jack led his friend down the hall.

"Yeah, but you said this was important." Wes followed, trying not to step on Henry's prancing feet. "He hasn't changed."

Jack entered the study and shut the door behind them. "Look, Wes. I appreciate you driving all the way up here. I didn't want to do this anywhere near the station. Other than you, I don't know who I can trust." Too wound up to sit, Jack leaned a hip on his desk. "I have some information for you, but you have to promise to keep the source confidential."

"You got it," Wes answered without hesitation.

"OK. What do you know about Richard Baker?"

Wes looked thoughtful. He rubbed his fingers on his chin. "Congressman Richard Baker?" When Jack nodded, he continued, "Rumor has it he's being groomed for higher office. He was big in the news last fall when his wife went missing. She had some mental illness. Nobody ever did find her. I looked over the bare facts of her disappearance a couple of months ago. Had a Jane Doe in the morgue that fit her general description. Baker came down to the morgue and viewed the body. It wasn't her. Why? What do you know about him?"

Jack paused. "I know where she is."

Wes straightened in his chair.

"I've spoken with her." Jack gave him Beth's version of her marital history.

Wes stared at him. His mouth hung open. "Shit. That's some story. Be difficult to prove, though. She doesn't have a copy of the DVD?"

"No."

"Too bad. Would've made good leverage." Wes scratched his chin. "Does she have any proof Baker faked the suicide attempt?"

"No."

Wes fell back in his chair, his shrewd black eyes fixed on Jack. "Jack, even if I believed every word, I can't investigate a congressman without hard evidence. It's her word against his. The guy has powerful friends. He's the Republican Party's new golden boy. Some people say he'll be president someday. People are going to get pissed if I start digging around in his private life. I'll end up back in a patrol car. I'll be directing traffic for the next fifteen Thanksgiving Day parades. You know I hate standing out in the cold, Jack. His father plays golf with the governor, for Christ's sake."

"He's dirty, Wes."

Wes waved a hand in the air. "He's a politician. They're all dirty."

"You're becoming awfully cynical."

"Comes with the territory."

"I want you to meet her," Jack said.

"She's here?" Wes asked incredulously. "Elizabeth Baker is here?"

"Yeah, she's here. She's my new caretaker." Jack paced back to the window, turned his back to Wes. He knew his face was giving up too much, especially to Wes. He took several deep breaths.

"Let me guess. Beth Ann Markham." When Jack nodded, Wes sat back in the desk chair and tapped a pencil on the desk.

"Somebody tried to run her off a cliff. With Beth's accident and the disappearance of a local woman, I've been keeping everyone close to home." Jack walked to the window and stared out across the lawn.

"I heard about your missing waitress. She fits the Killer's victim profile."

"Yes, she does. Feds haven't made it official, but that's what they're thinking, too. I got that feeling in the pit of my stomach standing out there at the scene."

They were both silent for a minute. Wes would never doubt Jack's gut.

"Anyway, back to Beth. I want you to meet her." Jack led his shocked friend from the room.

Beth and the kids were sitting at the kitchen table playing an ancient game of Scrabble they'd found in one of the closets.

Wes stopped and gaped at Beth.

Beth met Wes's scrutiny with a direct stare. Ben appeared to sense the tension in the room and shifted closer to his mother. Katie shrank backward. Her tiny hands began to shake. Jack's heart tightened. He moved around the table and scooped her up.

"This is Wes. He's my friend. He's going to help us."

She settled down, leaning on Jack's chest, except her lower lip still trembled a bit.

When Wes sat down in one of the kitchen chairs, Jack knew they'd won him over. Wes was as much of a sucker for scared kids as Jack.

Jack nudged Ben and nodded toward Katie. Reluctantly Ben took his sister by the hand and led her out of the kitchen.

"OK, Wes, what do you want to ask her?" Jack leaned his elbows on the table, reached for Beth's hand, and covered it with his.

Wes stared at their joined hands for a second, then blew out the breath he'd been holding. "I'm in."

"Thank you," Beth said.

Wes flushed. "Don't get too excited. This'll take some time. I don't know who I can trust. Probably no one. These are very powerful people. I'll call you if I come up with anything." There was nothing left to say. Wes excused himself and politely said good-bye before heading out the door. Jack followed him to his car.

"I've got to get this guy, Wes. I won't let him hurt her again." Jack clenched his jaw in frustration. "I'm pretty sure I'm in love with her."

"No shit. I already figured that out for myself. I'll do some sniffing around, see if there's any dirt under the congressman's manicured nails. Don't hold your breath, though. If there were anything really juicy, some political rival would probably have found it by now." With a wave, Wes drove off.

With some regret, Jack wondered if he'd put his friend's life at risk, too. He shook off the guilt and returned to the house. Wes was a cop. Getting creeps off the street was what he did.

Beth was still in the kitchen, sitting at the table, staring at its pocked surface. Her shoulders were bowed against the weight of her memories, her expression bleak. While Jack couldn't remove her burden, at least he could share the load.

"Hey." Jack squatted down in front of her, lifting her chin with his hand and looking into her sad eyes. "Wes is a good guy. He'll help us."

She nodded, as if speaking took too much effort at this point and she didn't have the energy.

"I have one more favor to ask. You need to level with Chief O'Connell, too. After your accident and Mary Ann's disappearance, Mike's going to run background checks on everyone in the town. It's only a matter of time before he finds out your name isn't Markham. He's a smart cop. We have a better chance of getting his cooperation if we approach him with the information."

"I'll think about it."

"Think fast. You're a newcomer to Westbury. If you were a man, no doubt he'd already have you in for questioning."

– – –

Jack's eyes blinked in the pale gray of predawn. Beth stirred against his chest. She was warm and soft and naked. What was a man to do?

He slid a palm up to her breast, then stroked her creamy skin lightly all the way down to the curve of her hip. One sleepy moan, and his heart kicked into a gallop. When her back arched under his hand, his dick twitched toward her like a divining rod seeking water.

Her eyes fluttered open, and she smiled up at him with complete confidence. His chest ached, and he needed to be joined with her as much as he needed air to breathe. His hand slipped around her hip and between her legs.

She'd woken up soft and wet for him.

Desire coursed through his belly. His erection pressed against her thigh, and his balls cheered it on.

He rolled her onto her back, parted her legs, and covered her. To mate, to claim, to brand her as his. He slid into her tight heat. Her legs shifted and wrapped around his waist, letting him burrow deeper. He'd slept with a number of women in his lifetime, but being inside Beth was like having an electric current run from the tip of his dick to the base of his spine.

He lowered his head and claimed her sweet mouth. Her tongue answered his in a mating dance that mimicked their bodies.

The tension built, clenching his muscles from the arches of his feet all the way up to his eyeballs. She started to tighten; then his hands were grasping her ass and he was pumping harder, faster, sliding her up the bed beneath him as her heat clamped down on him from base to tip. Just before the top of his head blew off he came in a freight-train roar of sensation that robbed his lungs of air and his head of blood flow.

He nearly passed out from the intensity and literally collapsed onto Beth's body.

Holy Christ. What just happened to him?

Exhausted, drained of every ounce of tension, his body went limp. Breathing hard, he rolled off Beth and dragged her to his chest. He lay in the pale morning light, speechless, as his lungs caught up and his head stopped spinning. Beth's fingertips stroked his biceps. A heaviness settled over him.

– – –

Beth stroked Jack's chest as it rose and fell evenly. While he was exhausted from their lovemaking—no wonder considering the Olympic effort he'd put into the event—she felt charged up, as if he'd somehow transferred all his energy to her. There was no way she'd be able to go back to sleep now. She needed to move. She slid out from under his arm and left the warmth of his bed. After dressing quickly, she let herself out of the silent house and strode toward the barn. She'd stay close to the house and keep the ride short, but if she didn't get out of the house, she'd go mad.

Twenty minutes later, Beth adjusted her seat in the creaking saddle. Mist hung over the meadow, like smoke, in the gray dawn. Dampness muffled the sound of Lucy's hooves as she ambled across the field toward the forest path. A soft sucking sound accompanied each hoof as it lifted from the soggy ground. Beth held the mare to a walk, lulled by the gentle swaying of the horse's back.

Her early morning ride was all the solitary time she had each day, since she and the kids hadn't left the estate since the accident. It had been nearly two weeks since Wes's visit, and they'd heard nothing from him. There'd been no sign of the black sedan. Jack theorized that Richard's men were holding back because of the increased police and federal agent presence in the area due to the waitress's disappearance. Beth knew it was only a matter of time before Richard's men came back to finish the job. They were out there, waiting for an opportunity.

There'd been no sign of Mary Ann Spencer, either. Beth felt as if her world were hanging in a state of limbo. All of these terrible events were hovering over her, over the whole town, like a storm gathering force.

The clean scent of pine filled her nose as they neared the forest path. The trail changed from soggy grass to a thick carpet of pine needles, and Lucy's hoofbeats were reduced to a faint rustle.

The only positive emotion rolling through her head was her love for Jack, still not proclaimed verbally, but in her heart just the same. He hadn't said it either, but the passion in his lovemaking this morning told her he returned the feeling.

The kids loved him, too. They'd been so relieved to learn they no longer had to conceal their real identities.

The sound of water rushing over rock soothed Beth's ragged nerves. She relaxed in the saddle with a deep, cleansing breath.

The breeze shifted. Lucy's head snapped up. Her nostrils flared as they entered the shadows of the woods. The scent of something decayed drifted past Beth's face for a second before the wind shifted again and it was gone. The mare neighed, shrill and lingering in the morning silence. Beth gathered up the slack reins, her bowels knotting with apprehension.

Beth stroked the base of Lucy's neck. The horse's skin twitched, and she chomped nervously at the bit. Although spirited, Lucy wasn't normally skittish.

"Easy, girl. What's the matter?" Big ears swiveled back to listen to Beth's voice. The creek appeared as they rounded the bend in the trail. Lucy stopped short, long legs splayed, nostrils and eyes wide-open.

Something was wrong. Something was out there. The knot in Beth's belly tightened as she pulled the mare's head around, preparing to turn back, when she saw the form in the water. The breath rushed from her lungs as if she'd been struck. Although obscured by thick foliage, Beth knew exactly what it was.

The woman's body lay facedown, tangled in tree roots and partially covered in organic debris at the water's edge. There was no need to look for signs of life. The skin was gray and bloated. Dark hair floated in the muddy water like a soft, brown halo around the woman's head. Flies buzzed around the corpse. In the gentle current, a dry leaf drifted off the shoulder, revealing a small butterfly tattoo.

Lightheaded, Beth grasped the pommel of the saddle. The trees spun. The woods closed in upon her, abruptly claustrophobic.

The wind shifted once again. Beth could smell it again, more pungent this time, the putrid scent of rotting flesh. Bile rose in the back of her throat and she gagged. She dug in her pocket for the cell phone Jack had given her, praying she wouldn't drop it. Turning on the phone, she held down number two with shaking fingers, speed dialing the house.

She heard the phone ring, then Jack's voice, still raspy from sleep, a few seconds later. "Where the hell are you?"

"I'm all right, so don't get upset." She tried to steady her voice, but it caught and quivered anyway. "I'm in the woods. I think I found Mary Ann Spencer."

"Beth, I want you to get out of there. Come back to the house. I'm on my way."

Beth hung up and turned Lucy's head to point the mare toward home. Tears gushed hot from her eyes, and she blinked to clear her blurred vision. Luckily, Lucy knew which way to go and headed back down the trail at a brisk trot. Beth concentrated on maintaining her balance as her head swam with grisly images. The sound of buzzing flies echoed in her head.

The mare broke into a canter when they broke free of the forest. Beth pulled her to a stop as soon as she saw the Explorer bumping across the meadow toward her. Sliding off of the horse's back, she leaned against the big animal for support. She stood there wobbling until she felt Jack's strong arm around her waist, catching her as she slid toward the ground. The reins dropped from her grip. Her body was cold from the inside out. Breathing hard, she gasped for air to fight the increasing dizziness.

"You're hyperventilating. Take a deep breath and hold it." Jack opened the tailgate of the truck and helped her into the back. He pushed her head down to her knees. She didn't seem to have any control over her trembling extremities.

"Exhale. Again. Deep breath, hold it." Once she had her breathing under control, he handed her Lucy's reins. "Can you hold on to her? If not, I'll let her go. She'll head for the barn, right?"

"I'll take her," Beth whispered and wiped her forearm across her eyes. He cupped her cheek with his hand, stroking a tear off the side of her face with his thumb. The sorrow she saw in his eyes was a reflection of her own.

"I'll be right back." He turned away, using his cane to limp toward the trees.

Freezing, Beth clenched the leather reins in her fist. Her uncontrollable shaking faded to shivers and left nausea in its place. She pulled her knees up to her chest in an upright fetal position, and rested her forehead on her jeans. Good thing she hadn't had breakfast yet. Lucy, in tune with her mistress's moods, butted her head against Beth's legs.

Jack reappeared, his face hard, his mouth set in a grim line as he sat next to her on the tailgate. "I called Mike."

She only nodded in response. Her initial hysteria subdued, an overwhelming sadness filled Beth. Seeing that young girl dead, discarded naked in the slime and mud, filled Beth with more despair than she had felt even at the peak of Richard's torment. She thought of Robert Spencer, whose entire world was going to come crashing down on him this chilly, damp morning. She knew from experience he would want to see his spouse before he would believe it was Mary Ann.

Brian had suffered mostly internal injuries in the accident that killed him, and his face had looked normal, too normal, when she saw him on the viewing screen in the morgue. She remembered that moment with a stab of renewed loss. How would Robert possibly view Mary Ann's bloated, rotting body, see what some animal had done to the woman he loved, and survive?

Death was final. There was no time for a final kiss or caress, to apologize for a harsh word or argument. The world imploded with no warning. Beth knew what it was like to experience the loss of your spouse, your best friend, your lover, all at the same time. To be alone, dealing with the worst event of your life without the one person you always expected to have at your side to help you through the rough patches. The sheer weight of the emptiness was enough to suffocate a person.

Her brother's and parents' deaths had nearly been the end of her. Thank God she'd met Brian. He'd given her new hope. When Brian died, Beth had a baby to care for, and Ben's grief to worry about, which took precedence over her own despair. At least during the daylight hours, she was busy, her mind occupied with formulating coping strategies for Ben, her body dealing with the demands of an infant. At night, though, the loneliness nearly crushed her.

Robert had no children to distract him, to force him to rise and face each day. Adding to his trauma was the cruelty and horror inflicted upon his wife. How would he ever close his eyes again without seeing the wounds on the body he'd made love to, feeling the pain and terror she suffered? The media would make sure the public knew every detail of his wife's horrific death. He wouldn't be able to escape it.

Jack's arm came around her shoulders, breaking both her trance and the thin layer of numbed control she'd been sustaining. Blood roared in her ears. The chattering of her own teeth echoed in her head. Her brain briefly registered flashing lights before all sights and sounds faded to black.

She opened her eyes to find herself flat on her back in the bed of the Explorer, her feet propped up against the window. A fleece blanket was tucked around her body. She could hear Jack's voice and turned her head toward the sound. He sat on the tailgate next to her. She felt the weight of his hand on her thigh. Lucy was tied to a nearby tree.

"It's her." Chief O'Connell was standing a few feet away. He'd removed his hat and was running his hand through his short red hair. "You better get her up to the house. I'll need a statement from *Ms. Markham* later. I have to wait for the crime scene van, so I don't know how long I'll be tied up here." The cop turned and stalked back to his car.

He knows.

Beth blinked a few times to clear her vision. Images came rushing into her head with painful clarity, the grotesque shock rising in her throat, choking her. She felt Jack's arm around her. He helped her onto the passenger seat, and then drove back to the house.

"Easy. I don't need you fainting again."

Fainting? She had never fainted in her entire life, not even when she'd found her father. She'd gone numb instead.

By the time they made it back to the kitchen, the kids were up. The smell of freshly baked biscuits turned Beth's stomach. Mrs. Harris took one look at her face and handed her a glass of ice water while Jack delivered the bad news. Beth hated for the children to have to hear about it, but she wouldn't be able to conceal the police activity at the house today.

"Is it the lady that's missing?" Ben asked tentatively. "The waitress?"

"The person hasn't been identified yet, Ben," Jack explained. "Chief O'Connell is down there now, and he's waiting for a whole lot of other policemen who are going to help him find out."

Katie's eyes were troubled. She climbed up in Jack's lap instead of her mother's and took his face between her palms. "It'll be OK, Jack. The bad men never catch us. Mommy's too smart for them."

Mike O'Connell walked into the kitchen as those words left the child's mouth. Beth knew she should have been nervous, but her brain and body were utterly depleted. The big man stood still in the entryway for a minute. He glanced at Jack before accepting a cup of coffee from Mrs. Harris and taking a seat at the table.

She patted his broad shoulder as he glanced backward at her. "There's a fresh pot of coffee for anyone who needs it."

"Thank you, ma'am."

Mrs. Harris retreated from the kitchen. Jack met the chief's gaze and stood, lifting Katie with him. "Come on, Ben. We'll all go down and feed the horses." They went out the back door, leaving Mike and Beth alone.

Mike sipped his coffee, eying Beth over the rim. "Feeling better?"

"Yes."

"OK, then. Who are you really?"

The police chief wasn't going to beat around the bush, which was good. Beth had no energy for verbal sparring either. "My name is Elizabeth Baker."

Chief O'Connell's red eyebrows shot up. "As in Congressman Baker?"

"Yes." Beth met the chief's gaze straight on.

"Let's start with your statement about this morning and work our way back to your vanishing act."

Beth didn't leave anything out. She'd already told her story to Jack and Wes. Each time the retelling seemed to get easier.

The chief took notes in a small notebook. "Jack's a good man, and he's my friend. You're not going to run out on him are you?"

"If I was planning to run, we wouldn't be having this conversation." Beth summoned strength from deep within, strength she didn't know she possessed, and looked Mike straight in the eye. She didn't feel like the same woman who'd fainted out in the field. "I've gotten very good at disappearing."

The big cop sighed and scrubbed a hand over his face. "I bet you have. Unless I find out any of this relates to my case, I'll keep it quiet. But you need to understand that I can't withhold information from the FBI."

Beth nodded.

"Please don't go anywhere. I'll be back. "

CHAPTER TWENTY-NINE

"I can't believe it was that easy." Beth felt like all the air had been let out of her lungs. Sitting next to her on the small couch in the study, Jack placed a hand on her knee and squeezed.

"I don't know if *easy* is the word I'd use." Jack's obscenely expensive lawyer, Carlyle Hughes, picked a dog hair off his navy blue pinstripe suit and dropped it on the carpet. "When I met with him this morning, Congressman Baker adamantly denied your accusations. He claims to be devastated by the divorce request but has no desire to force you to remain married to him. Mind you, he didn't look all that devastated, but it was only the two of us. Had there been a camera in the room, I've no doubt the congressman could have looked as broken up as he deemed necessary." Carlyle steepled his manicured fingers. A gold Harvard Law School ring winked, and the light glinted off hair the color of polished silver.

Beth was amazed at the security money could buy, like the high-powered attorney sitting across from her. Carlyle had been old friends with Danny O'Malley. If it hadn't been for the personal referral, Beth would have thought of him as an old shark, predatory and cold.

She summoned a smile. If Beth wanted to fight fire with fire, she needed Carlyle Hughes. Since Wes and Sean had been unable to unearth any dirt on Richard, she had only two options:

to remain in hiding or confront her husband. She hadn't taken Sean's offer to "remove" the threat seriously.

"Still. It doesn't feel right." This was good news, so why did she feel so vulnerable? "I didn't expect him to give up this easily."

"Well, he didn't just agree. There are conditions," Carlyle said.

Next to her, Jack tensed. "What kind of conditions?" He rose and crossed to the credenza. "Can I interest you in a scotch, Carlyle?"

"It's a bit early, but if it's the thirty-year-old Macallan Danny stocked, then I can't resist."

Jack flipped two tumblers then hesitated. The bottle hovered. His mouth tightened as he poured two fingers of amber liquid into only one glass and handed it to the lawyer.

Carlyle sipped. "Excellent." He set the glass on the end table and opened his portfolio. "Here's the deal. If the congressman agrees to the divorce, withdraws his claim of Mrs. Baker's mental instability, and removes his petition for guardianship of her children, he expects a signed liability waiver and confidentiality agreement. No appearances on *Oprah*. No memoirs on her married life. No Lifetime Network TV movie. Not a peep to anyone. Ever. And Mrs. Baker must agree to relate a plausible story to the press that will enhance the congressman's political image."

"He wants to put a positive spin on this? Unbelievable." Jack began to pace the small room, but Beth noticed, despite his anxiety, he did not head back to the credenza.

In the leather wing chair, Carlyle crossed his legs. "Really, Jack, Mrs. Baker—"

Beth interrupted. "Please don't call me that. Beth will do."

"I think Mrs....er...Beth should strongly consider the offer. She has no evidence from the time in question, while the congressman has medical reports and testimonies from numerous top-of-their-field doctors. She spent a week in a psychiatric ward after a documented overdose. Baker called an ambulance and arranged private care in one of the best medical facilities on the East Coast. Outwardly, it appears as if he's done everything humanly possible for his wife. Filing charges against the congressman under these circumstances would be unwise. He's fully prepared to pursue guardianship of your children. No judge or jury is going to believe the congressman orchestrated the entire event."

"It's the truth." Beth's stomach turned over. She was going to have to choose between recovering her life and restoring her reputation, the latter of which could place her children in jeopardy. Not acceptable. Nothing was worth even the possibility of Richard getting custody of her kids.

A brief flicker of desolation passed over Carlyle's face. "The truth is only relevant if you can prove it."

And wasn't that a sad fact of life?

Unwilling to accept the limited choices, Beth's mind whirled. "But what about all those physical and psychological evaluations last week? Don't tell me I went through all that for nothing." Although Quinn had set her up with a matronly internist with the bedside manner of a grandmother, letting Dr. Miller poke and prod her had been the very last thing she wanted to do. Wait. Check that. Letting the psychiatrist in on her own private hell had been far worse.

Carlyle gave her a wry smile. "Those reports are the only reason you got an offer this good, believe me. At this point I believe the congressman simply wants to control the impact on his career. He's been playing the devoted spouse a long time. His constituents would turn on him in a second if they thought they'd been lied to. Baker sees himself in the White House someday."

Beth couldn't imagine being free. What would it be like not to constantly look over her shoulder? To sign her kids up for school and join the PTA? Did it really matter what other people thought? She glanced over at Jack. His lips tightened in a thin line as he waited for her decision. She knew he'd support her no matter what she chose to do. The hell with it. Her image wasn't that important. Jack's opinion was the only one that mattered. "If he'll leave us alone, I'll sign whatever he wants."

"That extreme won't be necessary. Baker may control the legal arena, but we still have media exposure on our side. *Oprah, Jerry Springer, The View*. Any one of those producers would sell his soul to the devil to expose the congressman. If he isn't reasonable, you don't sign the confidentiality agreement." Carlyle rose, smoothed his trousers, and tugged on his French cuffs. "Don't worry. I'll handle everything."

Beth didn't trust her voice. She nodded.

Beth followed as Jack walked the lawyer to the door. "Thanks, Carlyle."

"You and Beth have nothing to worry about."

God, was it true? It didn't seem possible that it was over.

Jack closed the door. Draping an arm over her shoulder, he led her to the kitchen. "Everything's going to be OK."

It sure seemed that way, but Beth's stomach wouldn't settle. She supposed it was going to take some time to adjust to *not* being a fugitive.

She filled the teakettle and turned on the gas burner. "Tea?"

Jack sighed. "Sure."

Her heart swelled. She knew he'd much rather have a scotch, and that she was the reason he wasn't indulging. The house was quiet. Mrs. Harris was playing bingo at the Methodist Church, and the children were in bed.

As she pulled two mugs and the box of chamomile tea from the cabinet, Jack stepped up behind her and wrapped his arms around her waist. Leaning back against his hard chest, she absorbed his body heat. His heartbeat pulsed through her body.

"Beth, have I told you I—" The ringing of the phone interrupted him.

Jack reached for the cordless and squinted at the Caller ID display. He frowned. "It's the police chief." He stabbed the talk button with his finger. "Hey, Mike." Jack's eyes opened wide as he listened for a minute. His eyes lit up with interest. "No shit?"

A few minutes later, he returned the receiver to its stand. "Mike's arrested Will Martin for Mary Ann's murder."

"Really?"

Jack nodded. They were both silent as the sadness of the waitress's death hung between them.

The teakettle whistled, and Beth poured water into one of the mugs.

"He wants some advice." Energy vibrated from Jack.

"The police chief needs your help." She smiled. "You'd better go."

"Are you sure?" His feet were already pointing toward the door as he asked.

"Positive. The situation with Richard is settled. The Riverside Killer's been arrested. I'm going to drink my tea, watch something mindless on TV, and try to put all of this out of my head for a while." She didn't believe that was possible, but she'd felt Jack's pride surge at the police chief's request. He needed to go.

"OK." He leaned down to kiss her. "Lock the door and set the alarm after I leave."

She nodded. Outside the French door, Jack leaned on his cane and waited until she'd secured the house. Though the danger had passed, they were all going to be paranoid for a long while.

Jack hadn't been gone for more than a half hour when Beth returned to the kitchen. She rinsed her mug and placed it in the dishwasher, glancing out the French door to the brightly lit lawn beyond.

"Oh, no."

CHAPTER THIRTY

Four horses grazed in the back yard, which was lit up like a football stadium with the new security lights. They must have broken the gate or a fence board. Not an unusual occurrence for big animals, but she was too tired to deal with their antics tonight.

Too bad no one else was home.

She scribbled a note and left it on the counter in case anyone came looking for her. Grabbing Henry's little-used leash, she listened for the sound of his dog tags but heard nothing. Henry had gone to bed with Katie. Obviously it would take more than a few horses on the lawn to disturb him.

With a sigh, Beth reset the alarm, stepped out the door, and locked it behind her before walking across the thick grass. She passed under the massive oak tree in the center of the yard. Above her head, branches swayed in the cool, wet breeze that promised rain. In the gunmetal gray sky, patchy clouds drifted in front of a nearly full moon.

Using the leash, she trekked the three geldings back to the pasture one by one. As she'd expected, the latch on the gate was broken. She looped her belt around the posts to hold it closed. Lucy was limping, and Beth led her directly to the barn. She passed through the bright circle cast by the barn's new overhead light, opened the heavy sliding doors, and led the mare into the building, flicking on the light switch in the aisle as she passed.

The empty stable smelled of hay and dust. Something to her left rustled in the straw. Beth paused mid-stride and made a mental note to visit the pound for a couple of big tomcats as soon as possible. Rats could get out of hand in a flash.

"Now, Lucy. What did you do to yourself?" Standing in the bright aisle, she focused her attention upon the horse's leg. Blood ran down the bronze foreleg from a stitch-worthy cut above the knee, which must have happened when the mare busted through the gate. Beth put Lucy on the crossties and went into the tack room for the first-aid kit. She punched the vet's number into the new phone on the wall while gathering the necessary first-aid items in a clean bucket. Dr. White's machine picked up. Beth left a detailed message. The vet would show up as soon as he could. In the meantime, she'd clean and bandage the wound.

She stepped back out into the aisle, bucket loaded with gauze pads, soap, and a leg wrap. An arm snaked out from the next stall, wrapping around her neck and jerking her backwards into the dark. The bucket clattered to the floor.

A scream rose in her throat, but the pressure from the viselike grip strangled the sound. She twisted, but another arm circled her shoulders, arching her backward and pinning her arms to her chest. Her lungs screamed from lack of oxygen as she kicked ineffectually against her attacker's shins.

With both hands she grabbed at the thick arm encircling her neck and pulled down. She managed to relieve enough pressure to suck in a lung full of air. She threw her head backward. A grunt sounded in her ear as she connected with his chin, but his grip remained strong.

He shifted. The arm fell away from her shoulders. Before she could break free, something sharp pricked her cheek. Hot blood trickled along the side of her face. Beth froze.

"Stop it, bitch! It's not what I had planned, but I'll cut your throat right here." Even in whispered tones, she knew that cold voice. Richard pressed his lips to her ear. "Why didn't you just run when my men cut through your ladder or ran you off the road? God, you're a pain in the ass."

Hatred and anger thickened his speech, but his grip loosened slightly as he spoke, allowing her to gulp the moist air greedily. Beth's eyes darted around the dark stall, looking for some weapon, anything she could use to get away from him, but the stall was empty. Lucy moved restlessly in the aisle, tossing her head, jangling the metal clips on the ends of the ropes that connected her to the walls.

"There's no such thing as an acceptable divorce for a politician, no matter how my PR people spin it. Being a widower, however, will send my popularity ratings through the roof. Poor me, dedicated to my mentally ill wife, devastated when her dead body washes up somewhere. I'm practically a saint already." His hot breath burned her neck. "You promised to stay with me until death do us part. Guess which one of us is going to die?"

Richard loosened his grip around her waist, spun her around, and shoved her. Her back and head struck the wall. Pain lanced through her head. Nausea rose in her throat, and her vision blurred.

The noise startled the horse. Beth heard her bolt, breaking the crossties. Hoofbeats passed the stall door, then faded.

Three feet away, Richard waved the knife. Beth's heart pounded against her ribs like a trapped wild animal. She sidestepped toward the doorway. If she could just put some distance between them, she could draw her gun from its ankle holster. This close, she'd never get it out fast enough. In her pocket the pepper spray Jack insisted she carry pressed against her hip. It was her only chance.

The cold gleam on the blade reflected the evil glint in his flat blue eyes. He stabbed the knife at her face in a taunting arc. She blocked its thrust with her arm instinctively, barely feeling the blade slice through the skin. Warm blood ran down her forearm. He jabbed at her belly, and again she blocked the knife's path with her arm. Blood dripped from her fingertips into the straw.

Beth steadied herself, balancing on the balls of her feet and ignoring the pain, as he lunged forward again. She stepped aside, drew the pepper spray from her pocket, and sprayed it at his face. He was in motion, so she missed at first, but the tail end of the arcing liquid hit its mark. He threw a hand over his eyes, blinded by the tears pouring down his face.

"You're dead!" he roared, wiping his face on his sleeve.

Beth darted out of the stall, her feet slowed by the deep straw bedding.

– – –

"Thanks for coming, Jack."

"Glad to help." Jack shook the police chief's hand and lowered himself into the worn visitors' chair. He hung his cane on the wooden back, trying not to look too excited at the prospect of discussing a murder. But damn, his blood practically hummed. "What do you have?"

Across the scarred desk, the chief's leather chair creaked as he settled his bulk back into it. "Two long, dark hairs and a couple of drops of blood in Martin's trunk."

"No way." To say Jack was shocked was an understatement. Sure, Martin was scum, but a murderer? "Are you shittin' me?"

"No." Mike shook his head. "I got an anonymous tip that Martin's car was seen following Mary Ann out of the diner parking lot the night she was abducted."

The skeptic in Jack zeroed in on the key word. "Anonymous?"

"Yeah. I know. Convenient." Mike ran a hand through his thick red hair. His uniform was wrinkled. The bags under his bleary eyes attested to the number of hours he'd been working Mary Ann's case. "Call came in from the pay phone at the Stop 'N Shop."

The hair on Jack's neck stood up. "Security cameras?"

"Not on the pay phone. And nobody saw anything, of course." Mike pinched the bridge of his nose. "Along with the altercation he'd had with Mary Ann at the diner, it was enough to get a warrant. Found the evidence in the trunk right away. Lab put a rush on the DNA tests. State crime scene unit went to the house. We'll see when the results all come back in."

Jack scratched chin. "So, other than the suspicious nature of the call, what else is bugging you?"

"One, he has an alibi. According to his father, they were unloading a tractor trailer full of feed that night."

"Dad could be lying."

"I know." Mike rose and crossed to the window. "It's just a feeling, Jack. I don't think he's smart enough to be the Riverside Killer."

Jack didn't believe Martin had the gray matter to pull it off, either. "What's the profiler say?"

"Mixed feelings there. Even though he's never been charged, Martin's got a history of sexual harassment. He's the right age and race, a bully with a beef against women. On the other hand, he's thick as an ox, loud-mouthed, and has a whole horde of drinking buddies. Not exactly genius, solitary, serial killer material.

But profiling's not an exact science, as the FBI keeps reminding me."

"Does he have access to accpromazine?"

"He says he doesn't use it. His horse is a stud, and apparently Ace causes some sort of penile paralysis in stallions."

"Huh." Jack didn't have a reply to that one.

"It's not that hard to get hold of Ace, so that wouldn't necessarily rule him out anyway."

"Maybe he just copied the Killer to get Mary Ann," Jack suggested.

Mike turned back to his desk and sank into the chair. "That's one theory the profiler suggested, but until all the evidence from his house and car has been processed, who knows?"

– – –

Hysterical barking woke Ben. He rose from his bed and padded barefoot into the hall to listen. Downstairs, Henry was going ballistic about something. He glanced in his mom's room. Empty. After looking in Katie's room and making sure she was still sleeping, Ben quickly trotted down the steps.

"Mom?" He ducked his head in the living room, then the study. His mother wasn't in either room. Henry began to whine. Ben followed the noise to the kitchen where the big dog was digging frantically at the bottom of the French door.

His mom wasn't in the kitchen either. Where was she?

The hackles on the back of the dog's neck were raised. "What is it, Henry?"

At the sound of Ben's voice, the dog grew more agitated, looking from Ben to the door. He began to growl and snarl at the closed door.

The note on the counter drew his attention. Mom was down at the barn. Ben was suddenly certain something bad was happening. The hair on his neck rose to mimic the dog's.

He called his mom one more time. No answer. He picked up the phone and dialed Jack's cell, but Henry was making such a racket, he could hardly hear the ringing on the other end of the line. Scanning the yard quickly, he looked down at the insistent dog. After turning off the alarm the way Jack had showed him, Ben opened the door. Henry raced through the opening and headed across the back lawn toward the path that led to the barn.

Ben quickly closed the door and reset the alarm. No matter what happened, he couldn't leave Katie. He'd promised to take care of her.

"Hello?" Jack's voice came over the line, and Ben turned his attention to the telephone.

– – –

Beth took three awkward running strides in the barn aisle before Richard's hand clamped around her ankle and pulled her to the ground. She landed on her face in the packed dirt, kicking frantically at his strong grip with her free foot. He grabbed the other ankle and hauled her back across the floor toward him. Flipping her over, he straddled her thighs, shifting his grip to her wrists, now slippery with blood. Her blood.

He pinned a hand on each side of her head and moved his body forward onto her stomach. She kicked and bucked futilely under him. Adrenaline pumped through her veins, blocking out the pain of the knife wounds.

"Hold still. You're just going to wear yourself out. I'd rather not do this here. You're leaving with me." He was breathing hard with the effort of holding her down, and she realized she'd never fought back before.

If he thought she was going with him without a fight, he was the one that was delusional.

He pulled her hands over her head to hold both wrists together in one hand and brought his free fist down across her cheekbone. Pain exploded under her eye. The room went out of focus; images blurred and flashed before her: Richard's chiseled face contorted by rage, the gossamer cobwebs along the ceiling of the barn, the flash of light on the steel blade of the knife he'd set down next to his leg. She lost track of time. All she could hear was the rushing of blood in her ears and the drumbeat of her heart.

Her intention to fight like a demon leaked out like air from a slashed tire.

Taking advantage of her momentary stillness, Richard reached into his pocket and withdrew a hypodermic syringe. Her eyes focused instantly upon the needle. Charged by renewed fear, gasping for breath, she writhed in the dirt under him, trying to avoid the hand bringing the needle toward her leg. Near hysterical at the thought of being drugged and helpless with him, she bucked and twisted her body enough to bring her knee up and into his exposed groin. The closeness of their bodies prevented her putting any real force into the motion but it slowed him down. He grunted and his jaw tightened with pain.

He stuck the syringe between his teeth and punched her again. The pain burst through her jaw in a kaleidoscope of colors. Blackness crept around the edges of her vision. She waited for the prick of a needle, but Richard's weight jerked on top of her body.

"Ahh!" Snarling drowned out Richard's shocked cry. His weight jolted back down onto her legs.

Beth shook her head and blinked hard to clear her sight. A large tan and black shape hung from Richard's arm. She barely recognized Henry. His teeth were closed on Richard's biceps, ripping the fabric of his black shirt, knifelike fangs tearing through the flesh like a true predator. Blood flowed down Richard's tanned arm and over the gold Rolex on his wrist. Savage, guttural sounds came from the infuriated dog. Henry jerked his huge head from side to side, pulling Richard off Beth's body.

Beth scooted backward. Clawing at her hem, she yanked up her pant leg and pulled the Sig from its holster. The metal was slippery with her blood, and she fumbled with the gun. Richard screamed as the dog's sharp teeth shredded the skin and muscle of his arm. Beth gripped the gun in both hands. Richard tried to rise, pushing to his feet with the dog still attached to his arm. He stretched forward. His hand clamped around the hilt of the knife lying in the dirt. He raised the weapon over the dog.

Sighting on the center of his chest, Beth squeezed the trigger.

– – –

Jack leaped from the patrol car as the chief stopped in front of the barn. Mike's footsteps thudded in the dirt behind him. A mixture of screaming and snarling emanated from the barn. A gunshot. Then silence.

Ignoring the pain lancing through his leg, Jack broke into an awkward run. He drew his gun as his eyes took in the details: wide-open doors, interior lights blazing. Lucy stood at the far side of the barnyard, long ropes dragging from her head. Blood dripped down her slender foreleg.

Mike headed around back.

Heart slamming, Jack stepped to the door with his back to the wood, gun drawn up in front of his chest. Then he turned his head to look around the doorframe.

A man lay face up in the aisle. A large dark red splotch bloomed across his chest. Beyond the body, Beth sat against the wall in an upright fetal position—a gun in her two-fisted grip pointed at the body in front of her. Blood trickled down the side of her face and soaked her T-shirt and jeans. Next to her, Henry sat quietly. His head rested on Beth's knee.

At the other end of the aisle, Mike's head peered around the door. His eyes scanned the scene, held on Beth's gun.

Jack caught the chief's gaze and shook his head.

"Beth? It's Jack. I'm coming in," he called out as he eased around the corner. As soon as she saw him, she lowered the gun until it pointed at the floor. Either dead or soon to be, the man on the floor was no longer a threat. Barely glancing at him, Jack rushed to Beth's side. He dropped to his good knee and closed his hand around hers, gently twisting the gun from her limp grasp and engaging the safety.

She turned toward him, her eyes glassy with shock, while he attempted to determine the extent of her injuries. Long gashes in her forearms were smeared with blood and dirt. Her face was swollen and bruised. Blood dripped from a split lip.

Mike checked the rest of the stable with his gun drawn before kneeling down next to the man's body and pressing two fingers against the man's neck. "Holy shit! It's Congressman Baker."

"He dead?"

"Nope."

"Too bad."

Mike jogged out of the barn and returned a minute later with the first-aid kit from his patrol car in his hand and a couple of blankets over his arm. "Ambulance is on the way." But Jack ceased paying attention. He knew Mike had to apply basic first aid, but as far as he was concerned, the bastard couldn't die fast enough.

Jack grabbed some rolled gauze from Mike's kit and wrapped Beth's arms to stop the bleeding.

Henry whined softly and licked Beth's hand.

"Good dog." Jack's hand absently rubbed the dog's head.

"You're not kidding he's a good dog. Your K-9 reject really tore this guy up." Mike's comment drew Jack's attention. He glanced over at the congressman. Mike was applying pressure to the gunshot wound in Baker's chest, but the man's arm was mangled right down to the bone. Jack looked at Henry with renewed respect and gratitude. The big dog thumped his tail weakly and flipped Beth's hand with his nose. Blood matted in the fur around the dog's mouth and down his fawn-colored chest.

"You did good, Henry."

– – –

Jack followed Quinn into the private room he'd arranged for Beth under a false name. Once the details of the shooting were released, reporters were going to be all over the hospital like buzzards on roadkill. The kids had wanted to come with him, but Jack talked them into staying with Mrs. Harris at the estate. He didn't want them to see Beth in this condition.

He knew Beth was OK before Quinn had taken her away, but the sight of her still made his heart skip a beat. Bandages wrapped both arms from wrist to elbow. Her skin was nearly as white as the sheets, a consequence of shock and blood loss. An IV dripped into the back of one hand.

Jack approached the bed and stood still for a minute, watching her chest's even rise and fall. He let out a shaky breath.

"She's sedated. She'll probably sleep for a few hours anyway. I know she doesn't like drugs, but in this case, I think they're necessary." Quinn took a blood pressure cuff from the wall and wrapped it around Jack's arm. He pumped it up and frowned. "Either you calm down, or I'm getting you a sedative, too. I'll come back and check on both of you later."

Without taking his eyes off of Beth, Jack nodded. When he turned back to ask Quinn a question, his cousin was gone.

He slid down into the blue vinyl chair next to the bed and took her limp hand in his. Then the events of the night passed quickly through his head in a choppy sequence.

He leaned his head forward on the bed, resting his forehead on the top of her thigh. Tears streamed down his face as the tight rein on his composure finally broke.

– – –

Beth cracked her eyelids. Her head felt as heavy as a bowling ball, her mouth cotton-ball dry. Experimental movement sent sharp pain slicing through her arms.

She glanced around the hospital room, and then settled her gaze on Jack.

"Hey. It's OK. You're in the hospital. You're going to be fine." He reached up and stroked her forehead.

Warmed and reassured by his touch, her eyes quickly traveled around the room. She took in the hospital room, the bandages, the IV, Jack's weary face. Pain began to eat through the drug-induced haze. Her forearms felt like they'd gone through a meat slicer.

"Don't try to move. Let me get the nurse." Jack moved quickly to the door, one hand rubbing at the back of his neck as he stepped out the door. When he returned, a nurse followed him to Beth's side. After a rapid-fire assessment, she left, promising to bring Quinn and drugs shortly.

"Hurt?" he asked, gently rubbing the back of her hand. She nodded and tried to speak, but her throat was so dry, she could only manage a squeak. Jack reached for the cup of water by the bed and held the straw to her lips. Cool water slid down her throat.

She cleared her throat. "What happened?"

Jack shook his head. "I promised Mike we wouldn't talk about it until he took your statement. He's waiting outside. Think you're up to it?"

She nodded. "Just tell me if the kids are OK."

"The kids are fine. They're home with Mrs. Harris. I didn't think they should see you until you were ready?"

"Thanks." She shifted her position, grimacing as the pain shot up her arms again, almost making her wish she wasn't awake. This kind of pain could make her change her mind about being trapped in a drugged fog. Medication definitely had its place. Like here and now.

The door opened, and the police chief stuck his red head through the door.

"Ma'am. Jack." The chief gave her a nod. Rumpled and bleary-eyed, Mike looked like he hadn't slept in a week. "Do you feel up to making a statement?"

"I'll try." Beth reached for Jack's hand. He threaded his fingers through hers and squeezed gently.

Mike pulled out a notebook and sat down on Beth's other side.

Beth had thought it would be excruciating to revisit what had transpired in the barn, but she found herself so depleted, so utterly drained, that she just reported the gruesome facts, slowly and exhaustively, without a trace of feeling. When she'd finished, a muscle in Jack's face was twitching. His grip on her hand tightened.

"Did you find the needle?" She'd been stunned by the blow to her jaw and had lost track of it when Henry attacked Baker.

O'Connell nodded. "We found the syringe in the dirt. It's at the lab for testing. Press got wind of it, too. Media rumors are flying about Baker possibly being the Riverside Killer."

"What about Will Martin?" Jack asked.

"Damned if I know." The chief closed his notebook and stood. "I'm sure I'll have questions, but that'll do for now."

"Wait a minute." Beth put the head of the bed up a few degrees. As the pain sharpened, so did her brain. "What happened to Richard? Is he here?" She held her breath, waiting for the answer.

"Congressman Baker was stabilized here last night and airlifted to Hartman University Hospital." Mike sighed. "Last I heard, it was touch and go."

He glanced at Jack, then back at Beth. "That's enough for today. I'll be back when I have some more questions for you. If you remember anything else, call me." The cop nodded to Jack and Beth then left the room.

As soon as the door swung shut behind him, the nurse hurried through with some pills. Neither of them spoke until she left the room.

Beth absorbed the information. Richard was still alive. For now. But he could still die—because she'd shot him in the chest. Her brain told her she'd been very lucky, but she still had to live with the memories of that night and all the repercussions. If he didn't survive, how would it feel to know she'd taken a life? Even though Richard hadn't left her a choice, the possibility that she might have killed him weighed on her conscience. Her taxed mind couldn't comprehend how Richard could be the Riverside Killer, though. That seemed impossible. Time would tell, she supposed. He certainly hadn't had any qualms about killing her.

She shuddered at the images that swept through her mind. "If Henry hadn't showed up, Richard would have gotten me. Your dog tried to rip him to pieces."

"I'll never say another bad thing about Henry." Jack grinned. "He eats nothing but steak for the rest of his life."

"Where is Henry today? And what happened to Lucy? I forgot all about her."

"Henry is with the kids. And the vet showed up a couple hours later and stitched the horse up. I already called Jeff. He said he'd take care of Lucy's injury until you're up to it." Jack's voice faded along with the pain as the drug made its way through her veins. "Arms feel better?"

"Yes, I'm feeling numb." Her own voice sounded far away, and her eyelids grew heavy.

"Numb is good. Go to sleep."

CHAPTER THIRTY-ONE

The black Crocs squeaked on the speckled, commercial-grade linoleum. In navy scrubs, with a stolen hospital ID clipped to his front shirt pocket, he walked through the ICU with a purposeful stride. The tech whose badge he'd lifted was brown haired and ordinary looking. So was he. Unless someone looked very closely...

He raised the ID at the uniformed cop guarding the doorway of the private cubicle. The cop barely glanced at it.

After all, the patient was the prisoner, and it wasn't like he was going anywhere—except hell maybe, if there was one.

He grinned. Considering his own hobby, he hoped not.

No one else paid any attention to him as he ducked inside Baker's room. Hartman was a large teaching hospital with a state-of-the-art trauma center. As such, the place was teeming with medical staff and students at all hours.

He glanced at the industrial clock on the wall. Perfect timing. The seven o'clock shift change ensured the nurses were in patient review, getting ready to pass their charges on to the night crew.

It was a good thing the congressman wasn't still in Westbury's tiny community hospital. It would have been much harder to sneak into the smaller facility, where everybody knew everybody else.

He'd been there when his father had passed away in an impersonal cubicle just like this one. Serial killers were supposed to come from dysfunctional families and abusive parents. He had no such excuse. Sure, his mother had died when he was young, but his father had done his best to fill the void. There'd been life insurance. They hadn't been rich, but they'd never gone hungry either. All in all, aside from the fact that he'd spent a lot of time alone, his childhood had been ordinary. Out of respect for his dad, he hadn't indulged in his hobby until after he'd died. But as soon as the old man had passed, he hadn't let any grass grow under his feet. Some kids wanted to be doctors or firemen. He'd always been fascinated by Jack the Ripper.

He supposed growing up without a female role model could have prevented him from developing a normal affection for women, but he thought it more likely that he'd simply been born with a flaw in his conscience, a hole, like a baby could have in its heart at birth. But he'd leave the psychoanalysis to the shrinks. He had a job to do.

He set the plastic tote full of medical supplies on the bed and glanced around. All the machines were beeping the way they were supposed to. The ventilator hissed from its stand in the corner.

His gaze moved to the face of the man in the bed, the man who'd dared to mimic him—and badly.

Fluorescent light accentuated the congressman's pallor. Countless tubes, drains, and lines snaked over his body. This might not even be necessary. The guy looked like he might check out at any minute. He had to make sure, though. The congressman had poached on his territory. Beth was his prey. All his to enjoy.

Plus, that bastard hadn't only borrowed his name. He'd dragged it through the mud with that half-assed kidnapping attempt. Like *he'd* ever fail that abysmally. It just wasn't that hard to abduct a woman, as he'd proved time and time again. And would once more, as soon as he got the opportunity.

Besides, now that Beth was deeply entrenched at the O'Malley estate, she wasn't going anywhere. With Baker out of the picture, soon permanently, and the police convinced they had the Riverside Killer in custody, she'd grow more careless. Planting that evidence in Will Martin's trunk had been genius. Not that having that big oaf taking credit for his work was flattering, but a man had to do what a man had to do. But in that case, it had been *his* choice to sacrifice a bit of his reputation so he could make his next move.

Besides, it was only temporary. His image would be restored to its full glory after he took Beth.

The keys to achievement were discipline and planning, both of which Congressman Baker had botched. He deserved to die for his audacity alone. Then the asshole had gone and injured a horse. An unforgivable sin. Horses were noble and pure. Animals didn't lie or cheat or commit other sins like humans. They deserved better treatment than people.

People like Congressman Baker.

Lifting the sheet, he slipped the syringe from his pocket and quickly jabbed the needle into the large muscle of Baker's thigh. Delivering the drug intramuscularly would ensure he had time to make a hasty exit before the congressman's organs went apeshit.

He had maybe ten minutes.

Which was more than enough time.

He strolled down the hall and out the double doors with all the other employees leaving at the end of their shifts. Outside, the warm breeze carried exhaust fumes and the scent of rotting garbage. Philadelphia residents cursed and honked with abandon.

So much for the City of Brotherly Love. He walked the two blocks to the lot where he'd parked his car.

He kicked an empty beer can aimlessly as he unlocked his sedan. Disappointment weighed on him. Tonight's killing had left him distinctly unsatisfied. He'd never killed a man before. It wasn't nearly as much fun as being intimate with a naked woman. There hadn't been any struggle for life, no scent of panic, no eyes wide-open in terror, no recognition that *he* was the one in control. And leaving before Baker was actually dead had been downright anticlimactic. Usually, after such an event, he basked in a powerful afterglow, as if his batteries had been recharged. No such luck this time. But the job was done, and that was all that mattered.

He slid into his car and piloted it toward the entrance to the Schuylkill Expressway. Ninety minutes till home. He checked the dashboard clock. He'd be home in plenty of time to watch the ten o'clock news.

He smiled to the empty car. He looked forward to watching some breaking news in the saga of Congressman Baker and his estranged wife.

CHAPTER THIRTY-TWO

Jack set two mugs of coffee on the patio table and slid into the chair across from Beth. Despite the warmth of the late-morning sun, she was burrowed in a huge sweatshirt of his. It made her look as vulnerable as a child. Following her gaze to the horizon, he scanned the view. Over the mountains, the sunrise painted the sky pink, and he sincerely hoped the whole "red sky in morning, sailor's warning" saying only applied to the weather.

'Cause they could sure use a freakin' break.

Reaching across the scrolled metal table, he curled his fingers around Beth's hand. Just above her wrist the fabric hid the thick bandages that covered dozens of stitches. Three days ago he'd almost lost her. The memory welled up in his throat. A sip of coffee helped him swallow the lump.

She turned toward him, exposing the battered left side of her face, her bruises another reminder of how close she'd come to being killed.

"You feeling OK?"

Her smile was a little crooked due to the swelling. "Yeah. Just restless. I'm not good at sitting around."

Jack feigned surprise. "I never would've guessed."

"And I miss working with the horses."

He deadpanned, "No worries. You'll be back to shoveling shit in no time."

"I hope so." Her smile widened.

He raised her hand to his mouth and kissed her knuckles. "I didn't get to finish what I was going to say the other night, but I love you."

"I know." She smiled. "And I love you, too."

A grin stretched across his face. "I've never said that to a woman before. Now you're going to have to marry me."

Her face froze. The smile faded. "I think I'd better get my life sorted out first, don't you? That may take a while." She pulled her hand out from under his to pick up her coffee. Averting her gaze, she lifted the cup to her lips.

Was that a yes or a no? Maybe?

Well, shit. It hadn't occurred to him that she wouldn't accept. He'd thought it was a given. He was the one with the commitment issues. Right?

"We'll get through it. It'll be fine. Have some faith in Carlyle. He looks like a nice old gentleman, but in reality, he's as vicious as they come." Jack faced her and recaptured her hand, clasping both of his around it. The sun was warm on his back, but her fingers were cold, her face pale and drawn. "We love each other. That's all that matters. I'm sticking with you through this whole thing."

"Even if I go to prison?" Her voice quivered on the last word. She kept her face turned toward the mountains.

He shook his head, rubbing the back of her hand with his thumb. "You're not going to prison."

Still she didn't look at him. "We don't know that, Jack. Richard's father has a lot of clout. You have no idea what those people can do."

Didn't matter. He wouldn't let it happen. "But—"

Beth interrupted him. "Stafford will talk the prosecutor into pressing charges against me for attempted murder. I've accepted that. It's really just my word against Richard's, and you can bet as soon as he can talk, the first thing out of his mouth will be a well-crafted lie. Richard can spin anything."

Jack's oatmeal condensed to a ball in his stomach. He hadn't considered that he could lose her to a legal system skewed toward a powerful politician. "Then we'll talk to Carlyle about finding the best defense attorney."

Beth nodded, and she finally turned her wide green eyes to him. Her gaze was level and straight. "It's the kids I'm worried about. They have no blood relatives. Richard and his family would get custody of them if I went to prison."

"Then we'll talk to Carlyle about that, too." It sickened Jack that Beth had prison on her mind just a few days after nearly losing her life. The possibility that she was right about the situation hammered home all the reasons she'd been hiding in the first place. She hadn't had a choice. On her own, she'd have been at Baker's mercy. Without his money, Uncle Danny's fancy lawyer, and Mike O'Connell's integrity, she'd probably already have been arrested. Mike would never take a payoff or bow to political pressure, but a former senator could go over his head faster than a 747.

Even with the congressman out of the picture physically, the risk to Beth was still there. Damn it, would she ever be really safe? Would it ever be over?

Next to him, Beth lifted her face to the sunshine and closed her eyes as if appreciating something that might be in short supply soon.

Lost in thought, Jack started when the door behind him opened and the police chief stepped out. Jack had been expecting a follow-up visit, but from the worried expression on Mike's face, this didn't look like a routine call. Something must have happened. The police chief didn't sit, Jack's second clue that some new shit had hit the fan.

Mike walked to the edge of the patio and stared out toward the lake. Beyond the trees, its surface was a sheet of glass in the still morning. "Have you seen the news since last night?"

"No, sorry. We've been keeping the TV off." Seemed like every hour, the media had an "update" on Congressman Baker's condition or some new speculation on the estrangement between Baker and Beth. Or worse, someone had commented on the perils of having dangerous, mentally ill people on the loose. "The coverage has been brutal."

The public was behind Congressman Baker one hundred percent.

Mike sighed, turned, and pulled out a chair. Metal scraped against rough stone. "I don't know how to tell you this, so I'll just say it. Congressman Baker is dead."

The silence that descended upon them was broken only by a pair of tweeting sparrows.

Jack shifted his gaze from Mike's face to Beth's. A tear spilled from her eye and rolled down her swollen cheek. For Baker? Or for what his death meant to her?

The chair squeaked as Mike leaned back and rolled his head on Atlas-like shoulders. "The autopsy will be this afternoon. He was in critical condition, but stable enough that the doctors were surprised when he kicked. A nurse had checked his vitals twenty minutes before he coded. Nothing indicated he was checking out."

Mike pulled out his small black notebook. "I have to ask where both of you were last night."

The lump in Jack's throat swelled, and his heart skipped a beat. "We were here all night." He'd questioned many people in his career, but he'd never been on the wrong side of an interview. His life had done a complete about-face.

"Any witnesses?" Mike asked.

"Just the kids and Mrs. Harris." Jack stared at the police chief. "You can't think Beth is in any condition to have driven down to Philadelphia last night?"

"It's a possibility. I have to cover all the bases, Jack." Mike scrubbed a hand down his face. "But I admit, given Beth's physical condition, you'd be the more likely candidate. Those bruises stand out. Be hard for her to sneak into his room." Mike paused. "The congressman died around seven thirty. Was Mrs. Harris here at that time?"

"Yeah." Jack nodded. "We'd just finished dinner."

"I'll get her statement on my way out." Mike closed the notebook and shoved it into his breast pocket. "I'd find the best criminal defense lawyer you can, Beth. Stafford Baker is on a media rampage against you."

The last remaining bit of color drained from Beth's pale face.

The police chief paused in front of the door. "If the autopsy's clean and his cause of death is officially determined to be the gunshot wound, this time the charge would be murder."

"If Baker's autopsy is clean, Beth could be on the hook for his death. But if the autopsy turned something up, then I'm a suspect in his murder."

"Yeah." Mike nodded. "Either way, you're fucked."

– – –

A blue ribbon scrolled across the bottom of the television screen in James's plush room at the Bellevue Hotel in Philadelphia. The words *Congressman Richard Baker, dead at forty-three* caught his attention. He set his coffee down and turned up the volume to better hear the breaking news report.

A pretty newswoman stood outside a hospital emergency room entrance. In the background, an ambulance pulled up to the door, red strobe lights flashing.

"We're outside Hartman University Hospital, where Congressman Richard Baker was pronounced dead last night from a gunshot wound to the chest. The congressman was shot three days ago by his own wife, Elizabeth Baker—the same wife he'd been searching for since her mysterious disappearance last fall. According to sources close to the Baker family, Elizabeth was a former mental patient at this very hospital after she attempted to commit suicide..."

Blah, blah, blah. James tuned her out. An official account from anyone close to the Baker family was total bullshit.

The screen shifted to an interview with Stafford Baker. The former senator sat in a swiveling chair in the newsroom. A microphone was clipped to his navy suit jacket. For a man whose son had just died, Stafford looked immaculately groomed in a navy suit and blinding white shirt, with the prerequisite red power tie. Although polished and pressed, the strain was evident in the paleness of his skin, the repetitive clenching of one fist, and the puffy flesh around his eyes.

The interviewer turned to his guest. "Mr. Baker, you claim that the congressman was attacked by his estranged wife. She says he attacked her."

Stafford Baker shook his head and frowned. "My son had recently located his wife. He wanted nothing more than to bring her home and get her help. He lived in fear for the children for almost a year. I've no doubt those ridiculous accusations against Richard will be dropped. He did nothing but try to be the best father and husband possible under the circumstances. Unfortunately, my daughter-in-law has a long history of mental illness. It runs in her family. Her father committed suicide. Without the proper medication, she's a dangerous woman. Depressed, paranoid, and delusional. Her diagnosis was one of the reasons my son campaigned so hard for mandatory health-insurance coverage for treatment of mental illness. He realized that, given the cost of his wife's inpatient stay, many uninsured or under-insured Americans would be unable to obtain professional help."

The reporter leaned forward. "Then how do you explain the injuries Mrs. Baker suffered?"

"Elizabeth must have hurt herself. It wouldn't be the first time." Stafford eyes filled. "My son was a great man, destined for great things. He's the victim here." He took a shaky breath. "I bear my daughter-in-law no ill will. She's sick. But for the sake of public safety, she needs to be locked away where she can't hurt anyone else. It's time this country stopped allowing potentially dangerous, mentally ill people to roam the streets."

"Mr. Baker, before your son was killed, you'd been considering making another run for the Senate. What are your plans now?"

Baker straightened his shoulders. "I can't make any decisions right now. My family needs time to grieve."

Unbelievable. The bastard was still campaigning. He'd just shifted his focus from his son to himself. He was one smart son of a bitch, had covered his ass every way from Sunday. Beth couldn't win. If she agreed with the doctors, she was nuts. Denying her official medical records made her look even crazier. Hell, if James didn't know her, *he'd* believe Baker. Conspiracy theories were always hard to swallow.

But James knew Beth, and now he knew the Bakers as well. Both father and deceased son were rotten down to their stunted souls. Beth needed someone to play hardball for her, someone who'd play dirty. O'Malley was too much of a white hat. People like Stafford Baker didn't play by the rules.

James fingered a flash drive barely larger than a stick of gum, the results of his extensive surveillance on Richard Baker. While the pictures and videos James had recorded with the tiny camera he'd hidden in the heating vent weren't evidence of any illegal activity, he was pretty sure Stafford wouldn't want these movies uploaded to YouTube any time soon.

Unless they wanted to change the name of Capital Hill to Brokeback Hill.

Now the only question was how to get a message to Stafford. If James could get the former senator to lay off Beth, she'd be OK. James glared at the distinguished-looking man sucking up media attention on the screen. A few full-color glossies of Richard riding his aide like a show pony would keep Stafford Baker off Beth's case forever.

She'd be safe.

James paused. The dream hadn't come for a few days. Maybe she already was safe. Only time would tell. Of course, his gift only honed in on violence. He doubted he'd be warned if she were going to be arrested.

James slid a disc into his laptop and clicked on backup. By the time he'd showered, the disc would be ready. Then he'd be ready to contact Stafford. He could use one of his anonymous webmail accounts. No. An e-mail could be intercepted by staff. He eyed the disposable cell phone he'd picked up at the mall. Untraceable. Probably the best way to go.

He stripped off his shirt on the way to the bathroom and then stepped out of his shorts, dumping the contents of his pockets onto the vanity. Beth's silver pendant gleamed in the light. His hand stretched for it automatically. In the interest of her safety, he'd gone for zero contact since they'd separated. His gift was the only way he could check up on her.

The vision slammed into him before he even touched the silver disk. Darkness and fear instantly swamped his senses, blocking out his sight. A room opened in front of him, dimly lit by a bare bulb in the ceiling. Plywood covered a few small rectangular windows high up on walls of raw cinderblock.

In the dream he couldn't move. He twisted his body on a flat, raised surface. Pain lanced up his arms and through his head and face. He wasn't paralyzed, but his limbs were restrained. Light glinted off steel. The blade of a knife arched slowly toward him, nicking the skin on his chest. Blood trickled.

Blind, James tripped over the lip of the shower. His feet went out from under him, and he pitched forward, striking his head on the marble floor.

His last thought before blackness descended was that he'd failed.

He was going to die before he could save Beth. Pain and violence were headed her way. Now.

CHAPTER THIRTY-THREE

"Are you sure you don't want to come?"

Beth set her tea mug on the patio table. "I'm really not up for it. Sorry." The police chief's morning visit had sapped all her strength.

"You sure?"

"Oh, yeah." Jack had hovered over her all afternoon. His concern was out of love, but a half hour alone was what she really wanted. She gave him a reassuring smile. "I haven't showered in three days. I'm cranky, dirty, and tired. Definitely not fit for human company."

Jack leaned over and pressed his lips gently on the unmarred side of her mouth. "You still taste good."

"Thankfully I can still brush my teeth." Richard had only bruised her jaw and cheekbone. The resulting swelling and variegated collage of purples were ugly but temporary. Two weeks or so and she'd be good as new. Other than the localized pain in her arms and face, plus some additional body bruises from her wrestling match with Richard, she felt surprisingly fit. The pain wasn't anything a couple of ibuprofen couldn't handle. If only she could be assured the rest of her problems could be just as easily solved.

"Stitches'll be out in five more days. Then you can shower all you want. I'll help." A spark lit up his eyes. He seemed determined to keep her spirits up, and had spent a good part of the day on the phone with Carlyle, who was confident his team of lawyers could handle Stafford Baker's vendetta.

Beth had her doubts, but she kept them to herself. "I'll bet." Putting one hand on the side of his face, she kissed him back. "I can't wait."

He straightened and frowned. "Maybe we shouldn't go."

"Jack, you're driving the kids to Quinn's house to spend the night. I doubt you'll be gone an hour. Please, the kids are excited, and they really need a little normal. It would be wonderful for them to get away from all this craziness for a while. Plus, I don't want them with us tomorrow for the press conference." Quinn had promised the TV at his house would be unplugged at nine o'clock the next morning, when the press conference was scheduled to air.

Carlyle had decided that it was high time Beth started using the press instead of letting Stafford Baker get all the media attention. And her lawyer insisted Beth get on television while her face was still battered and bruised. She didn't like the idea of letting the world in on her most private shame, but Carlyle was right. If she didn't speak up, people would naturally believe Baker. And geez, she couldn't look more vulnerable and pathetic than she did right now.

"I could get Sean to come and get them."

"That's silly."

"I guess you're right." Jack sighed. "You have your cell phone on you, right?"

Beth nodded and tapped the front pocket of the sweatshirt. "Yup."

"Need anything else?"

"No. I'm fine." She shook her head. "Thank you. The kids've been cooped up too long. And they're looking forward to seeing the other kids. Especially Katie." Sean's girls were also spending the night at Quinn's house. Jack's cousins were treating her and her kids like they were now part of their family. If only life could be that simple.

"OK. Mrs. Harris is inside. I'll be right back."

Ben and Katie slipped through the doors and hurried across the patio. Katie latched onto Jack's thigh. The little girl had been bouncing off the walls since breakfast, when Jack asked her if she wanted to go to the sleepover. Ben was trying to play it cool, but he'd packed his bag five minutes after Jack made the announcement.

Both kids kissed her good-bye and ran down the back lawn to the garage. At her side Henry whined.

"Come on." Jack slapped his thigh. "You can ride along."

With an enthusiastic "woof" the dog raced toward the kids.

"Wait up." Cane in hand, Jack limped after them as fast as he could manage.

Beth's breath caught in her throat. The scene was painfully ordinary. Almost as if they were a real family. Jack would be a terrific father for her kids, and he seemed to want the job. If only...

A couple of minutes later Jack drove around the house. The truck disappeared.

Beth leaned back into the chair and closed her eyes against the slanting light of the setting sun, which was dipping a bit earlier now that September had arrived. A warm, dry breeze rustled the leaves on the huge oak in the center of the lawn and sent the smell of freshly cut grass wafting across the patio. She'd have to address the issue of school for the kids. She'd already looked into homeschooling, but hopefully there'd be no need for it soon.

"Hey, Beth."

She shaded her eyes and squinted. "Hi, Jeff. What's up?"

"Is Jack home?" Her neighbor slouched and stuffed his hands into the front pockets of his jeans. "I wanted to ask him something."

"No. He took the kids to his cousin's house."

"They should enjoy that." Jeff smiled.

"What did you want to ask him? He shouldn't be too long."

"I was going to get him to call the vet. I was just looking at Lucy's stitches. The cut might be getting infected. Do you want to take a look?" Jeff narrowed his eyes at her and frowned. "You're probably not up to it. I'll just call Doc White. You look tired. I shouldn't've bothered you." He turned away.

"No. Wait. A stroll down to the barn is just what I need." Beth stood and stretched. Seeing the horses just might take her mind off her troubles. "I'm going a little stir-crazy. I'll just let Mrs. Harris know." She stepped to the door and opened it. The whir of a vacuum drowned out her attempt to call the housekeeper. "Oh, well. We won't be long."

"Are you sure?"

"Yeah. Nothing wrong with my legs. I just can't touch anything." She raised a sleeve to reveal the edge of a bandage.

"OK, then."

They strolled across the back lawn and along the path to the barn. Movement loosened her muscles. By the time they stepped into the barn aisle, she was tired, but her spirits were up.

Jeff led Lucy out of her stall and removed the bandage on her foreleg. "What do you think?"

The barn was dim. Beth bent over to get a closer look. The cut looked just a little red around the edges. "I see what you mean."

Pain exploded in the back of her head and everything went black.

- - -

Today was Jeff's lucky day. Seriously. He'd go right out and buy a lottery ticket—if he didn't already have plans for the night.

He actually *had* gone up to the house to ask Jack if he wanted him to call the vet. But Jack hadn't been home. Jeff's hope had bloomed like a bloodred rose. When Beth hadn't bothered to go into the house to tell Mrs. Harris where she was going, her fate had been sealed. Destiny decreed that tonight was the night.

He'd been prepared to wait weeks, or months even, for the right opportunity.

Jeff placed Beth in the back of his jeep and hurried around to the driver's seat. His heart skipped with excitement as he turned the key and shifted into first gear. Despite his eagerness, he kept the jeep's speed slow so he didn't jostle Beth around too much. She was damaged enough. Nothing he could do about that, though. Her spirit wasn't broken. That was the important thing.

With the thought that Beth had shot her husband fresh in his mind, he stopped the jeep in his yard, reached back, and patted her down. She was dressed in ugly sweat pants and a gigantic hoodie. The outfit wasn't flattering like her usual worn, snug jeans, but he had to admit, it made searching her for a weapon easy.

She wasn't armed. Why would she be? Her husband was no longer a threat. Everyone thought the Riverside Killer was in jail. Big LOL on that major coup.

Everyone in town thought Chief O'Connell walked on water, but Jeff had proven Mike was just a big dunce.

He lifted her into his arms and carried her toward the house. He wouldn't fling this woman over his shoulder like a sack of grain. No, Beth would be treated with reverence.

Shifting her weight, he unlocked the front door and went straight for the cellar. His workspace was meticulous. While he hadn't expected to have Beth so soon, he'd been prepared. Good to know those years in the Boy Scouts hadn't been a total waste.

He set her down on the stainless-steel table and took a moment to just look at her. Even with the bruises and swelling on the side of her face, she was beautiful. He turned the damaged side of her face to the table so he could view her perfect profile. Lovely.

The fact that she was smart and strong heightened his excitement. Beth possessed a rare strength that singled her out from the rest. A spirit he couldn't wait to test. Finally, a challenge worthy of all his years of practice.

It felt like Christmas in September. Beth was a great big present just waiting to be unwrapped. But just like Christmas, he'd have to wait until the right time. There was no point in starting until she was fully conscious.

With a contented sigh, he secured her ankles and wrists to the four corners of the table with the leather straps already in place.

Now he just had to bide his time until she woke. Shouldn't take long. He hadn't had to use a tranquilizer on her since it had been such a short ride.

He jogged up the steps to the kitchen for a bottle of water and an energy bar. He'd have to hurry. She wouldn't be unconscious for long.

– – –

James opened his eyes and quickly shut them against the bright bathroom light. His head throbbed. Raising a hand, he located the source of the pain: a fist-sized goose egg on his fore-head. James winced. Prodding it turned out to be a bad idea.

He moved his arms and legs. A few mild tweaks told him nothing was broken except his pride and his stupid head. How the hell had he fallen?

He levered his torso up and leaned back against the wall. The marble room spun around him. The floor was like ice under his bare ass.

A vague feeling of panic crawled up the back of his neck. Something wasn't right.

Beth's pendant glinted from the vanity. The vision came back in a whoosh. He pushed himself to his feet and swayed. Nausea rose in his throat, and he sagged down to the floor again.

Ah. Fuck it.

James crawled across the carpet on his hands and knees. He grabbed his cell phone off the nightstand and turned it on. Sitting on the rug with his back pressed against the bed, he flipped through the pages of his worn address book to the letter O. His finger found Danny O'Malley's number, labeled only as DO.

It took several tries to dial as his vision kept splitting into double images, and for the first time in forty years, his hands were shaking. But at last the line was ringing.

"O'Malley residence."

– – –

Beth opened her eyes and blinked hard. Her vision blurred for a few seconds and then cleared. Her hand tried to move toward her head but was restrained by something. She tested all four limbs. Pain sliced through her arms as the straps around her wrists bit into the stitches.

Panic crawled through her insides. She was tied spread-eagle on a stainless-steel table. She tried to bend her right arm, but there was no give in the thick leather straps. The rest of the bindings were just as strong.

Sweat broke out under the heavy shirt. Her heartbeat began to pound in her ears. The throbbing in her head echoed the beat.

She raised her head. Her prison was a dusty and damp basement. A bare bulb with a string switch was the only source of light. The small, high windows had been covered to block the light and, she supposed, prying eyes. On her right was a wooden staircase. To her left, on a workbench against the wall, light reflected off the shiny blade of a knife. On the other side of the room, another short flight of steps led to bulkhead doors. Her gaze fell to the concrete floor. Large, rusty, red splotches decorated the cement in a camouflage pattern.

Her breath locked in her chest as the truth hit her. She'd been with Jeff Stevens at the barn.

The Riverside Killer had been living right next door.

Footsteps sounded from the room above her. The old floors creaked and groaned. The hinges squeaked and the door opened. A thin strip of light fell in a slanted yellow rectangle on the staircase as a menacing figure loomed in the doorway, silhouetted by the brightness behind him. He watched her without moving for a long moment before starting down the stairs. His footsteps paused ominously on each individual tread.

Her breathing accelerated as he came closer. The scent of fear rose from her skin, a distinct pungent mix of sweat and hormones. Because of the light behind him, she still couldn't see his face, but it didn't matter. She knew who he was.

He stepped off the last tread and onto the concrete, taking his time to cross the floor.

"My lovely Beth." His fingers trailed along her cheek. She arched her back and pulled as far away as she could as he reached down to touch her again. Movement intensified the pain. Fire streaked across her arms as she pulled against the straps. "I'd tell you it's useless to fight, but it would be so disappointing if you just lay there."

Beth went still. Her breaths came faster. She was light-headed; her heart hammered in her chest; blood rushed in her ears.

Jeff's eyes, cold, black, and lifeless, bored into hers. "And there'd be no point in keeping you alive." He hummed under his breath as he moved to the workbench and picked up the knife, pausing to switch on an iPod player. Light glinted off the blade. "I made a special playlist for you."

Willie Nelson began to croon "Always on My Mind."

He kept his gaze leveled on her eyes as he moved back to the side of the table. "Now, let's get you out of those awful clothes."

He lifted the sweatshirt with one hand and, with the knife in the other, sliced through it in one cut. Despite her efforts to remain silent, to deny him the thrill of hearing her cry out, a whimper escaped her lips as the sharp tip nicked the skin of her breast.

– – –

Jack parked in the garage and stepped out of the truck. A night at Quinn's kid-filled house would be therapeutic for Ben and Katie and would keep them away from the press tomorrow. He wasn't looking forward to the media shit storm that would surely follow Beth's statement. The kids might have to stay at Quinn's for a couple of days.

His phone rang as he climbed the hill to the house. Henry raced ahead of him, wagging his tail at the door. The patio was empty. Beth must have gone inside.

"What's up, Mike?" Jack let the dog inside and then sat in her vacated chair.

"Got a bit of news for you. The liquid in Baker's syringe was acepromazine."

"Isn't that the same drug the Riverside Killer uses?"

Mike's exasperated sigh was audible across the line. "Yeah."

Jack scratched his head. "So now what?"

"I've no fucking idea. But he had a knife and the same tranq used by the killer. I can tell you this much. We'll be going through Baker's house with a fine-tooth comb as soon as the warrant comes through."

"I guess the possibility that Martin was just mimicking the killer to get Mary Ann looks even more likely," Jack said.

"That's the current theory. Talk to you when I have more." Mike disconnected.

With Mike's news rummaging around in his head, Jack let himself into the kitchen. Empty.

"Beth?" Silence greeted him. No Beth. He started down the hall. The house phone rang, and Jack heard Mrs. Harris answer it in the living room.

"No. I'm sorry. Danny died two months ago."

Jack stepped into the room and waited for her to finish the call.

She held up one finger. "You're looking for Beth?"

Startled, Jack motioned for her to give him the phone. "Who is this?"

"This is her Uncle James." The voice on the other end was male—and weak. "I need to speak with Beth immediately."

Jack covered the receiver with his palm and mouthed to Mrs. Harris, "Where's Beth?"

The housekeeper's brows knitted. "I saw her walking toward the barn with Jeff about a half hour ago. Isn't she back?" Mrs. Harris spun and hurried out of the room, calling for Beth as she hurried up the hall.

Fear snaked up Jack's spine. He uncovered the phone. "Why do you need to speak with her?"

The man on the other end was out of breath. "Who is this?"

"I'm Danny's nephew, Jack."

The line went quiet for a few seconds as Beth's uncle mulled something over.

"Beth's in terrible danger. Right now. I can't explain." Uncle James coughed. "I'm in Philadelphia. I can be there in ninety minutes, but that may be too late."

"How do you know she's in danger?"

James paused. "I just do."

OK.

"I'll find her." Jack tossed the cordless phone on the couch and tried to keep calm. Beth was fine. She'd just gone for a walk down to the barn to check on the horses. Hadn't she said she missed them this morning? And how could her uncle in Philadelphia possibly know she was in danger?

Mrs. Harris stuck her head in the doorway. "She's not in the house."

"I'm going down to the barn." Panic surged in Jack's belly as he grabbed his cane and tore out of the house. Henry raced behind the golf cart as Jack floored it on the path through the copse.

The stable was empty. Jack's gut tightened as he stood behind the barn looking out over the meadow. Jeff's farm was just over the hill, closer as the crow flies than by the road. Tire tracks showed the route from the spot where his neighbor usually parked his old jeep when he came over to feed the horses.

The realization struck Jack in one blow. It'd been Jeff all along. He'd set Will up. Jeff had killed Mary Ann and all those other women.

Jack jumped into his cart. Henry leaped up beside him. Driving with one hand, he punched Mike's number into his cell with his thumb. When the chief answered, he relayed the situation.

Jack parked the cart behind a small clump of trees and slid out of the seat. Henry jumped down and looked at Jack expectantly. With a hand signal, he motioned for the dog to follow him. Henry fell in silently at Jack's heels. The hackles on the dog's back were raised, but he remained miraculously quiet.

Jeff's jeep was parked in front of the front steps. Jack had driven by Jeff's place before, but he'd never visited. Missing the gun he no longer habitually carried, Jack circled the house. It looked like a normal farmhouse, nothing fancy, but clean and well maintained. The cellar windows were boarded up. Not a good sign. Jack peered in the ground floor windows. No Jeff. No Beth. Music played softly, muffled by the glass.

He tried the front door. Locked. Jack picked up a rock and punched it through the sidelight, hoping the music would muffle the sound. Reaching in, he turned the lock.

Henry skulked soundlessly beside him as they moved through the rooms, more slowly than Jack would have liked. But walking quietly with a cane was no easy feat, and Jack didn't want to tip Jeff off to his presence.

They circled the ground floor and stepped into the kitchen. Two closed doors. Jack froze and listened. The music came from the door to his left. Jack signaled Henry to sit. The dog obeyed.

Ears forward, he waited for Jack's next command. Jack turned the knob slowly and opened the door an inch to reveal a wooden staircase. The music's volume increased. Jack stooped for a better view.

Jeff's back was turned to him, partially blocking his view of Beth. Holy Christ. She was tied to a steel table. Jack's stomach flipped as he watched Jeff slip a knife through the fabric of her sweatshirt, exposing her naked breasts.

Stevens was going to die today.

Jack paused in the doorway, torn. Mike wasn't here yet, but there was no way he was waiting another ten minutes for the police. By the time he hobbled down there, however, Jeff could easily kill Beth. Even now, the blade hovered just inches above her skin as Jeff leaned closer to her and whispered something.

Henry nudged his leg. Jack glanced at the dog, still sitting beside him. Henry's eyes were fixed on Jack's face, waiting.

He pulled the door open and motioned the dog through.

Henry tore down the steps. Jeff turned, surprise barely registering on his face before the dog latched onto the hand with the knife, exactly the way he'd been trained. The weapon clattered to the floor. Screams echoed through the air as Jeff tried to shake Henry free. The dog hung on, his body swinging from Jeff's waving arm. Flesh tore under Henry's powerful jaws. Blood splattered on the cement as Jack hurried down the steps.

Jeff squatted and reached for the knife with his left hand, trying to drag the canine with him.

Jack brought his cane back in a two-handed grip and swung it like a baseball bat. He held nothing back, connecting solidly with Jeff's head. Something cracked. He hoped it was Jeff's skull.

The killer went limp on the floor, the dog still attached to his arm.

"Release."

Henry disengaged and sat, his gaze fixed on Jeff's prostrate form. Jack threw the "on guard" command over his shoulder as he turned to Beth. Fury surged in his chest as he took in the cut on her breast and the blood seeping through the arms of the sweatshirt where the leather straps had torn her stitches.

He should have let Henry tear off an arm.

He released her and gathered her in his arms. He wrapped the torn shirt around her torso and let her sob on his chest, trusting Henry to watch Jeff until the police arrived.

Not that it mattered. Jack was pretty sure the Riverside Killer wasn't breathing.

Sirens approached. Henry didn't move.

CHAPTER THIRTY-FOUR

Beth reclined on the couch. Her hand drifted down to settle on Henry's ruff. His tail thumped on the carpet. The dog had refused to leave her side, blatantly ignoring Jack's command to do so. Quinn had made a house call to repair Beth's stitches, saving her the trauma of a trip to the emergency room. Henry had watched every move the doctor made, and Beth suppressed any urge to wince in case the dog misunderstood and thought Quinn was hurting her. Upset with her refusal, again, to go in for a CAT scan, Jack's cousin had taken up residence in a guest room for the night to keep an eye on her. The press had already swamped the small community hospital, and Beth didn't want her picture on the evening news just yet.

Her arms ached despite the local anesthetic the doctor had administered. After everyone left, she'd probably break down and take a pain pill. Then maybe sleep for a week. She'd never been so tired in her life.

It was completely dark before the police chief finished taking their statements and rose to leave. "I have to sort out the mess with Will Martin. The FBI thinks Jeff planted the evidence in Will's trunk. Oh, and Baker was killed with Ace. The Feds are looking for a connection between him and Jeff."

"Well, that's strange, but it's a relief." Jack stood and shook the cop's hand. "Thanks for the help, Mike."

"Same here." Mike turned and slapped him on the shoulder. "You gonna give Henry back to the force now that he's given away his secret?" The cop nodded toward the dog, who Beth swore turned and stared right back at him.

"No way." Jack laughed. "He's part of the family. And he only works for Beth."

Jack was following Mike out of the room when the doorbell rang.

A few seconds later, Beth was startled as James rushed into the room just ahead of Jack. His Paul Newman–blue eyes locked on her as a huge breath rushed audibly from his lungs. Without a word he strode toward her. Henry stood, positioning his body between Beth and the approaching stranger.

"It's OK, Henry."

The dog settled back down but kept one eye on James as he sat on the couch next to her. He pulled her close and wrapped his arms around her for a few seconds. Releasing her, he straightened. His eyes were moist. "You're a mess."

"You said it." Beth laughed. A tear rolled down her cheek, and she wiped it away. "I missed you. What are you doing here?"

"Would you believe it's a coincidence?"

"No." Beth held up a hand. "Don't say it. You can't explain." She touched the red lump on his temple beneath his white buzz-cut. "What happened to you?"

James shrugged. "Getting clumsy in my old age."

"Not you." Beth shook her head. James moved like a cat.

"I have something for you." He shifted and reached into his pocket, drawing out her lost pendant, the medal of St. Florian, patron saint of firemen, that Brian had always worn. For years it had been her talisman.

Beth closed her hand around the disc, but she didn't put it around her neck. "I think I'm ready to give this to Ben."

Mrs. Harris came in with the cordless phone, her hand firmly over the receiver. "You have a call. Dr. Miller. Do you want me to tell her you'll call her tomorrow?"

Beth's stomach lurched. Whatever news the doctor had for her had to be important if she was calling this late. Across the room, Jack's mouth tightened as he glanced at his watch. "No. I'll take it." She moved to push herself up, but James put a hand on her shoulder. "You stay put. We'll give you some privacy."

The room emptied in seconds and Beth put the receiver to her ear. "Hello. This is Beth."

"Beth, your tests result came back in today." The doctor paused. "Everything's OK, but you're pregnant."

Shock numbed everything, including her brain and vocal cords for a second. "Has to be a mistake."

"We can do a follow-up, but all the blood work is consistent. Are you unhappy about this?" The doctor's voice was soft.

"No. Just surprised." Shocked, stunned, freaking blown away. "I was told that wasn't possible."

"Guess they were wrong. Wouldn't be the first time." The doctor laughed. "Congratulations. Let me know if you need a referral for an obstetrician."

Beth hung up the phone, wondering how the hell she was going to break *that* news to Jack.

– – –

Jack led Beth's uncle into the study and poured them each a scotch. He kept his own to a single shot. "You OK?" He nodded toward the egg on James's temple.

"I'm just fine." James accepted the glass and wandered around the room, checking out the pictures on the walls. "O'Malley really got around."

"That he did."

"How'd he die?"

"Had a massive heart attack a couple of days before Beth got here. It was quick."

The older man nodded. "Not a bad way to go."

Jack supposed that when he was that age, he might have the same attitude.

James stopped in the corner where Uncle Danny had hung his Vietnam photos. He peered closely at the shot with the edgy group of men gathered round the helicopter. Raising a finger to the glass, he pointed at one of the figures. "I remember when he took that shot. We were waiting for the all-clear."

Jack rummaged in the desk for his uncle's black-handled magnifying glass. He moved to James's side and examined the image. The man leaning on the side of the chopper was a young James.

"A couple of days before that," James tapped the photo, "my men and I rescued your uncle and his unit from a POW camp. Afterward your uncle gave me his name and address stateside and said if I ever needed anything I could call him. I'd only seen him once or twice since he retired, and not at all in the past thirty years, which is why I sent Beth here. I knew no one would connect O'Malley and me. Hell, I didn't even know if he'd remember me. He did." James held his drink up. "To Danny." He downed the shot in one swallow.

Jack raised his glass to follow suit.

"Jack, can I talk to you for a minute?" Beth stood at the open door. Her face was tight.

Jack set his untouched drink on the desk, rushed to her side, and took her arm. "Sit down."

"I'm OK, Jack." She protested but sank into the chair anyway. Blowing out a hard breath, she looked up at him, uncertainty in her eyes. "I'm just going to say it. I'm pregnant."

Holy shit. Jack felt his jaw drop. His brain went blank, but just for a few seconds. He dropped to his good knee and took both her hands in his. "Now will you marry me?"

Beth stared. "I thought you might be upset."

"Why the hell would you think that?"

"Because I told you—I thought—"

"OK, I admit, it's kind of a surprise, but the good kind." Jack gripped her hands tighter and planted a gentle kiss next to her bruised mouth. "Well, shit. A baby."

He glanced over his shoulder at the old man leaning against the desk, grinning. "You'll stay, right? Someone has to give the bride away." In fact, seeing James had made Beth so happy, Jack would think of a reason to keep him around permanently.

He turned back to Beth.

The smile slid from her face. "If only Stafford Baker would leave us alone."

Across the room, James cleared his throat. "You don't have to worry about Baker anymore."

Beth's brow furrowed. "What do you mean?"

"You have a good lawyer?" James asked. At Beth's nod, he leveled a serious gaze at them both. "Well, I have a present for him. A little video the Bakers definitely won't want made public. Stafford Baker won't be bothering you anymore."

Beth's eyes lit up with understanding.

Jack swallowed a laugh. The old guy was staying.

Beth leaned forward and kissed him. "It's over then."

Jack kissed her back. "No. It's only the beginning."

THE END

ABOUT THE AUTHOR

 More than ten years ago, Melinda Leigh abandoned her career in banking and never looked back. Since then, she has won numerous writing awards for her paranormal romance and romantic-suspense fiction. When she isn't writing, Melinda is an avid martial artist: she holds a second-degree black belt in Kenpo karate, studies Brazilian Jiu-Jitsu, and teaches women's self-defense. She lives in a delightfully messy house with her husband, two teenagers, a couple of dogs, and one neurotic cat. For more information about Melinda and her books, please visit www.melindaleighauthor.com.